The Release

Escape From Torment

Ralph Nelson Willett

*"**This story is captivating from beginning to end.** The author presents a realistic case of a woman trying to escape the man that abused her, something we see happen all too often. At one point I was so caught up in the story I had tears in my eyes for Carrie and a few times I had to remind myself that this was fiction! The story goes on to show us how big our God is and how big His mercy and grace are.*

I can hardly recommend this book enough."

Denise Moore,
Board Secretary of the Van Buren Domestic Violence Coalition

Can I Ask A Favor?

If you enjoy this book, please consider providing a review on Amazon for it. Reviews help readers decide if they would like to purchase a book or not and is useful for the author when making decisions on what to write for his next book.

Here's the link where you can add your review:
www.NorthernOvationMedia.com/therelease/review

Thank you.

Want Free Books?

From time to time the author offers his Kindle books for free to those who are interested. <u>These offers are highly temporary.</u> If you'd like to know when you can get his books for free, please sign up for his mailing list at:
www.NorthernOvationMedia.com/freebooks

~~~

This book is a work of fiction. Names, characters, places and incidents are either the product of the author's imagination or are used fictionally. Any resemblance to actual persons, living or dead, or to actual events or locales is entirely coincidental.

Copyright © 2017 Northern Ovation Media. All rights reserved. Including the right to reproduce this book or portions thereof, in any form. No part of this text may be reproduced in any form without the express written permission of the author.

Acknowledgments

There are several moments in my life where I can look back and say "God did that." The launching of my writing career is one of those times. He brought a group of wonderful people into my life to encourage me to complete the book you are now holding. And now I have an opportunity to thank those people here.

I'd like to thank Theressa Ruppert for her contribution and input into the story. Much of the events surrounding the main character, Carrie, can be attributed to her input. Thank you, Theressa.

I'd like to thank Dan Diekema for taking his time to patiently answer many of my questions regarding police response and interrogation. In many ways he helped to make the implausible plausible. Thank you, Dan.

I'd like to thank Beth Steere, who's support and suggestions helped to make a better product. Thank you, Beth.

To Pastor Milan Bittenbender, thank you. Without your initial support this story and many others would not exist.

To my readers, thank you for your support. I can't begin to express how grateful I am to have you spend your time with me.

Lastly, but most importantly, I'd like to thank my wife, Sherri. Without her acting as my first line editor, and encouraging me when I needed it the most, nothing would ever come to fruition. I have no words that can express the gratitude I have for being blessed with you in my life. I love you. Meeting you is another instance where I can look back and say "God did that."

The Release

Escape From Torment

Ralph Nelson Willett

Chapter 1

Keeping off from the main highways, Carrie Rhodes continued north. She had been driving for the past two and a half hours and was already exhausted. Only sheer determination kept her going. She wasn't sure where she was at the moment, but it did not matter. She just needed to be as far north as possible before eight that evening. It would have been faster to take the expressway, but felt that would have been expected and too much of a risk. It was better to take the back roads.

She did not expect the first call until just after eight. That's when he would understand that she had left him and taken everything she owned with her. Then he'd call. Over and over again she ran the scenario through her mind. Her phone would ring, she'd see his name, and she'd refuse to answer it. Carrie could imagine how he would explode with anger as he realized that she wasn't going to take his call. This time it would not matter. She was gone. She'd be north, far north.

The time on her cell phone had rolled forward an hour as she crossed into the Eastern time zone at the Michigan border. She had until Eight o'clock Michigan's time before he found her missing. That was if he didn't stop at the bar before going home. She hoped he would, but that still would not give her much time.

The road she was traveling on seemed to be tucked between high hills. She caught glimpses of houses surrounded by trees, barely visible, hiding like she wanted to be. Trying to calm herself, she tried to focus her thoughts on other things. How much gas did she have? Where was she going to stay tonight? Was she hungry? Did she forget anything? Could he find her? She could feel the tension rising again with that last thought. Could he find her? He'd look, she knew that, but could he find her?

Turning the radio on, she began sifting through channels trying to find anything that would distract her thoughts. The only channels she found were all Chicago channels. That was the last thing she wanted, something more to remind her of Chicago. She turned the radio off.

Leaning back in her seat, she brushed her hair back with her hand, took a deep breath and let it out slowly. The hills and trees were giving way to flatter land where some tall bushes were planted in long parallel rows. She wondered what was being farmed there.

Suddenly, without warning, the engine of the car stopped. The power steering failed. She grasped the wheel with two hands wrestling it to the right shoulder of the road while pushing on the brakes with both feet. She eventually brought the car to a stop just off the edge of the pavement.

What was wrong? She checked the gas. There was still half a tank. The check engine light was lit red, but that told her nothing. She tried to start it again. The engine turned over and over without so much as a pop. She pumped the gas pedal hard as if by the sheer force of her will she could bring the engine back to life again.

Panic began to set in. She didn't know where she was and there certainly would not be anyone here that she could call.

She swore as she hit the dashboard with the palm of her hand several times. She swore again and tried to start the car. The engine seemed to be growing tired as it turned over more slowly with each passing second. Eventually, she turned the ignition, and the only result was a disappointing series of clicks.

Her mind raced frantically as she wondered what to do. Where was she? Where could she go? She needed to calm herself down so she could think. As the panic slowly subsided, it was being replaced by feelings of hopelessness. It was all over. There was nothing more she could do. She placed both hands on the top of the steering wheel and rested her head on them. Staring out of the passenger side window, she saw the rows and rows of bushes in the field next to her and recognized them. "Blueberries," she thought. "They're blueberries." Taking in a deep breath, she blew it out slowly. "And this is where I die," she said aloud. "by the blueberries." She no longer cared.

~~~~

Alarm bells began ringing in Chi's head the second he saw the woman slumped over the steering wheel of the car. Something wasn't right. She was facing away from him as he drove past her and all he saw was the back or her head with its long blonde hair draped down. He slowed his truck to a stop along the side of the road and tried to get a good look through his rear view mirror. There was no movement.

Putting his truck in reverse, he turned looking over his right shoulder and began backing up until he was within a few feet from the front of the small blue car. Still no movement. Climbing out of the truck, he walked back to the driver's side door. The front license plate told him that she was from

Illinois. He could see the car was packed loosely with clothing and other personal items that appeared to have been thrown in haphazardly. He knelt down until he could see the driver. She was resting her head on her hands.

He tapped the window. Still no movement. He tapped again but this time using the heavy ring on his right hand. It made a sharp, distinct snapping sound. A moment passes and finally there was movement as her head raised slightly. Slowly she began turning towards him. Her hair hung over her face. Using her left hand, she pulled it back and tucked it behind her ear.

Chi's first reaction when seeing her face was an internal shock. Someone had worked this woman's face over. Her left eye was swollen nearly to the point of being closed. Her lips were swollen and broken in places. She rested her head on her hands again, this time facing him. He could not see her right cheek but assumed it was equally as bruised.

Setting aside his initial shock, he spoke loudly enough for her to hear him through the closed door window. "Are you alright?" He had known the answer to the question before he asked it but it still needed to be asked.

She slowly reached down with her left hand and rolled down the window. Placing both hands on the ledge of the door, Chi squatted outside the open window. "Are you alright?" he asked again.

"My car died." Her voice was quiet, nearly without emotion. Her eyes looked downward, unfocused. Chi had seen this look before. It was the look of someone who had given up. Given up trying. Given up caring. Given up hope.

"Can I take a look?" Chi asked.

"Sure." There was still no movement in her eyes. Her voice signaled a level of indifference he had seen before. This was someone on the verge of suicide, someone that had given up any desire to live.

"Can you pop the hood?"

Raising her head just enough to see the hood latch, she pulled the lever. The hood made a loud pop as it released. She then laid her head down on her hands again.

Chi walked slowly around to the front of the car. His eyes scanned the surrounding area for anything else that may seem out of place. The only thing unusual was this car. Unlatching the hood, he lifted it and looked around. He wasn't a mechanic but was looking for anything that would suggest what the problem might be. There was nothing. He pulled at and twisted the battery cables. They were secure.

"Try to start it," he said loudly to her.

Without lifting her head, she turned the key. Chi heard the clicks. He knew the battery was dead and thought for a moment about what the options would be. There were jumper cables in the back of his truck cab. He could try and jump start it, but something inside him told him not to.

He closed the hood, walked around to the driver's side door and knelt down again. She glanced at his face briefly and then looked away. Chi noticed the far away look in her eyes.

"Can I call a wrecker for you?"

"Sure."

Chi stood, and taking out his cell phone stepped behind the car. He selected a number out of his contact list and dialed it.

Jessie answered, "Hi, Chi. What's up?"

"Hey, Jess. I've stumbled on a small problem. Can you bring a wrecker over?"

"Your truck? What did you do?"

"No. It's not my truck. It's someone else. Small car."

"Where you at?"

"Right around Blue Star and 16th. You'll see my truck."

"Alright. I'll be a few minutes. I need to go get the truck."

"Thanks, man."

"Sure thing. See you in a few."

Chi disconnected the call, put the phone back into his shirt pocket and again looked around for anything unusual. Nothing stood out.

He returned to the driver's side door. She still had her head resting on her hands. "I've called for a wrecker. It's going to take a few minutes before he gets here." She remained silent as if she hadn't heard him.

He looked her over again. She had been badly beaten. He tried to gauge how recent it was. A few hours ago perhaps. He could not tell if she had other injuries or not but from what he could see he thought it likely. "Hey, maybe I should get you to the hospital."

She looked at him, "No." This time her voice carried some emotion.

He nodded at her. "Is there anything you need?"

She looked away off into the distance, still with unfocused eyes and murmured, "no thank you."

He nodded, stood up and walked towards the back of the car. Looking again at the contents of the car, he now assumed she was running from someone. He tried not to make assumptions. That was contrary to his training, but at times some things seemed too obvious. He assumed she was running from whoever had beaten her and she left in a hurry.

Chi recognized the car that rolled past in the opposite direction as belonging to Peter Sender. It slowed to a stop, made a U-turn, pulled up behind the small blue car and turned off the engine. Pete stepped out and walked up to Chi.

"What's up, Chi?"

"Car's dead. Jess is on his way, but you need to take a look at this girl. She's been beaten up pretty badly."

Pete stepped up to the car. The woman was now sitting back in her seat and looked up at him. Her eyes then fixated on the weapon holstered at his side. Squatting down, Pete watched her eyes as they followed the pistol down until her view of it was blocked by the car door.

"Hi," he said. "It's OK. I'm a South Haven police officer." He gave her a smile as she looked up into his face. "You wanna tell me what happened?"

"Not really," she said just above a whisper as she looked away.

"What's your name?" he asked.

"Carrie."

"Hi, Carrie. I'm Pete. Carrie, we can put whoever did this to you away for a long time. He won't be able to hurt you anymore."

"I'm fine."

"You don't have to let anyone do this to you."

"I'm fine." She was looking away from him, out towards the blueberry field.

"OK. But at least let me connect you with some people that can help you. There's a place in Paw Paw that helps with domestic violence."

She turned her head slowly toward him and looked him in the face. "What makes you think this was domestic violence?" Her voice had taken on a stern tone.

"Am I wrong?"

She turned away again and spoke brusquely, "I'm fine."

Pete pulled a business card from his wallet. As he held it out to her, he said, "Here, please take this. You call me if you change your mind."

She took the card, placed it on the passenger side seat and turned away from him. Pete stepped back to talk with Chi. "She won't let us help her." Chi nodded but said nothing. "How long before Jess get's here?"

"I'd think about another fifteen minutes."

"OK. We'll wait. Do you know if she's got a place to stay?"

"I don't know anything about her," Chi answered. "When I first saw her she was slumped over the steering wheel. I had to knock a couple of times on the window before she even looked at me."

Pete nodded. They stood shoulder to shoulder behind the car facing it. They could see that Carrie had leaned her head against the headrest. "Her name is Carrie," Pete told him.

The two stood silent for several moments and finally Pete spoke, "I've seen this type of thing a few times. It really makes you mad. All too often the woman won't press charges. They finally changed the laws so that we don't need her to."

"I'd suspect this happened out of state," Chi replied.

"I'd say so."

"Anything you can do?"

"Not without her cooperation."

Chi tucked his hands into his pockets. It wasn't often he felt like he needed to do something but could not. He hated that feeling. "I've got some water in my truck. Let me see if she wants some." He walked up to the passenger side of his truck and pulled out a bottle of water and walked it back to Carrie. He offered it through the window. She accepted.

She struggled to try to loosen the cap. To Chi, she looked weak and broken. Finally, the seal broke, and she raised it to her lips and drank. Her hands trembled as she lifted the bottle. Water spilled on her shirt as she swallowed, her swollen lips not able to seal well around the bottle. She drank half of it, put the cap back on and tried to hand it back to Chi.

"No. Keep it. You need it."

She pulled the cap off again and drank half of what was left. "Thank you," she said quietly.

"Carrie, my name is Chi. You know, like the tea, just spelled different." He smiled at her broadly as he tried to distract her with mild humor. She stared vacantly at him without acknowledging it.

"Hi, Chi. My name is Carrie." The response was so automatic and reflexive it was as if she did not realize that Chi already called her by name. She turned, looking distantly down the road.

"Carrie, is there anything I can get you?"

"No, thank you," she replied weakly.

"Is there anyone we can call for you?"

"No."

"Where are you headed?" Chi asked. Pete joined Chi at the door as she answered.

"North."

"Where 'bouts?"

Carrie didn't answer. The reality was she didn't know. It was just north.

Pete spoke up, "Carrie, do you have a place to stay?"

"I'm fine."

"Carrie, I don't think you are fine. I think you're in trouble. We can help you."

"No. I'm fine."

Pete and Chi looked at each other. They badly wanted to help, but she was refusing everything they could do.

Jessie's wrecker pulled up on the opposite side of the road. Leaning his head out of the window, he shouted at them, "Is this the car?"

"Yeah," Chi shouted back.

"Alright. Move your truck so I can hook up." Jessie drove on a few yards more until he could make a U-turn and then turned around. He pulled up behind Pete's car and waited for Chi to move his truck. After pulling his truck up enough to give Jessie room to connect up the tow truck, Chi walked back to join Pete at the car.

Jessie parked his tow truck a few feet in front of the blue car and stepped out to join the others. He shook Pete's hand. "Hey, Pete. What's going on here? A party?"

"Not quite."

Jessie saw that neither man returned his smile, so he asked again in a more serious tone, "What's going on?"

Pete responded, "Her car is dead. She's been beaten up pretty badly."

Jessie looked over at Carrie but could not see her face. "What do you mean 'beat up'?"

"Somebody beat her up. Looks like they did quite a bit of damage but she's refusing any help."

Chi was squatting down beside Carrie again. "You're going to have to get out to let the tow truck do its job."

Panic flashed across Carrie's face. Her body stiffened, and her head shifted side to side as she tried to process what she was going to do. She did not want to get out of the car. She could not get out of the car. She began taking quick short breaths, and her hands fumbled for things automatically and without reason. She picked up the business card that Pete had given her and then put it down again. She grabbed her purse off from the passenger seat and hugged it to her and then set it back down. She twisted herself towards the back seat and grabbed a handful of clothing and put it on the passenger seat.

Chi tried to calm her, "Carrie, it'll be alright. All your stuff will be safe. You can ride with me to the shop if you'd like or if you want, you can ride with Pete or even in the tow truck with Jessie."

Grabbing the steering wheel with both hands, she settled down some and tried to calm her breathing. She was looking straight forward with wild eyes at the tow truck. Moments went by, and she finally calmed enough to look at Chi.

"Where's he taking it?"

"To his garage. He can take a look at it and see what it will take to fix it."

She looked at Jessie who was talking to Pete, back at the tow truck and then slowly back at Chi. She felt trapped. There was nowhere to run and nowhere to hide. Resignation burrowed in even deeper. She tried to open the door, but it was locked. Unthinkingly, she tried again and again to open the door. Chi finally stepped in, "Here, let me help." He reached in and pushed the unlock button on the door. The button popped up with a quiet click. There was still enough juice in the battery to unlock the doors, thought Chi as he opened the door for her.

She kept her face pointed downward and away from Chi as she stepped slowly out of the car. Jessie was maneuvering the hoist into position. She watched him connect up as if she were watching a movie. She felt dazed and outside of herself.

"Would you like to ride with me?" Chi asked.

She looked over at him, made a small shrugging gesture and nodded almost imperceptibly. He held her arm in an attempt to steady her as they walked past the tow truck to where his truck was parked. Opening the passenger side door, he helped her in and closed it behind her. As he walked around to the driver's side, he waved back at Pete and Jessie to signal them that he would stay until they were ready to go.

After sitting behind the wheel and closing the door behind him, he handed Carrie another bottle of water. She took it from him and held it in her lap as she stared vacantly at the dashboard. "Have you had anything to eat today?" he asked her.

She could not remember if she had eaten today. She didn't think so. She tried to remember the last thing she ate but could not. She shook her head. "No."

"I'll tell you what, it's still going to take them a couple of minutes before Jessie gets all hooked up and can get your car to his shop. Let me take you to the McDonald's drive through and get you a burger."

"OK." She hung her head even lower.

He pulled out his cell phone and rang Pete to let him know his plan. He then started the truck and headed off. Carrie kept her head down staring toward the floorboard. Pulling into the drive through, he asked her what she wanted.

"Just a cheeseburger."

"Pop?"

"Sure."

At the order kiosk, Chi ordered two cheeseburgers and a small Coke. As they drove up to the pickup window, she faced away from him towards the right side of the truck. When the burgers and Coke were handed to him, he brushed her arm with it and passed it to her. She took the bag without looking and then the Coke. It wasn't until they drove out of the parking lot that she finally looked forward and opened the bag.

She ate the first burger carefully and painfully and washed it down with half of the Coke. She removed the second burger from the bag and offered it to him.

"That's yours," he said. Carrie unwrapped it and ate it more quickly. She then finished off the Coke just as they pulled into the garage parking lot. They had arrived sooner than the tow truck there, so they waited quietly in the truck.

"Thank you," she said.

"For what?"

"The burgers."

"No problem. You looked hungry."

She nodded. She hadn't realized how hungry she was until she started eating the first burger.

Jessie pulled into the parking lot with Pete following close behind. The tow truck backed the car up to one of the stall doors and parked. Pete parked beside Chi's truck, stepped out and then stepped over to where Jessie was working.

"Can they fix it today?" she asked Chi.

"They're closed right now. I don't know what Jessie can do tonight. We'll see."

She watched as her car was lowered to the pavement and disconnected from the tow truck. Jessie parked the truck on the other side of Pete's car. He went to the front door of the garage, unlocked it, stepped inside and raised the stall door.

"Let's go see what's going on," Chi told her while exiting the truck. Carrie unfastened her seat belt and let herself out. She walked alongside Chi towards Pete who was standing beside her car. Her steps were short and shuffling and Chi noticed what seemed to be a slight limp.

Jessie came out and spoke to Carrie, "Why don't you have a seat in the waiting room while we push your car in here so I can have a look at it."

"OK," she said quietly without moving. It appeared that Carrie hadn't understood him. Jessie glanced at Chi and then at Pete. No one said anything.

Reaching in through the driver's side window, Jessie put the car into neutral. "OK, help me push this back." The three men pushed the car back into the stall, and Jessie popped the hood.

Chi stepped back beside Carrie. "Come on," he said. "Let's let Jessie do his thing, and you and I can wait together in the waiting room. He offered his arm to her. She glanced at his arm, then at her car. She ignored the arm he offered to her and walked slowly into the waiting room.

Carrie sat staring vacantly at the floor. After sitting for a few moments, Chi tried to strike up a conversation. "Where're you from, Carrie?" No answer. He repeated the question, again with no answer. Moments passed, and he felt that his attempt at conversation had completely failed.

Finally, barely loud enough for Chi to hear her, she said, "Chicago."

"Chicago," he repeated. "Where're you headed?"

"North."

"Traverse City?"

"Sure."

Chi knew she had no plans. She was just running, just headed north. "Carrie, is there anything I can do for you? Anything?"

"No, thank you. I'm fine."

She stood up and pulled a magazine from a rack, sat down again and pretended to read. Chi recognized this as a way to avoid further conversation, so he sat quietly with her and waited.

It wasn't long before Jessie stepped into the waiting room with Pete following behind him. He was holding a small part about the size of his hand and stood in front of her with it. "This is the problem."

She winced as she stood to look at it. "It's the control module," Jessie said. "It's fried. I won't be able to get a replacement until tomorrow."

She looked up into his face and then looked away as her eyes darted wildly around as she tried to plan what to do next. Jessie continued, "The part is two hundred dollars."

She looked up again at him, over at Chi and back down to the floor. Her shoulders visibly dropped. She then slumped back down into the chair. The look of defeat was complete. If she had looked defeated to Chi before, the depth of it now seemed even greater. The three men glanced around at each other. The look on each of their faces conveyed that they wished they could do something more, anything.

Chi squatted down in front of her. She continued staring at the floor. "You can't pay for this can you, can you?" he said quietly. She shook her head. "You don't have a place to stay either." Again she shook her head only slightly. Chi nodded slowly and looked down at the floor, too. He then looked up at Jessie and Pete, stood, walked out of the waiting room and signaled them to follow him.

"She doesn't have any money. You know that, right?" Both Pete and Jessie nodded.

"We can get her to the women's shelter in Paw Paw," Pete reminded them.

"That's the best option," Chi agreed. "But for some reason, she doesn't want to go there. We can offer again, but if she refuses, then there isn't much we can do. I could buy the part for her but even if I did how far do you think she'd get?"

"A couple more hours I would think," replied Jessie. "But then what?"

"Exactly," Pete agreed.

"Look, here's what I'm going to do," Chi said. "I'm going to offer, again, to take her to the women's shelter. If she refuses, then I'm going to offer to let her stay at my place until her car is fixed."

"Whoa!" Pete was holding his hand palm out towards Chi. "As your friend, I'd have to advise against that. You've no idea what you're getting yourself into."

"Then what? You think we should just leave her out here? I can't do that. Not in her condition. I don't even think she had eaten anything in a couple of days until I bought her McDonald's. No. That's what I'm going to do. Hopefully, she accepts the offer to go to the shelter. Then one of us can take her over there."

Pete was shaking his head, "Don't do that. This has bad mojo written all over it."

Chi nodded, "I know. But it's the right thing." He stepped past Pete and Jessie back into the waiting room. Carrie hadn't moved and was still staring at the floor. Her eyes seemed to droop beneath the swelling. Pete and Jessie followed Chi and watched.

"Carrie," Chi began. "Let me take you to the women's shelter in Paw Paw. They can put you up until we can get your car fixed."

She looked him square in the face. "No." Her voice carried weight behind it.

"OK. Then I'll tell you what. If you like, you can stay at my place tonight. I've got a spare room that you can stay in and get cleaned up. Would that be OK?"

"No," she said softly.

Chi took on a firmer tone, "That's not an option. I will not have you sleeping on the street. Do you understand me? You need a place to stay for the night, and I've got a room for you. I'm not going to argue with you. The other choice is Pete will have a uniformed officer come here and arrest you. Is that what you want?" He lied about the uniformed officer. That wasn't an option, and he knew it. He hoped she would not call his bluff.

She looked up at him again. Tears were welling up in her eyes. "OK," she said weakly, almost inaudibly.

"That's 'OK' for going with me or 'OK' for going to the women's shelter?"

"Going with you." She stood but kept her head down staring at the floor. "Can I get my stuff out of my car?"

The three of them transferred all of her belongings into Chi's truck bed, and then Chi helped her back into the cab. As Chi was closing the door, Pete met him and spoke quietly to him. "Again, I have to advise you not to do this."

"Pete, is there really a choice here?"

"There's always a choice."

"What's the choice, Pete?" Chi was looking at Pete with a stern intensity.

Pete took a deep breath and let it out. He looked around as if searching for a better answer. As he watched Jessie lock the garage, he said, "OK, but please be careful. You have no idea what you're getting into."

"Prayers, Pete. Lots of prayers." Pete nodded and walked back to his car. Just before climbing in he asked, "Do you want me to follow you home and help bring her stuff in?"

"I think I'm OK. Thanks." With that, he climbed into the cab and headed home.

Chapter 2

Carrie stared forward as Chi drove them to his home just outside of town. To Chi, she appeared to be living in a fog. She was with him in body, but her mind had checked out. Neither one spoke as he drove but he would glance over at her every once in a while to be sure she was OK. Driving across the expressway overpass, she turned and pressed both hands against the window and tried to look as far southward along the expressway as possible. She then looked over at Chi. Chi gave her a kind smile as she brushed her hair from her face and sat back against the seat while still turned towards him.

Chi had turned back to face the road, but Carrie remained facing him, looking at him with passive eyes. Her stare was uncomfortable. He would look back and forth from the road and then to Carrie. She seemed to be trying to read him in some way, trying to understand him. She then took her eyes off his face and looked over the rest of his body. She completed her examination just as he turned into his subdivision.

Carrie sat up straighter as she saw the homes within the neighborhood, with their well-watered yards and neatly trimmed landscapes. To Chi, she seemed amazed at what she saw as she took in the view of the neighborhood. He slowed his truck to fifteen miles per hour and watched her as she put her hand on the passenger side window, turned and faced outward. She looked back at him wide-eyed and seemingly confused. He returned a smile. This was a nice subdivision and one of the newer ones, but it wasn't the most expensive in the area, and to Chi, it certainly did not warrant the type of reaction that Carrie was having at the moment.

He turned left at the next road and slowed to a stop to wait as a couple of children moved out of the street where they had been kicking a soccer ball around. They exchanged waves as they drove past. As he pulled around a curve Chi pointed to a house at the end of the cul-de-sac. "That's mine," he said as he began to reach up over her head for the garage door opener clipped to her visor. Carrie flinched causing Chi to pause. Seeing that he was only reaching for the door opener, she relaxed again, and Chi completed his reach and pressed the button.

The garage door opened. He pulled in slowly to the center of the garage and parked. Carrie could see a motorcycle parked in one corner, a snow blower and shelving packed with various items. He reached for the garage door opener again, more slowly this time. Carrie watched, moving only her eyes as he pushed the button causing the garage door to close behind them.

"OK, here we are," he said looking at her. She returned his look but didn't make any attempt to get out of the truck. "We'll take your gear in and stow it in the guest bedroom. There is a bathroom and shower there you can use to get cleaned up if you want. Then if you're interested, I can try to make you a more proper dinner if you're still hungry."

"OK," she said softly. Chi could not determine what the tone of her voice conveyed this time. It wasn't fear. It wasn't excitement or even gratitude.

Chi opened his door first and then as if given permission, Carrie opened hers and climbed slowly out. She still held the water bottle that Chi had given her, but she didn't appear conscious of it. As Chi stepped over to the interior door of the house and unlocked it, she looked into the bed of the truck where her belongings had been put. When it was in her car, it looked like there had been so much more, but in this truck bed, it seems to be so little. It felt to Carrie as if her life had now boiled down to just a handful of clothes and nick-knacks. She looked back at Chi who was standing on the step to the door watching her. He nodded at her, stepped down and over to where she was standing, reached in and pulled out a garbage bag full of clothes. He handed her a smaller one, pulled out a second bag and began leading her into the house.

As she stepped in, she stopped at the door. She stared wide-eyed at the most beautiful kitchen she had ever seen. It had what she thought looked like white marble counter tops and white cabinetry. There was an island with a stainless steel sink that matched all of the appliances. A couple of bar stools stood on one side of the island where someone could eat and sit comfortably if they chose. For the most part, the counters were bare except for a coffee maker and a knife rack. To Carrie, everything seemed too clean, too shiny, and too new.

Chi turned to see if she was following him and saw that she had stopped at the door. "We're this way," he told her. Her attention returned, and she followed him. He stepped to a closed door and slid it sideways. The door tucked into the wall. Carpeted stairs led downward, and he was halfway down before Carrie reluctantly began to follow. The stairs turned sharply to the right at a landing and then down another four steps opening up into a large open area.

Carrie stopped at the landing to look around as Chi walked ahead. On one side there was a counter with a small sink and a small refrigerator. Near it was a large window covered with wooden blinds. Opposite of that, against the wall, was a large flat screen TV with a sound system the likes of which Carrie had never seen before. Facing the TV were two, leather easy chairs, a sofa and matching end tables between them. At the far end of the room was a door that she assumed to be a guest room. It appeared that Chi was leading her there. Next to it was an open door to a bathroom. On the other side of the open area, near where she was standing was another closed door. She assumed this was a second guest room. The entire lower level was bigger than her apartment, she thought. It was like a second house under the main floor.

Chi opened the door to the bedroom, turned on the light and stepped in. Carrie followed behind and glanced around. On the far side of the room was a large window with Venetian blinds. The wall to the left had two smaller windows near the ceiling with blue fabric curtains that were closed. The bed was queen size with a large wooden frame and a large headboard. There were no sheets or blankets on it. There was a nightstand on either side with matching lamps. Near the window, there was another flat screen TV, not as large as the one in the outer room but still much bigger than the one she left behind. Next to it was a large armoire with two large doors and two drawers underneath. Near the bedroom door was a large closet and a rocking chair with a reading lamp. This *guestroom* was almost as large as her apartment, she thought to herself again.

Chi set her bags down next to the closet and turned to look at her standing in the doorway. She looked stunned and out of place. "I'll let you make up the bed while I bring the rest of your gear down. You'll find sheets, blankets and pillows there in the armoire." She nodded at him and stepped in as he walked past her to go upstairs for another load.

Carrie set her bag down next to the ones that Chi had brought down and looked around some more. This felt unreal. She put her hand on the bed and swept it slowly across it, palm down.

Opening the armoire she pulled out a bottom sheet from the shelf and carried it to the bed. She began stretching it out but found her right hand wasn't cooperating the way she needed it to. The throbbing pain made it difficult even to unfold it. She finally had it stretched out to the point that she could fit the corners around the mattress, but her attempts at lifting the corner and fitting the sheet around it were failing. Her hand was too weak to either lift the corner up or to pull the sheet around it. She pulled it down half way and stood back. That would have to do. Stepping to the next corner of the bed, she saw Chi standing in the doorway with another load. He had been watching her.

She looked at the corner where she tried to fit the sheet and then back at Chi. "I'm sorry. I can't."

Chi stepped in and placed his load next to the rest of her belongings. "No need to apologize. I understand." He stepped up to the bed and quickly and easily fit the sheet around all four corners. He then placed the top sheet on and tucked it in. It was swiftly and expertly done. The sheets looked impressively tight as they stretched across the bed. Next, he put two blankets on, tucked them in and topped it off with two pillows.

"All done," he said.

"Thank you," she replied meekly. Chi had made the bed so quickly, and with such precision, she could not help but somehow be impressed.

"Would you like to put your gear in the closet while I bring the last load down?"

"Yes. Thank you."

"OK. I'll be back in a minute. Just one more load."

She opened the closet and looked inside as Chi walked away. There were places to hang clothes, drawers to put things in and shelves to stack things on. She brought one of her bags over to the closet and set it on the floor. Her hand hurt as she tried to untie the knot she had in the bag but she willed herself through the pain. She pulled the clothes out, put them in a drawer and then set the empty plastic bag aside. She was halfway through the second bag when Chi returned with two stacked boxes and a pile of clothes on top still on the hangers. Then entire pile came up to his chin.

"That's the last of it." He set the pile down next to the closet.

"Thank you," she replied quietly, as she looked down.

Chi took the clothes on the hangers and hung them on a rod. "Can I help you with the rest of this?" he asked.

"No. I'm fine," she said. "But I think I'll leave the rest of this for later if that's OK with you."

He looked around. Only a small portion of Carrie's gear had but put away, but he could see she was hurting. "How about you come upstairs with me and let me get you some Ibuprofen?"

She looked up at him and clenched her hand opened and closed twice. She could use something for the pain. "OK."

She followed him back upstairs and took a seat on one of the bar stools. Chi reached up into one of the cupboards and pulled down a large bottle of Ibuprofen and opened it. "How many do you take?" She looked at him as if she did not understand the question. "You look like you're hurting, so I'm going to prescribe four." He shook four tablets out from the bottle and handed it to her. He then pulled a glass from another cupboard, filled it halfway with water and handed it to her. She took the pills and washed them down. The water in the glass magnified the trembling in her hand.

He leaned back against the counter looking at her. "Would you happen to still be hungry?"

"A little, I guess," she replied quietly.

"I need to eat something too. I was going to make up a bit of chicken and rice. Pretty simple but I wasn't expecting company."

"That would be nice. Thank you."

He pulled a chicken breast from the refrigerator and set it on the counter. He measured out water, put a couple of chicken bouillon cubes in it and put it in the microwave to boil.

Carrie watched him as he cooked. She took notice of him for the first time. He stood about six foot two she guessed and was quite muscular. His back was to her as he made dinner and it had a "V" shape to it, broad at the shoulder and narrow at the hips. His arms were muscular but not in the way she had seen body builder's arms. He was wearing a T-shirt and the sleeves seemed to want to curl up above his biceps. His hair was cut very short in a crew cut, and he reminded her of what she thought someone in the military might look like. He certainly looked athletic, she thought. She tried to guess his age and decided he must be about thirty.

Chi cut the chicken into strips, put it in a pan along with a bit of olive oil and began cooking the chicken. He measured out instant Rice, placed it in a medium sized bowl and waited for the water. Once the water came to a boil, he poured it into the rice, stirred it and then covered it. When the chicken was finished cooking, he uncovered the rice, stirred it a couple of times, diced the chicken strips into smaller pieces, mixed it into the rice and then covered it again.

He set a couple of plates at the dining room table along with forks. "Would you like something other than water to drink? I've got Coke, Sprite, Dr. Pepper, Diet Coke."

"Beer?"

"No. Sorry. That I don't have." Chi thought he saw her shoulders drop slightly.

"I'll have a Diet Coke, please," she said meekly.

He pulled the soda from the refrigerator, poured it into a glass and set it on the table. He poured himself a glass of water. Bringing the bowl of rice and chicken to the table, he said, "All set. Let's eat."

She sat down at the plate he had placed across from him and waited for him to sit. As he set down, he held both hands across the table as if he were expecting her to take them and said, "I'll say grace." She looked at him and hesitated. He waited. Finally, she hesitantly took both of his hands. He bowed his head and said grace. It ended with 'In Jesus's name, amen.' She watched this unfold as if it were surreal, a dream.

He released her hands and picked up the bowl of chicken and rice. "Hold out your plate, and I'll dish it out." She held out her plate unsteadily with her left hand as he dished it out.

"Thank you," she said when enough was on her plate. He then filled his own plate and began to eat.

She ate slowly while watching him. The prayer he said over dinner seemed odd to her. She could not get it out of her mind. It seemed so natural to him as if he thought everyone in the world did the exact, same thing. Her father used to say grace. It always seemed long, drawn out and complicated. But Chi's prayer was simple. It seemed almost quaint and childlike.

"How's the chicken and rice?" he asked.

"Good. I like it. Thank you for making it."

"I'm not much of a cook. What about you?"

"Pizza. I can cook frozen pizza," she said. Chi saw her try to smile through swollen lips. It looked painful.

"I can't say I eat much pizza. Once in awhile. Just not very often."

There was a moment of silence as neither knew what to say. Finally, Carrie broke the silence, "I like your house."

"Thank you. I bought it a year ago when I moved back to South Haven."

"Where'd you move from?"

"Virginia."

"What did you do in Virginia?"

"Just stuff. So where were you driving to today?"

"North."

He looked at her to read her expression, but she looked away. "You really had no plan, did you? You were just running from whoever it was that did this to you. Will you tell me what happened?"

"It's none of your business."

"You're right. I know. But I also know that anytime I see someone get hurt like you are I want to step in and help."

She waited a moment then quietly said, "You can't help."

He regretted bringing the topic up and he was now searching for something else to talk about. She let him off the hook and changed the subject for him. "What city did you say we're in?" she asked adding confidence to her voice.

"South Haven. Right on the lake shore."

"What's in South Haven?"

"Beaches, lighthouse, state park, shops. Normal stuff I guess."

"So why did you move here?"

"I grew up here. I have family here. My Mom lives here."

"You got brothers and sisters?"

"I have a sister. She's in the Navy, married and living in Florida. What about you? Do you have brothers and sisters?"

"No. I'm an only child."

"Did you grow up in Chicago?"

"No. I grew up in Illinois. Small town west of Chicago. Nothing special."

"What took you to Chicago?" The question seemed to make Carrie uncomfortable. She fidgeted slightly in her chair.

"I guess I wanted to get out of the small town, to be free of small town attitudes and small town minds."

"What does that mean?" Chi asked her.

"I don't know. It's not the same now. I don't know what it means." She looked away. "What time is it?" she asked.

Chi looked over at the clock on the microwave. "About 8:30."

She looked out the window at the fading light. "7:30 Chicago time," she said flatly. "How'd it get to be so late already?"

"Time flies when you're having fun I guess."

"We're having fun?" she asked quietly as she continued looking out the window. To Chi, it looked as if she were waiting for something to happen.

Chi didn't respond but followed her gaze out the window.

"Are there any jobs here in South Haven?" she asked.

"I really don't know."

She took a deep breath and blew it out slowly puffing out her cheeks. She looked around the room at the pictures on the wall. Her eyes fixated on a picture of Chi and a woman. Both were smiling broadly.

"Who's that?" she asked pointing to the picture.

"That's my fiancé, Susan."

"Where's she at?"

"Dallas this week for work. She'll be back Wednesday."

"Does she live here with you?"

"No. She lives with her parents in town."

Carrie nodded. Small town attitudes, she thought. "So when you getting married?"

"June."

"Nice... June... Nice."

They sat there moments more in silence as Carrie stared out the window with her shoulders slumped. She looked as if her mind was a million miles away. "Why don't you go sit on the couch while I clean off the table," Chi said as he pointed to the sofa in the living room. Carrie stood slowly, pushed her chair in, walked over and sat down as Chi began clearing the dinner plates away.

She looked around the room. There were more pictures in here. One was of a woman in a Navy uniform that she assumed was his sister and then another with the same woman in a wedding dress along with a man in a tuxedo. There was a picture of Chi with his arm around an older woman in front of someplace that looked like a school and another prominent picture of Chi's fiancé.

She noticed there wasn't a TV in this room. It seemed odd to her that there would not be a TV in the living room. There was a small two shelf bookcase, and she could see several paperback books lined up neatly. On top of the bookcase was a Bible and a couple of other books. She came to the conclusion that this must be the reading room. That's why there wasn't a TV in here. It was reserved for reading.

'Rich people could do that.' The thought popped into her head unexpectedly. Chi certainly must be rich. He lived in a rich neighborhood with rich houses. She wondered what he did, where he got his money.

She looked around the room some more. On the end table next to her a paperback book caught her attention. She picked it up and looked it over. It was new and did not look like it had been cracked open yet. She read the title, 'Love's Obsession.' She nearly laughed out loud. This book was a romance novel. The picture on the cover was of a bare-chested muscular man kissing a woman wearing a long flowing dress that appeared to be blowing in the wind. She looked back over at the bookcase and suddenly realized that there must be a dozen romance novels on the top shelf all lined up together.

She had visions of Chi sitting in this very room reading romance novel after romance novel. The thought struck her funny, Chi curled up on the sofa with a tiny teacup in one hand and a romance novel in the other. She realized that the books probably belonged to his fiancé. Still, she enjoyed that momentary vision of this big, muscular, athletic looking man that drove a big macho truck and owned a motorcycle sitting at home at night alone reading romance novels. It just seemed all too absurd to her.

Chi had finished clearing the dishes away and wiped everything down. He stepped into the living room and sat down across the room from Carrie. "Is there anything you need?"

"I don't think so."

"OK. Let me know if you do. If you get hungry or anything at night feel free to help yourself to anything you need. I'll leave the Ibuprofen out where you can see it or if you want, take it downstairs with you."

"Thank you."

"You look like you're feeling a little better."

"I am, I guess." She flexed her hand. "Yeah. It's a little better."

Her phone rang, and she reflexively and quickly pulled it out of her back pocket. Her eyes widened as she stared at it. Panic began to set in, and it suddenly felt hard to breathe. A second ring and she took a slight gasp for air, and her eyes widened still more. A third ring and her right hand began to move slowly as if she no longer controlled it, toward the answer button.

The phone was suddenly pulled from her hand, and she saw Chi standing directly in front of her. She looked up at him realizing how close she came to answering the call. He was checking the name, Kevin, and then he silenced the ring.

"I'll keep this if you don't mind," Chi said as he tucked the phone into his front left pants pocket. She looked away from him. He didn't look angry with her but more like he was taking control. "Tomorrow we can change your number or get a new phone or something. But you're not keeping this number."

She nodded. It was 9:15. 8:15 Chicago time. Kevin would have just begun to understand that she was gone. He would have found that she had moved out and taken everything she owned with her. She wasn't sure if he'd be flying off in a rage, sitting down and crying or bragging to his friends. All of that was possible.

Chapter 3

Kevin first realized something was wrong when he noticed that Carrie's car wasn't parked in its usual space. She knew he wanted her home when he came home from work, he thought to himself. He didn't feel like starting the night out annoyed at her already.

He walked up to his third-floor apartment carrying two six-packs of bottled beer and swore under his breath wondering where she was. He let himself in and looked around. Something more was amiss. He wasn't sure what it was, but he could feel it. As he sat the beer down on the kitchen table, he called out for her, but there was no answer. He stood in the doorway of the bedroom. Her pillow was gone. He looked the room over. Anything that Carrie called hers was now missing. Small bits of trash were scattered around. His first thought was that she should have cleaned the room before she left.

His jaw clenched as he realized what was going on. He opened the door of the closet. There was a gap on the rod where her clothes once hung. He stood staring into the empty side of the closet. His muscles tensed, and his teeth made a popping sound as he ground them together. He could feel his anger slowly rising.

He closed her side of the closet and opened his. Pulling a wooden box from the shelf he opened the lid, verified that his bag of weed was still there, closed it and put it back from where he'd taken it. She knew better than to take that, he thought.

Kevin stepped out of the bedroom and stood at the kitchen table. He cracked open a beer and drank deeply from it as he looked around the apartment to see what else might be missing.

"She'll be back," he said aloud. He thought about where she might have gone and almost smiled at the thought that there wasn't any place that she could hide that he could not find her. He knew all her friends; he knew where her parents lived, and he knew all the places she might hang out. He even had connections at the women's shelter she was likely to go to again. She had no place to run.

He finished the beer quickly and opened another. Putting one of the six packs in the refrigerator, he took the other one and sat with it beside him on the sofa. He drank half of the second beer in four swallows and stared at the bottle as he lifted it up, looking through the brown glass towards the window. His breathing was becoming short and shallow as he alternated between clenching his teeth and relaxing his jaw.

With his free hand, he pulled out his cell phone from his shirt pocket, unlocked it, found her name in the contacts and dialed her number. One ring. Two rings. Three rings. No answer. He continued to let it ring until it went to her voicemail and then hung up his phone. He did not like being ignored. That made him angry, he thought to himself. He did not like it when she made him angry.

He sent her a text message, "Where are you?" Staring at the phone, he waited, finished his second beer and opened another.

He waited some more. He could feel his entire body tense as he lifted the bottle, swallowed, set it on his thigh and repeated the process until the beer was finished. Tossing the empty bottle onto the carpet, he opened another, stood and began pacing back and forth. His anger was rising. He then sent her another text: "Don't ignore me. Where are you?"

He was halfway through the third beer when he concluded that no answer was coming. He stood and stared out of the balcony door. Every muscle in his body tensed as the anger rose within him. He ground his teeth heavily then swore loudly. The anger swelled up in him until it finally burst out in a blind rage as he threw the bottle against the far wall. The bottle smashed against the wall, scattering foam and glass around the floor. He paced angrily back and forth from the balcony door to the kitchen table bursting out in strings of screaming profanity every few laps. Finally, stopping in the middle of the living room he stretched both arms outward and down to his sides and clenched his fist. He looked up toward the ceiling and screamed one long extended profane curse. His face turned bright red as the veins in his neck and forehead stood out as if ready to burst. He held that position for several moments then slowly relaxed. He lowered his head and looked around the room with angry eyes that shifted from side to side. Nearly out of breath he calmed himself further, sat down again and opened another beer.

Ralph Nelson Willett

Chapter 4

Waking Saturday morning, Carrie rolled over in bed and looked at the clock on the nightstand. 9:27. "8:27 Chicago time," she said out loud to herself. She lay without moving several moments and then pulled herself upright on the edge of the bed. She still felt stiff and sore. She tested the tenderness of her lips with her finger. Some of the swelling had gone down, but it felt strange, almost numb. After checking around the rest of her face, she looked at her right hand as she carefully flexed it. It felt a little better this morning. Its swelling had also reduced. Everything was still tender, but at least she felt better than yesterday.

She hunted around for a change of clothing and her hair dryer and headed into the bathroom for a shower. It was difficult for her to hold the brush as she used the blow dryer on her hair but she still managed after pausing several times to let the throbbing in her wrist pass. Looking at her face in the mirror, she could see that the swelling in her lips had almost gone away. Her eye looked better, but the bruising would take a while to fade. Touching her cheek just under her left eye, she tested it's tenderness as she pushed into it. She thought it would take a couple of days before the swelling went away completely but the bruises would take much longer. Makeup would help, but she wasn't sure if she would have enough to use for several days.

She made her way upstairs and stood at the top step and listened for Chi. He stepped into view out of a room adjacent to the living room, holding a mug of coffee.

"Good morning," he said. "You hungry? Can I make you some scrambled eggs?"

"Yes, please," she answered quietly. "That sounds nice."

"How about some coffee?"

"Yes, thank you."

She followed him into the kitchen and pulled up a stool and sat at the island. He poured her a mug of coffee and handed it to her. "Milk or sugar?"

"No, thank you."

He pulled eggs out of the refrigerator and scrambled them in a pan on the stove, mixing in cheese and pepper. He placed it on a plate and served it to her.

"Thank you," she said.

He pulled out a large container of whey protein. Mixing a scoop into a glass of milk, he drank it as he leaned back against the counter watching her eat.

"How'd you sleep last night?" he asked.

"Good. All the way through the night, actually."

"Well, you're looking better this morning."

She almost chuckled at the thought. "Thanks."

She finished her eggs and took a sip of coffee. "Do you think they can fix my car today?"

"I don't know." He shrugged. "But I've got a question for you."

He waited for her to look up at him then continued, "Can you pay for the work that needs to be done?"

Carrie looked down and stared at her empty plate. She did not have the money, having escaped with a total of sixty-three dollars. "Can I borrow some money?" she asked. She felt no need to look up at him and kept her eyes looking down at her plate.

Chi set the empty glass down and picked up his coffee mug again. He looked at her and shook his head ever so slightly side to side. She glanced up without moving her head to see the movement, her shoulders visibly slumped, and she resumed staring at her plate.

"Let me ask you something, and I want you to be completely honest with me," Chi said. "Can you do that?"

"I don't know," she said in a hoarse whisper.

"You need to be straight with me, tell me the truth. Will you do that?" Chi asked her.

"OK."

"How much money do you have access to?"

"Sixty-three dollars," Carrie replied.

"How far do you think that will take you?"

"I don't know."

"You told me you were going north. North where?"

"I don't know."

"So you have sixty-three dollars and no idea where you're going. Do you know anyone in Michigan?"

"No."

"So, Carrie, if I paid to have your car fixed and you headed north..." He paused and waited for her to glance up at him again. "then what?"

She had no plan beyond going north. She shook her head but didn't say anything. Chi nodded his understanding. "Don't you think it's better that you stay here awhile? Let's get you healed and back on your feet before you make any decisions on what you're going to do. You need a real plan. Just heading north isn't a plan."

She looked up at him, "Are you going to let me stay here?"

"For a while at least."

She smiled at him through her broken lips. "Thank you. But why? Why would you do that?"

He smiled back. "For now let's just say that I like coming to the rescue of damsels in distress." He took a big sip of coffee and continued, "There will be some house rules, though, that you'll need to follow while you're here."

Panic flashed through her eyes. "I'm not going to sleep with you," she said forcefully.

"That's not what I'm talking about." Chi's voice began to take on a sternness. "I'm talking about things like understanding that this is my home and that you are my guest. As my guest, you will conduct yourself that way. Is that understood?" He sounded like someone who was used to being in charge.

She relaxed. "OK."

"And I'd expect you to attend church with us on Sunday."

"Who's us?"

"My mother, my fiancé and me. We'll be attending LifeBridge."

She looked away and stared vacantly out of the patio doors. "I don't think I belong in church," she said quietly.

"That doesn't matter to me. But that is one of the stipulations of staying here."

"OK," she replied meekly.

"Besides, I actually think you'll like my church." He took the edge out of his voice. He was used to being in command and unquestioned. Sometimes he came off in a way he didn't intend to. He cleared the dishes and put them in the dishwasher. "Is there anything you need?"

"No, thank you."

"I need to go back in my office and do a little more work. You can make yourself at home." He poured himself another cup of coffee and walked into the side room he had come out of earlier closing the door behind him.

Carrie sat there a moment feeling awkward. Her host suddenly left her alone sitting at the kitchen island. She did not know what she should do next. Should she stay here on her stool? Should she go back to her room and stay? Finally, she stood, refilled her coffee cup, walked into the living room and sat on the sofa. She didn't know what was in store for her now. Her entire life seemed to be under the control of a complete stranger, this man she knew nothing about. He was correct in thinking that she had nowhere else to go. She had no choice but to do what he told her to do.

The romance paperback on the end table caught her eye again, "Love's Obsession" by Rachael Wallace. She picked it up, held it in her hand and looked it over, front and back. She had only read romance books a couple of times in her life. Just something to pass the time when she was bored. Opening the cover she flipped to the beginning and thought to herself, "I'm stuck here for a while" and she began to read.

~~~~

Chi's phone rang. He looked away from his computer and checked the caller ID. It was Pete. He put on his headset and answered it.

"Hey, Pete."

"Hi, Chi. Checking in. How'd it go last night?"

"Fine. She looks a lot better this morning."

"I've got to tell you something."

"OK," Chi felt a tension in Pete's voice.

"Rosie had a dream about you last night. She said that a bunch of guys were attacking you trying to kill you."

"OK. That's not a good thing. I'm not surprised, though. I think everyone is a bit tense after seeing Carrie like this."

"Chi," Pete hesitated. "I didn't tell Rosie what happened yesterday."

There was silence on the phone as Pete let Chi process this new information.

Pete continued, "Chi, you've got your permit. I think you should start carrying again."

Chi cleared his throat. "Pete..."

"I know. I understand. But you've got to know something, too. You're one of the good guys. It's not just you that may need protecting. It's anyone around you. You need to start carrying again."

"Let me think about it, OK?"

"Look, something happened yesterday that I don't think we understand yet and you're up to your eyebrows in it. If Rosie had a dream like that about me I'd take it as a warning and I'd have my weapon strapped on and one in the chamber."

"I know. I get it. I'll give it some thought. But I'll tell you what, send out an email to our life group. Be discrete. You don't have to go into all the details. I'm not sure what to tell them, but you'll figure it out and ask them to pray."

"Alright, Chi," Pete replied. "I've got a bad feeling about all this, and Rosie's dream doesn't make me feel any better."

"I know. But what else would you expect me to do?"

"I expect you to take care of yourself!" Pete had nearly interrupted him. He was speaking rapidly. Exasperation was coming through in his voice. "I expect that you'll be smart. I expect you to be safe. I expect that if you know anything at all that the police can take care of that you'll call me."

"OK, Pete. I get it. If I find something that can be addressed by the police, I'll give you a call."

"OK, Chi." Pete's voice began to calm. "I'm worried about you. This doesn't feel right."

"I'll be safe, Pete."

"You better, you massive jerk."

"Thanks, Pete. Love you, too," Chi responded.

"Alright. Call me if there's anything new at all, OK?"

"No problem. I'll call."

Chapter 5

Chi's front door opened unexpectedly, and Carrie stood to her feet desperately looking for someplace to run. She backed up close to the far wall and put her hands behind her on the window. Wide eyed she watched as a woman walked in holding a large plastic bag. The woman looked up and stopped just inside the door as she saw Carrie. She crouched slightly, muscles taut, face intense, looking as if she were about to attack. Her eyes were piercing. "Who are you?" the woman demanded.

Chi quickly came out of the side room and assessed the situation. Carrie looked terrified. She looked at Chi with eyes that appeared to be pleading. "Hi, Mom," he said as he faced his mother.

"Who's this?" the woman demanded without taking her eyes off of her.

"Come on in," Chi told her. The woman relaxed the tension in her body as she stepped in. He took the bag from her. "What's this?" he asked.

"I thought we'd have lunch," she replied as she glared at the woman standing at the far wall window.

Chi looked in the bag. It was take-out from a local Chinese restaurant. He took smaller packages out from the bag and set them on the island counter top. "Mom, this is Carrie. Carrie this is my mom, Margret," he said without looking at either of them.

Margret visibly relaxed. She nodded slightly and stepped over to Carrie holding out her hand to shake Carrie's. Carrie moved slowly and took her hand. Margret shook her hand with a squeeze. Carrie grimaced in pain and pulled her hand back.

"What happened to you?" asked Margret as she looked Carrie over.

Chi intervened. "Carrie had a little car trouble coming into town yesterday. She's going to be staying with me for a couple of days." Margret looked over at Chi. Carrie could not tell by her expression if she approved or disapproved. Margret nodded.

Margret stepped away into the kitchen. Chi and Carrie looked at each other as he gave her a slight nod. Carrie relaxed and sat back down on the sofa warily watching Margret as she pulled out plates and silverware, setting the table. Carrie looked at the clock. It was almost one o'clock. She hadn't realized how much time had passed since she had eaten breakfast.

Margret split up the food three ways on the plates and then poured three glasses of water. "Alright, let's eat."

Carrie looked over at Chi as if asking for permission. Chi nodded his head toward the table, and all three sat down. Margret held out her hands in the same way that Chi had the night before, one toward Chi and one toward Carrie. Chi took one hand and then held the other one out for Carrie. Carrie glanced between the two of them. They both waited patiently looking at her. She slowly reached up and gently took both their hands.

"Chi?" Margret said as she bowed her head. Chi bowed his head and said grace as Carrie observed the two of them.

"Dig in," Margret ordered.

Chi gave Carrie a faint smile as he began to eat. Carrie ate slowly. She wasn't hungry but felt compelled to eat as if Chi and Margret gave her no choice.

"So, Carrie," started Margret as she took another bite. "What happened?" She looked up at Carrie with a face not as intense as when she first saw her but still quite serious.

Carrie looked over at Chi to see if he was going to intervene. He wasn't. He waited for her answer also. "I got beat up," she answered.

"Boyfriend or husband?" asked Margret.

"Boyfriend."

"Did he kick you out or did you leave?"

"I left."

"Did he know you were leaving when you left?"

"No."

"Is he going to try and find you."

"I don't know."

"What do you know?'

Carrie hung her head. The questions came fast and direct. She was feeling interrogated but helpless to avoid answering. There was a sense of authority about Margret that compelled her to respond but what did she know that she could tell her? She knew he'd be angry that she had left. She did not know, though, if he'd be happy she was finally gone or if he would try to find her and bring her back. There was a lot she didn't know. "Not much," she finally said.

Chi broke in, "Her car broke down on Blue Star Highway. It's in Jess's shop now. Until she can get her car fixed, she's staying with me."

Margret looked him squarely in the face, "And how long is that going to be?"

"Until I say otherwise," he responded looking her square in the face. The two of them held each other's stare for a moment.

Margret stood up, "Excuse us, Carrie. My son and I need to have a private discussion outside."

Carrie looked over at Chi who stood up. His eyebrows were furrowed. She instantly worried about what was to happen to her next. Was she going to be kicked out of Chi's house and onto the street? Would she be allowed to stay? She watched as the two of them stepped out on the deck closing the patio door behind them. She could see them discussing her through the patio doors. Margret was several inches shorter than Chi, but she seemed equal to him in every other way. Her hands gestured towards him. He was nodding and speaking, leaning in towards her, but kept his hands tucked in his front pockets. His facial expression led Carrie to believe this was an argument between equals. They both appeared intense, nearly to the point of appearing angry with each other.

Finally, they both stopped and looked in through the door at Carrie. She saw them both visibly relax. Chi nodded, turned to his mother and said something to her. Margret nodded back at him. They both stepped inside and returned to the table.

Margret spoke first. She looked at Carrie with the same intensity that she saw when she was talking to Chi outside. "Carrie, you can't stay here."

Carrie's heart sank. She was being kicked out. She had no idea where she was going to go. "Why?" she asked quietly. For the first time, tears began to well up in her eyes.

"Because it's not proper. You both have reputations you have to protect."

"What? I don't understand." Her voice nearly cracked.

"You're moving in with me. You'll take Chi's old room for now."

She felt instantly conflicted. She felt both panic and relief as she realized she wasn't being kicked out onto the street but she did not know this woman either. Again she felt that her life was no longer under her control. "I can leave," Carrie told Margret. "You don't need to do that."

"No," Margret responded with authority. "You'll stay with me for a while. We'll have Chi bring your stuff over in his truck, and we'll move you in. There are some house rules though."

House rules again, thought Carrie.

"You'll attend church with me."

"OK," she replied meekly.

"You won't have any men over."

"OK."

"And you have to remember that it's my house and you're my guest. You'll need to act that way. No smoking or drugs."

Carrie remembered Chi using almost those exacts same words. "OK," she repeated quietly.

"But, consider it as part of your room and board that you are to help with dishes and house cleaning."

"OK." She was looking down at her plate resigning herself to whatever came next.

"One more thing, when you're well enough, you'll start looking for a job. After you get settled into a job, then we start looking for a place of your own. Agreed?"

Carrie looked up into Margret's face. It had softened as she was speaking to Carrie. The intense look had turned to one of compassion. Carrie looked between Margret and Chi. They both held the same look. She relaxed and wiped her eyes. Somehow this felt right, as if this were the way things should be. "OK. I can do that."

~~~~

Chi moved Carrie's belongings into his old bedroom at his mother's house. It still looked like a guy's room, but that was going to have to do for now. Margret had kept the room available for any guests she may have over, but those were few and far between. Carrie looked the room over. It was not even close to being as large as the one in Chi's house, but it was still nice. It was an older home in town and was kept up well. There was a lot of dark molding around all the rooms, and it had a feel of being lived in by generations of loving families.

Margret joined them in the room as Chi hung clothes in the closet. Carrie emptied trash bags full of clothes into dresser drawers. "How's it going?" she asked.

"Fine," Carrie replied. "Thank you for letting me stay with you."

"You're welcome. I'm glad I can help. Once we can kick Chi out of here, I'll show you around the rest of the place."

"Thank you."

"Do I need to leave now?" asked Chi.

"Finish what you're doing."

"I've got no problem leaving now," he teased back.

"Finish," insisted his mother.

Chi grinned at her and hung the rest of the clothes on the bar in the closet. "OK. Done. Anything else before I go?"

"No. That's it. We're good. You're dismissed, sailor."

"OK," Chi said. "I'll check in on you tonight sometime."

"Alright. Talk to you then," she replied.

Chi left the room and turned the corner away from view. "Wait!" Carrie stepped quickly out of the room to catch up with Chi who turned to face her. She stopped in front of him looking up into his face. "I just wanted to say thank you."

Chi gave her a crooked smile. It seemed only one side of his mouth was actually smiling. "You're welcome."

Carrie suddenly felt awkward, not knowing what she should do next, instinct took over and she rushed in and hugged him, burying her head into his chest. Chi also felt awkward at the sudden gesture but returned her hug, almost reluctantly. They held the embrace only a moment and then Carrie released him. "Thank you," she said again. She turned and walked back into the room with Margret as Chi watched.

~~~~

Margret showed Carrie around the house. There were three bedrooms. One that had been turned into a sewing room, the master bedroom, and Chi's old room. The house had a formal dining area as well as a kitchen with a small kitchen table. The front door opened into the family room. It had a large flat screen TV, a sofa, and a rocker recliner. On the wall hung several pictures. Margret pointed out several to Carrie.

"This is the picture of Chi when he first went into the Navy, just out of college," she said as she touched one of the pictures. "He looks pretty young there." She then pointed to a picture of a young woman. "That's his fiancé, Susan. They've been engaged for about six months now. Nice girl. Pretty and smart. Too good for Chi I think, but he done good."

She then pointed out another woman in a Navy uniform. "That's my daughter Diane. She's still in the Navy in Jacksonville, married with one son who's two years old now." She pointed to a picture of Diane and her family. "Her husband just got out of the Navy about a year ago and is playing stay at home dad for now. They're doing real good."

Carrie looked over some of the other pictures. There were more of Chi with his fiancé, along with more of his sister and family, and a couple of Chi's mother. There were several of Diane by herself and a few of just Chi. "Can I ask you a question?" Carrie asked.

"Sure."

"How did you come up with the name Chi?"

Margret laughed. "That's not his given name. That's his nickname. His real name is Cody."

"Then why is he called Chi?"

"I don't know. It had to do with something that happened in high school. Whatever it was you'll have to ask him, but the name just stuck." Margret chuckled again. "But I know for sure it has nothing to do with chai tea. He hates that."

Margret led her outside through the kitchen door, and they walked to the back of the house, to the back of the property lot. At the back of the lot was a deep ravine with a small creek. On the other side she could see the back of a home similar to Margret's.

Carrie liked the look of the ravine with its creek, mossy patches, and tall trees. There was nothing like this in Chicago that she was aware of. Margret told her that sometimes they would see deer walking down there. Once, she had even seen a very rare albino deer.

They sat down at a patio umbrella table close to the house and looked out over the back of the lot.

"I like it here," Carrie told her. "I've never heard of South Haven before yesterday. How long have you lived here?"

"We were married just after my husband Scott got out of the Navy. He had saved up so we could afford to buy a house right away. So we bought this one. He was good like that."

"What happened to him. Are you divorced?"

"No. I'm widowed. Going on four years now."

"I'm sorry."

"It's OK. You could not know. I still miss him a lot. It's hard when you lose your best friend."

"I didn't see any pictures of him on your wall."

"I know. I took them down. Chi and Diane weren't happy about that, but every day I saw his face it reminded me of what I was missing. Eventually, I'll get around to putting them back up. It just takes time."

There was silence between them for a while. Carrie could hear the wind rustling through the leaves of the trees and feel it blowing in soft puffs on her face and against her hair. She closed her eyes and took a deep breath in through her nose. Even the air felt pure here. She did not know if it was just Margret's house or South Haven, but she felt something different here, something better than she was used to.

When she opened her eyes, she saw Margret looking at her. Her brow was furrowed slightly. "Carrie, I know I said you had to come to church with me, but tomorrow I'm going to leave it up to you. With the bruises on your face like that, you may not want to go out in public."

Carrie nodded. "Thank you. I appreciate that. I'd rather not. I really don't like trying to explain all the time."

"OK. Next week for sure, though." Carrie nodded back in agreement. "I'll tell you what, though. I used to sell makeup. I know a bit about covering bruises. How about tomorrow after church, I go pick up some stuff, and we'll see what we can do to fix things up a bit. I wouldn't want to see you trapped here afraid to go out when it's pretty simple to cover things up."

"OK. That sounds good."

There was more silence as the two women enjoyed the breeze blowing across their faces.

"Carrie?" Carrie looked over at her. "I'm not a big believer in coincidences. I suspect your car broke down here in South Haven, at the right place, at the right time, so that Chi would be the one to come to your rescue. I'd be pretty sure that's a God thing."

Carrie nodded. "I'm not a big believer in God."

"That was my guess," said Margret. "But that doesn't change the fact. Where would you be right now if your car didn't break down? Where would you be if Chi hadn't driven by?"

"I don't know."

"It's not a coincidence. I see the hand of God."

"OK." Carrie's eyes took on that faraway, distant look. Margret knew Carrie could hear her, but she was now tuning her out. She let the conversation rest.

~~~~

It was 9:00pm. Chi sat at his desk staring into his computer as he worked. His phone rang, and he checked the caller ID.

"Hey, Pete," he said into the phone as he answered it.

"Hey, Chi. How'd it go today?"

"Fine. She's with my mother now."

"What are they doing?"

"I don't know. We moved her into my mother's house early this afternoon."

There was a long silence on the phone. Pete finally spoke. His voice was tense. "Why did you let her move in with your mother?"

"My mom insisted. No choice."

"But why would you do that after our phone call this morning?"

"What's the problem?" Chi asked.

Pete's voice began to sound on the edge of being angry. "I told you about Rosie's dream last night and then you move Carrie in with your mom?"

Chi waited a moment and then spoke. "I didn't forget. As a matter of fact when my mom and I were discussing our options I told her about it. You know my mom. She still insisted."

"Why would she insist that Carrie move in with her?"

"Mom's worried about what Susan would think, having a strange woman move in with me and all."

"Yeah, I get that but if you think I was bothered about you taking her in how do you think I feel about your mother taking her in? This isn't good."

"I know. I could have argued with Mom, but that wouldn't have changed things. She made up her mind and that was it. It was all over. Can you at least be sure someone drives by the house once in a while? It wouldn't hurt to have a police presence be seen."

"Yeah, I can do that." Pete hesitated a moment then continued. "Chi, I pray to God that this turns out all right. If something happened to Margret, I don't think you or I would be able to forgive ourselves."

Ralph Nelson Willett

Chapter 6

Carrie joined Margret at the breakfast table around 9:30. "What time is church?" she asked as she sat down?

"I'll go to the 11:01 service today."

"How many services are there?"

"Two. 9:01 and 11:01."

"That's an odd time," Carrie replied.

"Yes. It's been drilled into my head for so long I don't think I can just say nine and eleven anymore." She grinned at Carrie.

Carrie was drinking a cup of coffee using her left hand. In between sips she would rotate her right wrist slowly and clench her hand into a fist. The pain was going away, but it still felt stiff.

"How's the hand?" asked Margret when she noticed.

"Better." She put her hand down on her lap under the table hiding it from Margret. She took another sip of coffee.

Margret nodded but said nothing. She looked over Carrie's face. The swelling had gone down but the bruising was still there. It would take a week or two for the bruises to go completely away. Carrie saw her looking at her and they locked eyes. Margret gave her a reassuring smile that wasn't returned.

"Carrie, I'm not going to ask you to come with me to church today, but you're welcome to if you'd like."

"No thank you. I'm not into church so much anymore."

"That means at one time you were."

"At one time."

"What happened?"

Carrie didn't answer. She turned to look out the window. A look of sadness drifted over her just briefly and then vanished. Margret tilted her head slightly in wonder as she saw this and followed her stare out of the window. Margret finally spoke again, "It's OK. We'll go next week. I think you'll find that our church isn't like most churches."

Carrie looked back at her. A conflict raged in her mind. This woman had taken her in, given her a place to stay and fed her. All that she asked in return was that she attend church with her starting next week. But on the other hand, she had no intention of going to church – any church, no matter how different it might be. She wondered if Margret would actually throw her out if she refused to go. Finally, she asked, "What kind of church is it?"

"Well, we're affiliated with the Wesleyan denomination. We believe that Jesus is the Son of God. We believe that the Bible is God's word revealed to us."

"So are you Trinitarian?"

The question surprised Margret. It wasn't something that someone with little church experience would normally ask. "Yes. We believe that the Father, Son, and Holy Spirit are one."

"And do you believe that you must be baptized in order to be saved?" Carrie was looking directly in her eyes with intensity. Margret felt a tension she hadn't felt from her before.

"Carrie, I get the feeling that you were hurt in church once."

Carrie looked away again and resumed staring out of the window. She appeared as if the conversation was making her angry and was trying to suppress that anger. Taking a deep breath in, letting it out slowly as she ballooned her cheeks out, she visibly relaxed. "Once or twice," she finally said in a calm voice.

"You want to tell me about it."

"Not really."

"OK. But Carrie, please don't define God's love by how other people mess up. I've messed up before when I wished I hadn't. Everyone has."

Carrie then looked back at her and tilted her head. "OK. Then tell me, how do I define God's love?"

Margret felt at a loss for words. How did she define God's love? She knew all the standard Sunday School answers, but she felt sure that Carrie knew them too and had already rejected them. Romans 5:8 says "But God commendeth his love toward us, in that, while we were yet sinners, Christ died for us." Yes, she knew the Sunday School answers. She wondered if she could describe for her those times when she felt that God had just wrapped his arms around her in such a way that she simply just knew that she was completely and fully loved. Carrie obviously knew 'churchy' words and probably knew all the same churchy clichés she knew. So how could she define for Carrie God's love in a way that would be meaningful to her?

Margret squinted slightly as she thought. "Do you remember the conversation we had last night? The part where I told you that I'm not a big believer in coincidences? When I said that I saw the hand of God working when your car broke down at the right time and at the right place for Chi to find you and stop and help you?"

"Yes."

"I hope that I can show you God's love through us."

For a moment, Margret almost thought she saw the faintest of smiles cross Carrie's lips, but Carrie only nodded and took another sip of her coffee.

~~~~

Margret prepared to leave for church. Carrie sat on the sofa with her legs curled up under her staring vacantly out of the picture window into the back yard. She sipped her second cup of coffee.

"I'm going to stop at the store on the way home to pick up a few things. Is there anything you'd like me to pick up?"

Without turning from the window Carrie quietly replied, "No thank you. I'm fine."

"OK. I should be home around one."

Carrie looked over at her noticing how she dressed. She was wearing jeans, a long sleeve blouse and leather boots with three-inch heels. "Those are your church clothes?" she asked.

"Yes. These are my church clothes," she answered. "What were you expecting?"

Carrie shook her head. "A dress."

Margret chuckled slightly, "When I feel like it, but not today." She waved her hand as she exited the door.

Carrie finished her coffee and sat quietly. For some reason, she felt tense and angry but did not know why. She was confident that Kevin could not find her here so she did not think that was the reason. She thought that perhaps the coffee was making her tense. She needed to relax. She decided to try to meditate in the way that her friend Amber had once taught her, by crossing her legs in front of her, straightening her back, and resting the backs of her hands on her knees. She began by focusing her thoughts on the touch of her forefingers against her thumbs. She then tried to control her breathing and clear her mind, to think of nothing at all. Her breath became a slow rhythm of deep inhalations and exhalations as she opened her mind to emptiness.

Deep in meditation Carrie envisioned herself sitting in a soft, green, grassy meadow with the sun shining warmly down on her. She felt the tension melting away as a gentle breeze blew against her face. In her vision she opened her arms and turned her face towards the sun to let its warmth sink in.

A distant whisper caught her attention, and she listened to try and understand the words. As she listened, the sky began turning dark and the sun began to disappear behind dark storm clouds that were swiftly moving in. The grass around her turned quickly to weeds, withered, died, then turned a dark grayish brown. What light remained from the sun quickly faded leaving her in total darkness. She was suddenly afraid. Laughter from dozens of distant voices came closer to her from all directions, growing louder and louder to the point of almost overwhelming her. Something swooped at her from out of the darkness, and she instinctively ducked. A glowing finger faded into view and pointed at her as if accusing her of some great evil.

A lamb was thrown out of the darkness and landed on the ground in front of her, just inches from where she sat, making a dull thud. The lamb seemed to have its own light allowing her to see it in the darkness. It bleated piteously as it twisted and struggled, trying to stand. The laughter became louder still as she watched the lamb roll to its knees and then fall over again. The finger continued to accuse her.

A second hand swooped in from behind her close enough that she could feel a burning heat coming from it. She thought she smelled her own burning hair. Holding a large dagger that glowed as if on fire, it paused in front of her only a moment and then swung the dagger at her neck close enough that she could feel the heat burning the skin under her chin. The hand paused again directly in front of her face. Waves of heat washed over her. It vibrated heavily as if shaking with anger. She watched in horror as the hand shifted the dagger, pointing it downward and then turned its attention to the lamb. It brought the dagger down into the belly of the lamb, stabbing it and twisting. The lamb cried out in pain. It tried to crawl weakly away from its attacker, but the knife would plunge down again and again and then drag it back in front of Carrie. The lamb turned and looked at her with large pleading eyes as warm blood spattered on her face and began to drip down her cheeks. It bleated loudly as each wound stained its wool a bright red. Small pools of blood began to form beneath it. Carrie could feel its pain with each stab of the knife as if it were her very own. Death seemed certain, but the lamb accepted each violent thrust as it refused to die. Or could not die, thought Carrie.

She jumped from the sofa letting out a short scream of terror. Looking around in panic, her heart raced. She gasped for air as the laughter echoed in her ears and quickly faded away. The meditation was over, and she was standing back in Margret's living room. The smell of burning hair and blood was still in her nostrils. She crossed her arms and hugged herself, squeezing herself in tightly. Calming her breathing, she paced back and forth as her eyes darted around the room searching for any sign of the hand and dagger.

The exercise she used to try to relax had terrified her. The vision had frightened her beyond any fear she could remember. She was far more tense now than before she began. She vowed to herself to never attempt that again.

Carried paced back and forth in front of the picture window until she calmed herself enough to settle down. She still trembled. Turning, she faced the window, tucked her hands in her pockets and looked into the back yard. A couple of black squirrels darted around, and she focused her attention on them.

Moments had passed, she did not know how long, but her mind had drifted off as she watched the squirrels. Now they were nowhere to be seen. Carrie felt almost as if she had fallen asleep where she stood and her awareness was just now returning as she awoke. She felt calmer now, more relaxed. The terror she felt just minutes before was now gone.

Turning to look around the room her eyes were drawn to a book shelf. On it were several obvious religious books but there was also a grouping of paperback books that looked out of place among the others. She stepped over and pulled one out. It was a romance novel. She chuckled to herself. She found it amusing that Margret, who had to be in her fifties would be interested in reading romance novels. There must have been nearly a dozen books here and as she looked them over she realized that they were all by the same author, Rachael Wallace. She saw the same one she had started reading at Chi's house, "Love's Obsession". Pulling it out, she looked it over. It didn't look as if this book had ever been opened before. It appeared brand new. She leafed through it until she found the place where she had left off reading and sat back down on the sofa again and began to read.

~~~~

Margret returned home a little after one with a couple of bags from the store. Carrie stood to greet her still holding the book. "How was church?" she asked.

"Awesome as always," Margret replied, setting down the bags on the counter. "Chi said to say hi. So did Jess."

"That's cool," replied Carrie. "Tell 'em hi for me." Carrie realized that sounded silly since she did not expect Margret to be seeing them again anytime soon but Margret did not seem to notice.

Margret laid out several pieces of makeup on the counter and then put a handful of grocery items in the refrigerator. She noticed the book Carrie was holding. "You like the book?"

"Well, yeah. Kind of. I normally don't read romance books but I was kinda bored and needed something to do."

Margret smiled at her. "Now you're into the book aren't you," she stated.

Carrie smiled shyly. "Yeah. A little bit. You must like this author. You've got a lot of her books."

Margret chuckled. "I almost never read those books."

"Then why do you have all of them?"

"Chi gives them to me."

"Why would Chi give you romance books?"

Margret laughed this time. "I'm going to tell you a secret. It's probably the worst kept secret in South Haven." Margret hesitated.

"OK...," Carrie prodded Margret.

"Rachael Wallace is Chi's pen name. He writes those books."

"What?"

Margret laughed again. "Yep. It's true. He writes romance novels for a living. Does real well actually."

Carrie held the book up and looked it over. There was no hint that the book was written by a man. Margret continued, "He's written some other stuff. Science fiction, westerns, some spy stuff. But nothing took off like his romance books. He makes a lot of money off of those."

Continuing to look over the book Carrie said, "I'm never going to be able to look at him the same way again."

"Don't you ever tell him that I told you. He likes to keep it a secret. But like I said, it's probably the worst kept secret in South Haven."

"Well, now I'm going to have to read more. How many has he written?"

"I don't know. A dozen or more. I've only read a few that he's written. I just can't bring myself to read them because it just feels too weird, since he's my son and all."

"So do they all end happily ever after?"

"I think they do. Like I said I don't usually read them, but I do know he writes what sells. If happy endings are what sells, then that's what he's going to write. It was funny back when it became known that he was Rachael Wallace. There was a bunch of girls from his old high school class that just "so happened to be in town" and wanted to look him up. It seemed that because he was a successful romance writer that he would be really romantic in person. They all seemed to want a piece of that fantasy. He got pretty irritated with all that. I told him that it was the price of fame."

"When did he start writing?"

"He wrote his first book that never got published back in his freshman year in college. His second book was published when he was a Junior. He then wrote a couple while he was in the Navy in his spare time. I think it helped to keep his mind off things since he had to travel so much. He wrote his first romance novel just before he got out."

"What did Chi do in the Navy?"

"I really don't know. He doesn't talk about it. He just says he had to travel a lot and he was glad when he was done. Did I tell you his sister is in the Navy?"

"Yeah. You told me."

"Their dad was in the Navy too. We're a regular Navy family."

Carrie sat down at the kitchen table, and Margret joined her. "My dad was one of those super patriots," Carrie told her. "He always talked about supporting our troops and stuff but he never was in the military."

Margret looked at her thoughtfully, "Where are your parents?"

"Still back in Illinois, I think."

"Chicago?"

"No. A place called Bishop Hill."

"Never heard of it."

"No one has," Carrie replied. "It's about as small a town as they come."

"How come you didn't go there?"

Carrie looked down at the table sadly. "I wasn't wanted there." Carrie was searching for words and then continued, "They threw me out just after I graduated from high school. I haven't spoken to them or heard from them since."

Margret felt Carrie's pain. She felt it deep inside to the point where she herself wanted to cry. Carrie just looked sad. It appeared as if all the tears she had ever had over this had already been shed and there were no more.

"I'm sorry, Carrie."

"I'm fine."

"No. I mean I'm really sorry. Something like that shouldn't happen. I can't imagine how I would feel if that would have happened to me."

Carrie perked up and sat up straight looking Margret right in the face. She wanted to change the subject quickly so that she wouldn't have to think about this. "Hey. I thought you said you were going to fix my face with some makeup so we could go for a walk."

"Yes. I did." Margret reflected Carrie's sudden enthusiasm back at her. "But how about we eat some lunch first and then we'll play."

Chapter 7

Carrie felt good to finally be out in the sun. She and Margret took their time walking downtown.

"Where'd you learn to do makeup like that?" Carrie asked her.

"At one time I sold Mary Kay. I got pretty good at it. Then I got involved with the local community theatrical group and did makeup for them for a season. And it's not the first time I've had to cover a couple of bruises." Carrie looked over, expecting an explanation. "My daughter had a skiing mishap once when she was in high school. We did the makeup thing every morning for two weeks. Chi got a black eye once while he was still in high school, when he was doing all that karate stuff. He wore it like a badge of honor of some type. Showed it off. I think he was disappointed when it cleared up." Carrie showed a hint of amusement on her face as she listened.

They continued walking downtown as Margret filled her in on South Haven. She seemed proud of her hometown. Proud of its history, of what it is now, and of its people.

"How long have you lived here?" asked Carrie.

"All my life. Went to school here. Married my high school sweetheart. Raised my kids here."

"You've never lived anywhere else?"

"Nope. My husband and I married just after he got out of the Navy and we just settled here. Neither of us wanted to go anywhere else. It was just home for us."

"What happened to your husband?"

"He died, Honey. He's with Jesus now. I'll see him again." Margret had already told her she was a widow but didn't mind repeating it.

"I'm sorry," Carrie said.

"It's OK. It's been four years now. It was a freak accident at the plant he worked at in Holland. A forklift hit something that caused a metal bar to go right through his chest. Killed him instantly." Margret slowed her pace. Her shoulders drooped noticeably.

"I'm so sorry," Carrie said again.

They walked in silence for a while. Carrie now felt bad for asking about her husband, and felt that saying anything more would add to the awkwardness.

Margret tucked her hands in her front pockets and looked down at the sidewalk as she spoke. "I was so mad at God. I actually yelled at him." She chuckled to herself. "Imagine that: Me yelling at God. But that's what I did. And it didn't help that the church I was going to at the time kept telling me 'It's God's will' and all that. Like that's what I needed to hear. You know, someone actually told me that I was young enough to find another husband. How stupid is that?" She looked over at Carrie and for a moment, a spark of anger flashed through her eyes and passed just as quickly as it came.

"I stopped going to church altogether," Margret told her.

"Then what happened? You're going to church now."

"About three years ago I was feeling kinda bad and lonely. I was still mad at God. Diane was married, in the Navy and living in Florida and Chi hadn't moved back yet. It was late, so I got myself a glass of wine and just sat in the dark drinking. I remember I started crying. I told God how mad I was at him and kept asking 'why, why.' Then the strangest thing happened. I felt something different. It's hard to explain but I felt as if God just wrapped his arms around me and held me there. I felt like he just held me there for hours. And then I wasn't mad anymore."

"So what'd you do?" asked Carrie.

"I woke up the next morning on the couch."

"That was it?"

"Well not quite. That was a Saturday. I was thinking that I should go back to church but I just could not do it." Margret stopped walking for a moment and looked Carrie in the eye. "You know, that church I was going to never even stopped by to see why I wasn't coming anymore. Not once." She looked away and started walking again. Carrie said nothing.

"The more I thought about that the more angry I got so I said a little prayer. I told God that if he wanted me to go to a church then he was going to have to show me somewhere to go. That night I was in Meijer picking up some groceries when I met Pastor Milan. Just met him, right there by the milk cooler. He told me that he was a pastor of a new church that was meeting at the high school and he invited me to come. I had seen their signs all over town. Seems everyone has heard of LifeBridge, but I never gave them a moment's thought. Then I went over to Walgreens and met someone else there from that church who invited me. I took that as a sign: I asked God to show me somewhere to go and that same day two people invited me to LifeBridge."

"So?" Carrie asked.

"So, I liked it. A lot. I got involved. It was nothing at all like the last church I was in. We're actually in the community doing things and helping people. Sometimes we partner with other churches when we can, and support the things here that actually help the people here. I've seen lives changed in people you'd never think would have made it. People that everyone would have given up on but God didn't, and their lives were changed forever."

They had reached downtown and crossed the street to the south side of the main road. They paused to look in a store shop window that obviously catered to the tourists.

"How were these people's lives changed?" Carrie asked.

"All kinds of ways. Marriages were saved, drug addicts and alcoholics were able to get clean. There are people that had been in prison, but you would never know it because their lives have been changed so much. Our church has a book out called 'Transparency' that tells the stories of a few people. Stories of how God changed their lives. I'll try and get you a copy."

"Don't you think that their lives could have changed without a god?"

Margret looked directly at her. "No. Why would you ask that?"

Carrie looked her in the eye but said nothing. She turned and began walking slowly again as Margret walked beside her. Carrie noticed how many people there were downtown and the smells coming from the local restaurants and shops was making her hungry again. She stopped to look at a menu posted outside of a restaurant named Tello's.

"This looks good," Carrie said.

"It is. It's one of my favorites. We can plan a trip down here some night this week if you want."

Carrie looked at her surprised. "Really?"

"Sure. Why not?"

"I can't afford something like this."

"My treat." For the first time, Margret saw a large genuine smile across Carrie's face. She was glad to see it. "How about tomorrow for dinner?"

"I'd love that. Thank you." She turned back and looked over the menu excitedly as Margret watched her. When she finished she turned back to Margret. The smile faded as she said, "I've never been in a restaurant like that before."

"Never?" Margret could not hide her surprise. Tello's was a very nice restaurant but it wasn't so high end that it was out of reach for most people.

"No. Never."

"Oh my gosh, Carrie. We're definitely going to fix that tomorrow. We'll come hungry and eat lots." Carrie's smile returned.

They stopped in front of a small cafe that was closed. Margret pointed in the window. "That's the Living Room Cafe, a coffee shop. Our church sponsors that. It's generally staffed by volunteers and it's open Tuesday through Saturday."

"Volunteers?"

"Yeah. Our church has a vision of 'Extending the hope of a rich and satisfying life through Jesus Christ to everyone we meet'." She had raised her hands and flicked two fingers on each to indicate quotation marks. "This is part of that."

"So people come in and you preach to them," Carrie stated flatly as if she were annoyed at what Margret had just told her.

Margret chuckled as they began walking again. "No that's not what it's about. It's about being available to people who need you. There are people who come in and just grab a latte and leave, or just hang out for a while, but sometimes there are people that just need someone to talk to. People that are hurting. Sometimes people just like you. They don't always know that this is church sponsored, but God just seems to bring them in and we minister to them just when they need it the most. You never know how many lives are changed just because someone was willing to talk to them."

"No one ever talked to me," Carrie said softly.

Margret stopped walking so abruptly that Carrie took a step and a half before she stopped to turn back and look at her. Margret spoke softly, but her face became intense again, "Carrie," she said. "I'm talking to you."

Carrie worried that she had upset Margret. "I'm sorry. I didn't mean to offend you."

"You didn't offend me. I just want you to realize that I *am* talking to you. Just like when other people that are hurting end up talking to someone in the Living Room, you're talking to me now. I think God had brought you to me for just that reason."

Carrie nodded, and they continued walking towards the beach.

At the far end of town looking down the hill, Carrie could see that the sidewalk passed the marina and extended all the way down to the south pier where the South Haven lighthouse stood. She stopped and stood, taking in the view as she looked out over Lake Michigan. "Wow," she said. Her voice was almost a whisper.

"Pretty cool, huh?" Margret asked.

"It's beautiful," Carrie replied.

"Is there anything like this in Chicago?"

"Not from what I saw. I've never seen anything like this before." She looked at the boats docked at the marina. "Wow. Who owns all the boats?"

"I don't know. Local people, tourists, summer people. I really don't know."

"Do you know anyone who has one?"

"No. Not that I know of. Why?" Margret asked.

"I've never been on a boat before."

"Oh. Well let me ask around and we'll see if there's something we can do about that. There's a boat here that looks like a pirate ship. That's what I call it, the pirate ship. It sells tickets and takes people out every night. Maybe you can do that."

"Yeah. Maybe. Someday," Carrie said quietly in a tone that implied her doubt.

"Come on. Let's get to the beach," Margret offered.

They walked down the hill along the river and out onto the south pier along the river edge. Carrie walked with her hands in her back pockets close to the edge as she kept her eyes down trying to peer into the river's muddy water. Margret watched her every move. She felt as if everything was a new experience for Carrie but that she was trying to hide her amazement.

The sun was hot on their skin but the breeze coming off the lake made it comfortable. Gusts of wind would blow their hair back and Carrie would brush it from her face and smile at Margret. A larger gust of wind came up and Carrie spread her arms, raised her face to it and skipped once lightly into it. This made Margret smile. It reminded her of something she had seen her daughter Diane do once when she was much younger.

When they reached the lighthouse Carrie placed her left hand on it and then began to slowly walk around it as if she were feeling its texture, each ripple of the paint and every bolt in its steel. She then stopped, closed her eyes and took the moment to just feel and to listen. Margret watched, intrigued as to what may be going through Carrie's mind. This young woman who had suddenly come into her life so broken, seemed to be experiencing things for the very first time, things Margret had always taken for granted.

A smile came on Carrie's face and she opened her eyes to look at Margret. "I like it here," she said. "There's peace here. I can feel it."

"Yes. I can agree with that."

Carrie put her hands in her pockets and walked to the end of the pier and looked over its edge. The water was clear there. She continued walking around on the lake side of the pier and started heading slowly inland with Margret by her side. The water was very clear on this side of the pier away from the river. She could see the large boulders that lay beside the pier and several fish.

After a while, she looked up and over at Margret. "Thank you," she said.

"For what?"

"Taking me in. For this." She waved her arm around indicating the pier and the beach.

"You're welcome. I'm glad to have someone to walk with."

"Can I ask you something, Margret?"

"Sure."

"How old are you?"

"Fifty-six."

"You're older than my mother."

"Well, you'd be about my daughter's age. How old are you?"

"Twenty-four."

"Well, you're a bit younger. She's twenty-eight, twenty nine next month."

"I just look older. I know." Carrie sounded discouraged.

"I'm just not that good at judging age," Margret told her.

"It's OK. I've lived a hard life. I know I look older."

Margret didn't know what to say to this. It was true. Carrie did look older than twenty-four. When they'd first met, Margret thought her to be in her early thirties. They continued walking back to the shoreline in a contemplative silence.

Taking their shoes off they walked southwards along the shore dodging children and sandcastles. Small waves chased in and out, lapping at their feet.

"I've never done this before," Carrie told her.

"Done what?"

"Walked on a beach like this."

"You've never been on the beach before?"

"No. Never did. My dad wouldn't take us to the beach because there'd be women in bikinis there and I never went there when I was in Chicago."

"Oh wow. I'm so sorry. You've missed out on a lot."

"Yeah. I think I did."

Carrie thought for a moment as she walked, alternating between looking down towards her feet, looking far south down the beach and then out into the lake. Margret walked beside her. There was a sense of deep sorrow surrounding Carrie. She could feel her pain, a deep pain that appeared to have been buried for so long and was now just rising up.

Carrie spoke again quietly, "I envy you and your family, Chi and your daughter. I wish I would have had a family like yours. I remember when I was in school I'd see other kids that were happy. I wanted to be happy." Carrie looked over at Margret and looked her in the eyes and said again, "I wanted to be happy." She held Margret's gaze for a moment then hung her head down as she walked, trying to put words together to describe something she didn't fully understand. Margret could feel that Carrie was opening up. "Even the kids in my church seemed happy but anytime I thought I was happy then my dad would start yelling at me again, telling me I was going to hell for this reason or that reason and I'd end up crying all over again. I finally gave up trying to be happy."

"What about your mom?" asked Margret. "Where was she in all this?"

"My mom was scared of my dad," Carrie replied. She swore under her breath then added, "Everyone was afraid of my dad. He had a temper that would go off like a bomb. I saw him hit guys a couple of times. I never saw him hit my mom, though, never did."

"Was she nice to you?"

"She tried to be, but Dad would yell at her a lot too. Whenever she did anything he didn't like he'd pull out his Bible and preach something at her and tell her she was going to hell. The last time I saw her or talked to her was the day I graduated High School. She made me a cake to celebrate. When we got home from my graduation my dad went right out to the barn and started working right away again. You know he never said anything like 'good job' or 'congratulations' or anything. Anyhow, when he was working in the barn we never knew when he'd come in so my mom thought just her and I would have a piece of cake to celebrate so she cut us both a piece of cake. We ate it and were just sitting around the kitchen table when he walked in and saw us. He was so mad that we didn't wait for him. He yelled at my mom and started saying things like 'God made woman to be a helpmate for the man' and said that she was 'going to hell for not knowing her place.' I can still see my mom just sort of shrinking into her chair. She kept getting smaller and smaller as he kept yelling. I said 'It's just a piece of cake. There's lot's left. I'll get you some.' Then he lit into me. The only thing I remember him saying to me was if I didn't like it there then I could get out. Then he called me a whore. He called me a whore. He had no reason to call me that. I looked at my mom and it was as if she was trying to disappear into the kitchen chair. She could not help me at all. That was the last time my dad talked to me at all. I left the next day."

Margret stopped her by touching her arm and they both faced each other. "Carrie I am so sorry you went through all that. That's not right. That shouldn't have happened."

"I know. But it did."

Margret stepped in and gave her a hug. Carrie was surprised by the gesture, unsure what to do and then finally lightly hugged her back.

Chapter 8

Sunday evening Chi walked into his mother's house without knocking. Carrie jumped at the sound of the door opening but calmed herself as she saw Chi walking in smiling.

"Well?" asked his mother.

"Well, what?"

"What you been doing all afternoon?"

"Worked some and talked to Susan over the phone some." He sat down in a rocking chair in the living room joining the two of them.

"How's she doing in Dallas?" Margaret asked.

"She's bored. She has the day off so she just stayed by the pool and read."

"How come she didn't go sightseeing?"

"Probably because none of her friends are with her and she didn't feel like going alone."

"Chicken."

"Stop, Mom."

Margaret grinned at him. Carrie was amused at their interaction.

Chi turned to Carrie. "Missed you in church this morning."

"Your Mom said I didn't have to go today because of the bruises," Carrie said defensively.

Chi took a closer look. "Nice makeup job, Mom."

"I know. Pretty good, huh."

"Well Carrie," continued Chi. "You're welcome to come with me tonight to our life group meeting."

"What's that?" she asked.

"It's a way to get to know people. Sometimes when a church gets to be big enough people sort of fade into the background. A life group is a way to get to know each other better. We get together for Bible study and to have a good time together. It's basically a social group where we can all support each other."

"Not interested. But thank you, though," Carrie said as she turned to look out of the window.

"OK. But Susan will be here next Sunday and we'd like you to come with us."

"I don't think so."

Margret jumped in, "It would be good to get to know some people."

Carrie let out a slow breath. She kept her eyes focused outside. Her shoulders slumped. She did not like the pressure being placed on her and her body began to show it.

The doorbell rang. Carrie jumped. Her eyes flashed panic. Chi saw this and tried to reassure her. "The only people that know you're here are all friends. It's OK. You're safe."

Carrie relaxed as best she could but she was still breathing in quick, short breaths. Margaret began to stand but Chi stopped her. "I'll get it." He stood and walked to the front door. As he opened it Carrie could see Jess and a woman standing outside. Chi let them in.

"Saw your truck outside so we decided to stop in," Jess said. He turned to Carrie. "Hi, Carrie. You're looking better."

"Thank you," she replied.

"I'd like you to meet my wife, Becky."

Becky held her hand out to her. "Hi, Carrie." Carrie hesitated and looked to Margret for reassurance.

Margret nodded and said to Becky, "Her hand hurts. Maybe you all can shake hands later."

Becky pulled her hand back. "Oh. I'm sorry."

Carrie watched as Chi brought in two kitchen chairs for him and Jess. With a nod he directed Becky to sit in the rocker. Becky appeared to be about her same age and stood about the same height she did. She was wearing jeans with a light summer top and tennis shoes. Carrie caught a glimpse of something on her wrist. She kept directing her eyes at it trying to confirm what she thought it was. Becky noticed Carrie looking at her arm but said nothing about it.

"So how are you feeling today?" Jessie asked Carrie.

"I'm fine."

"You really do look a lot better than when I saw you Friday night."

"Thank you. What about my car?" she asked with a smile as she realized it was Jessie that had her car.

"Still there. Still waiting on the part."

"So where you from, Carrie?" Becky asked.

"Chicago."

"Did you grow up there?"

"No." She glanced again at Becky's arm.

Margret spoke up. "Carrie grew up in a small town in Illinois. She says it's even smaller than South Haven. Uh… What was the name of that town, Carrie?"

"Bishop Hill," she replied without emotion.

"Nice town?" asked Becky.

"I don't know. I didn't get out much."

"How come?"

Margret tried to steer the conversation away from Carrie for a while. "Becky's lived here all her life. She was a regular beach bum in her high school days." Carrie looked over at Margret but said nothing. "Jess did too," Margret continued. "Chi was just a couple of years ahead of Jess and Becky in school."

Carrie looked at Jess and then over to Becky again. They were a few years older than her but they both looked younger. Her eyes dropped again to Becky's arm.

Becky spoke up again. "What are you doing tonight?" she asked Carrie.

"I dunno," replied Carrie in a flat tone.

"How about coming to Life Group with us? We'd love to have you."

Again, Carrie glanced at Becky's arm. Life Group, she thought. This was another one of those church people. She felt trapped and wanted to leave, perhaps hide in her room. These people didn't know her or anything about her and they wanted her to go to church with them? No. That wasn't going to happen, she decided.

"No thank you. I'm not into church," she told them.

Jess broke in. "It's not church. There won't be any singing or taking money or anything like that. We're pretty much just hanging out. Seeing what's up with each other. We may have a Bible study but they're always really brief. But the best part is we're going to have food." He grinned at Becky who returned his smile.

Carrie looked at Chi who's face was expressionless. He leaned back in the kitchen table chair, cocked slightly to one side. He was looking outside as if deep in thought.

"Anyways, we'd love to have you," Jess continued.

Carrie looked directly at him. "You going to be doing a prayer thing?"

Jess opened his mouth to speak but Margret beat him to it. "Food," she said abruptly. Carrie turned to face her. "There's going to be food," Margret repeated.

Jess smiled. "Yep. There's going to be some really good food." Carrie turned back to him.

"Seriously," Carrie said. She hesitated a moment, squinted her eyes slightly and said to Jess in a lower tone, "Are you going to be having a prayer thing?"

Jess's face darkened. "If you mean 'do we pray there?', yes, there will be a prayer. That's part of it but usually, it's just one person. Not everyone has to pray."

Carrie tensed. "That doesn't work," she said with a building intensity. "And if you think it does then you're an idiot. I don't feel like wasting my time with you people." Her tone became harsh and direct.

There was silence in the room for a moment as everyone tried to come to grips with what was just said and the new tension in the room.

Chi, who was now facing her and fully attentive, spoke up. "I'm not sure what you mean." He sat straight in his chair and leaned in.

Carrie turned to face him directly, squaring her shoulders to him. She appeared ready for a confrontation. He continued, "I've been places and seen things and I know for certain that if prayer didn't work I wouldn't be here. I'd be dead." He let that sink in a moment. "I've seen lives changed, people changed and I've seen people healed. I don't know your life story but one thing I'm absolutely sure of is that you're here because prayer works." He pointed to her chair. "You're sitting here in that chair because prayer works." He looked her in the eye with an intensity that echoed hers.

Silence lingered in the room as Carrie and Chi held each other's stare. Everyone else exchanged uncomfortable glances between themselves. Margret cleared her throat to break the tension.

Carrie relaxed slowly and finally looked away from Chi's intense gaze. Kevin could be intense but the intensity that Chi showed had a power behind it that she wasn't familiar with. Not a dark power like Kevin's but more like a strength that challenged her to be his equal. A power completely under his control very much unlike Kevin's who could explode with rage at the slightest provocation. This was a power she did not have to fear but was still a power that demanded respect. Chi relaxed again.

Carrie again looked at Becky's arm and again Becky noticed. Becky suddenly became cognizant of what Carrie was looking for and turned her wrist over to reveal a small tattoo. It was a butterfly. Carrie stared at it a moment and then looked up into Becky's face. Becky gave her a small smile.

The tattoo confused Carrie. That was not what she expected from a church going woman. Her father had drilled it into her over and over again that any woman that let themselves be tattooed was a prostitute or tramp and was doomed to hell. From what she had seen and experienced in Chicago that all seemed to be true. But this woman, with this tattoo, had just invited her to church. Everyone in this room hung out in church together and the way that she had been treated by these complete strangers made a liar out of her father.

Carrie looked around the room. The tension began to fade but the silence lingered. Chi stood, stepped over to the kitchen island and poured a glass of water. She watched him, squinting her eyes as she jutted out her chin and sucked in her cheeks. She felt angry. She watched him as his face was changing from intensity to something that more resembled kindness. He stepped over to her and held out the glass of water to her.

Carrie was confused at the gesture. Why did he bring her water? He smiled at her with a genuine kindness as he held the glass out to her patiently.

Carrie stood abruptly nearly knocking the glass from Chi's hand. She looked Chi in the eyes angrily and then looked the group over, person by person. She walked with a quick deliberateness to her room and closed the door hard behind her. Everyone in the room had watched her walk away. In unison, they all turned to look at Chi. He stood motionless with only his eyes moving as he looked between the remaining three.

Margret stood and looked Chi angrily in the eye. "I'm not sure if you were being a jerk or not," she told him. "Why did you do that?"

"Do what?" he asked.

"What's the deal with the water? She didn't ask for anything."

"That wasn't intended to be anything other than getting her a glass of water. The way she looked at me when I was getting one for myself made me think she wanted one."

"I'll go talk to her," she said as she walked towards Carrie's room. She then turned around to face Chi again. "Stop trying to be nice. You're not any good at it." She gave a gentle rap on Carrie's bedroom door and then entered without waiting to be invited in.

Margret found Carrie sitting on her bed with her back resting against the headboard. Her arms were folded and she glared at the foot of the bed in a childish pout. Margret sat in the chair next to the bed.

"What is going on?" Margret asked her. Carrie didn't react. "Carrie, talk to me. What's going on? These people were only trying to invite you to join them at their life group."

Carrie turned to Margret, her face became angry. She swore at her using an expletive suggesting what they could do to themselves.

"Whoa," Margret said becoming angry. "What is the matter with you? They were trying to be nice to you. And I'd suggest that you don't talk that way to me again. Do you understand?"

Carrie calmed herself and turned away, resuming her stare at the foot of the bed. Margret watched as the anger in her face faded to a sadness. Margret also let the tension fade from herself as she shifted her posture in her chair. The silence lingered for several moments.

"Why don't you tell me what's going on?" Margret asked again.

Carrie sought words to describe what she was feeling. She had never examined what she felt about church to any depth. She only knew that anything to do with church, anything to do with God, was now out of the question of being considered.

Carrie began to speak. Her words came slowly with what appeared to be painful deliberation. "You have no idea what I've been through. You have no idea how many times I prayed to God for help and help never, ever came. God doesn't exist and never did. If you're trying to get me to buy into your fantasy you can forget it. I'm not interested in pretending anymore."

Margret let her words sink in. She took a deep breath in and let it out slowly in a loud audible whoosh as she looked away. Carrie slowly turned to look up at Margret, expecting to see her angry, ready to lash out at her but what she saw was compassion. It appeared as if Margret was trying to hold herself back from rushing in and hugging her. Carrie's body nearly crumbled into itself as she looked into Margret's eyes.

Margret stood and cautiously approached her sitting next to her on her bed. She put her arm around Carrie and pulled her into her. Carrie's body tensed at the gesture but Margret held her gently and tightly. The tension began to fade and Carrie relaxed, releasing her body into Margret's embrace. Margret held her without offering any words as she let Carrie rest in her arms.

"There is no God," Carrie said softly as if reminding herself. Margret held her.

~~~~

Margret came out of Carrie's room to find Chi sitting at the kitchen table. "Becky and Jess leave?" she asked.

"Yeah. About a half hour ago. She OK?"

"Yeah. That girl's been through a lot. I hope you don't take her behavior personally."

"I don't. Is there anything I can do?"

"No. I don't think so. She's OK now."

Margret pulled out a chair and sat across from Chi. "She reminds me of a whipped puppy. Afraid of just about everything. Scared of any interaction with anyone." Chi nodded and looked down. Margret continued, "I think the only thing we can do now is to pray for her."

"Yeah. Got that. Been doing that since Friday night. Becky and Jess will have our life group start praying for her. Becky said she's going to pop around this week and see her."

"That would be good. I think it would be good if someone her own age talked to her."

Chi nodded and they sat quietly for a moment. Chi began to stand. "Alright. I'm headed home. I'm already too late for life group and I could use the time to write some more."

"You know, Carrie was getting into one of your books. She thought it was funny that you're Rachael Wallace."

"Yeah, Mom. Thanks for telling her," he said with a touch of sarcasm.

"Worst kept secret in South Haven," she replied with a smile.

"Thanks to you. You know how to keep a secret."

"I can keep your secrets. It's the people I share them with that can't keep them." Margret chuckled at her own joke. "Besides, it's kind of hard to brag about your son when he's a woman."

He held out his palm at her. "OK. Enough. I'm headed home." He turned toward the door.

"You know, I'm a bit worried that once you get married all these romance stories are going to stop. Then what are you going to do for a living?"

Chi turned to her. A mischievous grin spread across his face. "I'm going to be even more romantic after we get married."

Margret chuckled again. "Famous last words."

Chapter 9

Carrie awoke Monday morning to find Margret at the kitchen table with her Bible opened in front of her. "Good morning," Margret said softly.

"Morning."

Carrie looked around the kitchen for the coffee pot and having found it pulled a cup from the cupboard and poured herself some. She sat down across the table from Margret. Margaret closed her Bible and a study guide that was opened next to it.

"How'd you sleep last night?" Margret asked.

"Pretty good, actually. It's been a while since I've slept that good." Carrie looked around for the clock on the wall. It was almost 10:30. "Ten-thirty," she said. "I slept a long time."

"You must have needed it. You know you fell asleep in my arms last night," Margret stated.

"Yeah, I know. Thank you. I think I must have been overly tired."

There was a moment of silence as both sought words. Finally, Margret spoke up. "What would you like to do today? We can fix you up with makeup again and go out."

"That would be nice. I wouldn't mind walking downtown again then out to the beach."

"Sure. I need the exercise. How about we go for a drive, too? I'll show you around."

"OK. That would be fun."

"Tonight we got a date at Tello's, don't forget."

"Oh yeah. That's still on?"

"Of course. You, me and dark red wine." Margret tilted her head slightly and looked down as if trying to remember something. "Isn't that a song somewhere? 'You, me and dark red wine'?"

"Roses and Rides by The Jimmy Layton Band. Rose to number 24 on the top 40 charts in August of 1979."

Margret stared at her for a moment. "How could you know that?" she asked. "You weren't even born yet?"

Carrie shrugged. "I have a good memory for things," she said. "I used to hide in my room and listen to a radio I had. My dad didn't know I had it."

"Anyhow," continued Margret. "We'll get some good food and relax a while."

"Sounds nice. I'd like that."

Carrie sipped her coffee as Margret stood and refilled her own cup. Carrie looked up into Margret's face as she sat down again. "Margret," she began. "I'm sorry about last night."

"I know, Hon. I know you've been through a lot."

"You've been so good to me and I shouldn't have treated you like that."

"It wasn't just me, you know. Becky, Jess, and Chi were there. But I can tell you that they understand, too. They may not know your story or what you've been through but they know when people are hurting and they're caring people."

"I feel bad I talked to them that way. Do you think Chi is OK?"

Margret chuckled. "Chi's fine. I don't think anyone but Susan could ruffle his feathers."

"It looked like he was mad at me."

"No. I don't think so. He may sometimes come off gruff but that's only because he's used to being in charge and not being questioned. He used to be an officer in the Navy. He's used to that kind of thing."

Carrie remained silent and focused her eyes on her cup of coffee that she held with both hands on the table. She lifted her right hand and rolled it around at the wrist testing its stiffness.

"How's the hand?" Margret asked.

"Better. It doesn't hurt like it did."

Margret looked her face over for the bruising. "Let's get you something to eat and then I can reapply your makeup."

"I'm not hungry but thanks."

"You need to eat something. You're healing and your body needs food to repair the damage. How about some eggs and bacon?"

Carrie relented and nodded. "OK. Just one egg, please. Sunny side up."

"Fine. Two eggs, bacon and toast it is," Margret said as she stood again from the table. "You need to add some meat on those skinny little bones of yours."

~~~~

After applying Carrie's makeup, she took Carrie on a walk to explore the town again with her. This time Margret took her across the river to the north beach. They walked down Dyckman Avenue until it ended at the beach and then walked the shoreline toward the north pier. Carrie could see the red lighthouse from where they were. The waves were much higher today than when they had walked the beach Sunday. They would crash over yards away from shore and then roll up to shore in bubbles and foam. They walked slowly just out of reach of the waves.

"When I was a kid we used to go swimming in waves like this," Margret told her. "Me and a bunch of the boys. The girls were too chicken. It was a lot of fun back then but I think I'd be too scared now. When you're a kid it never occurs to you that you could die." She pointed down the beach toward some kids in the water. "I'm pretty sure the red flags are out and they're out there swimming in it. If a rip current caught them it would pull them right out to the middle of the lake."

"What's a rip current?" Carrie asked.

Margret looked at her blankly for a moment. She found it hard to understand that someone Carrie's age wouldn't know what a rip current is. "It's when the waves push a lot of water up toward the beach. The water has to go back out somewhere and sometimes it all goes back out in the same spot. It's like a river pushing you back out. The problem is you can't usually see it happening. If you're in it, it will push you right out into the lake. If you're not a good swimmer you could drown."

Carrie looked over the water trying to see if she could see anything that might look like a rip tide. Margret continued, "When I was just out of high school, me and a couple of girlfriends went in. The waves weren't this high. It was probably yellow flags. I got caught in a rip tide and didn't realize it. I was trying to come back into shore and I wasn't getting anywhere. I had my feet planted on the bottom and I was pushing in but it seemed like the harder I tried the further back I went. When I finally realized what it was I went sideways to it along the shore and finally came out of it. By the time I hit shore I was exhausted. Never fight a rip tide, Carrie. Always go sideways to it."

"I'll try to remember that," Carrie said. "But I won't be going in the water anytime soon."

"It's nice to go swimming in the summer," Margret told her.

"I can't swim," Carrie told her. Her voice was just loud enough to be heard over the waves.

Margret looked at her. Carrie was walking slowly with her head down looking at the sand just ahead of her feet. Margret felt a wave of compassion come over her. "You don't know how to swim either?" Carrie shook her head. "What *did* you do as a kid, Carrie?"

Carrie took her time answering. She waded through thoughts of her childhood. What did she do as a kid? "I went to school, I came home, I did chores and I went to church." Carrie looked at Margret for her reaction. Margret didn't respond. She continued. "I wasn't even allowed to have any friends over. I never went anywhere and if I got to go to the store for anything I always had to be with my Dad. Even my mom always had to be with my dad when we went into the city to go shopping. The only time I got to go anywhere or see anyone was when I went to school."

Margret looked down and shook her head slowly. "I'm sorry to hear that Carrie."

"My mom was cool. She tried to make my life good but my dad made it hard. Sometimes my mom and I would talk for hours. I kinda miss that. I'm sure she loved me." Carrie remained silent for a moment and then continued. "I don't think my dad ever loved anyone."

As they walked along the beach Carrie noticed dozens of seagulls all facing the same direction into the wind. She reasoned that would be the best way for them to stand, facing into the wind. "That's funny how they all face the same direction," she told Margret.

"It's easier to face into the wind when you have a streamlined body, I suppose," Margret responded. "A lot easier than trying to stand sideways to it."

"I love the beaches here," Carrie said.

"Yeah. I like them too. I can't imagine ever living too far from them."

"And I can't imagine living here," Carrie told her. "This place seems so peaceful. Even with all the waves and the wind, it just seems so peaceful."

"That's part of what I like about it too," Margret replied. "I think that's what Chi and Diane like about it. My daughter Diane is in Florida now but she swears that when she gets out of the Navy they're moving back. I know her husband wants to."

They walked in silence for a few minutes toward the north pier. Carrie remained deep in thought. "Margret," Carrie said, finally breaking the silence. "Thank you for taking me in. You didn't have to do that but I don't know what I would have done if it wasn't for you and Chi."

"Well, I told you before that I don't believe in coincidences. You're here for a reason. I know your life has been hard but I think it's going to turn around for you here."

"How long will you let me stay with you?"

"Well, I guess we'll just have to see. I've no plans to kick you out but I think the best thing to do is for you to start looking for a job once the bruises heal and then once you're settled, move out on your own. You need to learn how to be independent. I can help you do that and I'll be here for you if or when you need me."

Carrie nodded her understanding. "What kind of job do you think I can get?"

"I don't know yet but I do know that God has something for you."

Carrie gritted her teeth but tried not to let her frustration with Margret for mentioning God again show. Just the word made her tense and angry. "I hope so," she finally replied.

They reached the North pier and looked down its length. The waves were not so high that they washed over the pier but she could see that on occasion a wave would crash against the pier wall and it would splash high in the air.

"Can we go out there?" Carrie asked.

"I'd rather not. I don't feel like getting wet."

Standing with her face into the wind, Carrie let the wind blow her hair back behind her as she watched the waves wash along the pier. Wisps of hair floated around in front of her and then blew back behind her again. She closed her eyes and let the sun soak into her face as she spread her arms out. She was smiling.

Margret watched her intrigued. She took the wind and the waves for granted. This was something she had known all her life but to Carrie, this was all new. Carrie raised her chin up higher into the wind and leaned into it. To Margret, it reminded her of the sea gulls they had just passed that all stood facing the same direction into the wind toward the lake and it's crashing waves.

"It looks like you're enjoying that," Margret told her.

Carrie didn't open her eyes. "I am," she responded. "It even smells good here."

"I'm sure you're going to like South Haven."

"I think so," Carrie replied as she pulled her hair back from her face. With her left hand, she held her hair in a ponytail to keep it from blowing in her face. She looked at Margret with a big smile. "The north beach is even better than the south beach," she said.

"Well, I think so. We used to hang out here when we were in high school. Scott and I would park his truck right about there and we'd sit on the tailgate just hanging out with our friends." She pointed to a parking space back up the beach.

"It must have been nice," Carrie told her.

"It was. We had a good time."

They started walking the sidewalk along the river up towards the north marina. Carrie let her hair blow in the wind again as it whipped around her face.

"We're going to have to get you a hat," Margret told her.

"No, I like this," she responded.

The further they walked up the river the more the wind settled down. Carrie pulled her hair back behind her. "Margret, can I ask you a question?"

"Sure, Hon."

Carrie hesitated a moment, looked at Margret and then down at the ground. "How did you feel when your husband died?"

"I was devastated. Why do you ask that?"

Carrie slowed their pace as she looked down in contemplation. "I think I would have been happy if my dad died or if Kevin died. At best I don't think I would have felt anything. I'm pretty sure I wouldn't have been sad."

Margret looked at her trying to understand the source of the question. "I was sad. Like I said, devastated. I was mad at the world, mad at God."

"Didn't that make you think there wasn't a God?"

"No. It didn't. It just made me mad at him."

"But if there was a God then why would he let an accident like that happen to your husband? If God is real then he's supposed to be all powerful. If he's all powerful and he could have stopped your husband from being killed and he didn't..." Carrie paused then continued, "then he's a murderer."

Margret stopped their walking and faced her. "Whoa. You need to stop right now. I know where Scott is at this very moment. He's in heaven with Jesus. That was going to happen sometime. We're all going to die. It just happened to him a little earlier than I would have liked. Just because I don't understand what God's doing that doesn't mean what he did wasn't the right thing to do."

"So you're saying he chose to kill your husband. That makes him a murderer."

"I said stop that," Margret said gruffly. "God is not a murderer. You need to be careful what you call the God who created this universe."

"That same God you say created the universe let me and my mother be abused for twenty-four years. You try to tell me about God's love but you can't explain what happened to your husband."

"First of all, your mother is a grown woman. She chose to stay with your father and keep you with her. She made her own choices and those choices hurt her daughter. Secondly, you left and got out of that as soon as you could which is what you should have done but then you chose to be in another abusive relationship. And let me tell you something else, it's OK to be angry with God. He understands. He really does and he still loves you."

"So where was his love for the past twenty-four years?"

"And as soon as you chose to leave that abusive relationship he brought you to us. Why did you wait so long, Carrie?"

Carrie looked at Margret expressionlessly. She turned and began walking again slowly. Margret walked beside her. Tears began to roll down Carrie's face but rather than wiping them she held her head up, looking forward into the distance, letting them roll down her face.

"You don't know me," she finally told Margret without looking at her.

Margret continued to walk alongside her. After several moments she asked, "Who does know you, Carrie?" Margret asked softly.

Carrie stopped and wiped her eyes while avoiding looking at Margret. She turned and faced out over the river, and leaned forward against the railing. She sniffed and ran her sleeve across her nose.

Margret stood against the railing beside her. They stood quietly. Finally Margret said softly, "Carrie, I love you."

Carrie looked at her and wiped her eyes again. "You love me? What does that even mean?"

"Is it OK that I want to see you healthy and happy? That I want to take care of you like I would my own daughter? Is it

OK that I feel your pain, that it hurts me when I know you're hurting? You're right, I know very little about you, only what you've told me. But I know what I've seen, I've covered your bruises with makeup. I've held you as you trembled. Last night when I went to bed, every time I closed my eyes I saw myself covering up those bruises and I could not help but cry. I cried myself to sleep last night, Carrie. Because I want to help you but there's only so much I can do. I feel kind of helpless."

"Why?"

"Why do I feel helpless? Because I can't..."

"No," Carrie interrupted. "Why do you care? Why would you do all this?"

"Well, because God loves me."

Carrie scoffed and looked away. "There is no God," she said sternly.

"Yes, Carrie. There is. And he loves you too. And he wants you to have a happy life in him."

She looked back at Margret again. "And what does *that* mean?"

"What? A happy life in him? What do you think it means?"

Carrie turned away again and waited several seconds before responding. "There is no God," she said again quietly.

Margret nodded. She wished she could break through her resentment, her pain, and her grief but Carrie was pushing back. She decided it wasn't her job to convince Carrie of anything. She'd leave that up to God.

"How about we head home, jump in the car and go bug Chi for a while?" Margret asked.

"Why? Do you think he's still mad at me?"

"Why would he be mad at you?"

"Because of what happened last night?"

"Ah. Well trust me on this. He doesn't get bent out of shape with such small stuff. He probably won't even remember it happened. Besides, maybe we can get him to pay for our Tello's dinner tonight." Margret grinned conspiratorially at Carrie. Carrie finally smiled back in return.

Ralph Nelson Willett

Chapter 10

Thump. Thump. Thump, thump. Margret and Carrie could hear the thumping coming from Chi's house as soon as they exited the car. The low thumping was clearly noticeable from outside but Margret didn't seem to take notice. It had a rhythm to it, two slow then two quick. Margret put a key in the lock, opened the door and walked in with Carrie following nervously behind her.

The thumping pattern changed, one slow then two quick. The whole house seemed to shudder with each thump. Carrie could feel it in her stomach.

"Let's have a seat. He's going to be a few minutes," Margret said as she found her way to the sofa.

"What is that?" Carrie asked.

"That's Chi banging on his punching bag. He's working out."

"Shouldn't we let him know we're here?"

"He knows. He probably knew the second we entered the subdivision. He's got some stupid, crazy security system, bunch of monitors and all."

Carrie sat on the opposite end of the sofa from Margret and anxiously looked around. Margret had picked up one of Chi's Popular Science magazines and began leafing through it.

Thump. Thump, thump. Thump, thump. The pattern changed again. Each thump made Carrie jump internally. She tried to calm herself but each thump sent heavy vibrations through her body. It was beginning to make her physically ill.

The thumping paused and she felt herself relaxing. A much heavier thump, one that made the windows rattle, was enough to make her gasp. Margret looked up from her magazine and looked at her. Carrie felt a rising panic and fear causing her to begin to tremble. Her face paled as her eyes widened. A second equally heavy thump shook the house again then it was followed by another in quick succession.

"You OK, Carrie?" No response. "He's doing his karate kicks now. It's kinda cool to watch him do that but he doesn't like it when I interrupt his workouts."

Carrie's breathing became quick and shallow. She sat on the edge of the sofa and folded her arms in front of her squeezing them in tightly around herself. She began rocking back and forth. Margret stood and sat down next to her putting an arm around her.

"What's the matter?" Margret asked her. "You're shaking."

Thummmmppp. Thummmmppp. The entire house shook. Margret pulled her in tightly. Carrie laid her head on Margret's shoulder. She held herself tightly and continued rocking slightly as Margret held her.

There was a pause again in the thumping. Margret could hear Carrie's labored breathing.

"Are you OK, honey? Do we need to leave?" asked Margret. Carrie's body trembled as she rocked back and forth in Margret's arms.

The thumping stopped. "I think he's done," Margret told her. Carrie didn't move for several moments. Finally convinced the thumping had stopped she reluctantly pulled away from Margret and sat up straight on the edge of the sofa.

Margret watched her as the fear in Carrie's face began to fade. Her eyes now had a wild look about them as her breathing began to return to normal. Carrie hung her head and looked down at the floor. "I'm sorry," she said quietly.

"There's no need to apologize, sweetie. It's OK."

Carrie relaxed and sat back on the sofa. The color returned to her face. She was now beginning to look normal again.

"You want something to drink or anything?" Margret asked.

"No thank you."

"Chi won't mind. He's got soda and water."

"No thank you," she repeated.

As she calmed herself, Carrie began to look around the living room. She noticed the romance book sitting on the end table where she had left it the previous Friday night. She wanted to pick it up but felt too shaken to move. Still trembling, she ignored Margret who remained seated on the edge of the sofa watching her.

Margret patted her knee. "It's OK. He's done. Do we need to leave?" she asked again.

"No, I'm fine."

Margret waited to see if an explanation was coming for what just happened but Carrie said nothing. She returned to the opposite end of the sofa again and resumed leafing through the magazine while keeping a concerned eye on Carrie.

After several minutes Chi emerged from the staircase that led to the lower level of the house. He wore a sleeveless shirt and light athletic shorts. He dripped with sweat and his clothes were drenched. He casually looked over towards Carrie and Margret as he walked into the kitchen.

"Hi," he said.

"Hey," Margret replied. "Did you hurt it?"

"Hurt what?"

"The punching bag. You were beating it up pretty good."

"Oh. Yes, it was whimpering like a baby by the time I finished. It wasn't as tough as it pretended to be." He almost grinned at her.

Carrie looked at him. She felt as if he was using a metaphor that was supposed to be her. Chi gave a thin smile to Margret and then to Carrie. Carrie looked away.

He pulled out a large container of protein powder and mixed it with juice in a large glass. Leaning back against the counter he began drinking it as he faced them in the living room. He spoke to his mother between large gulps of his drink. "What are you doing here?"

Margret didn't look up from the magazine. "We've come to see if you wanted to invite us out to dinner tonight at Tello's."

"Ah. So what you're saying is you want me to buy you dinner."

Margret pointed at him and winked. "Yes. That's it. How could you turn down an invitation like that? Thank you." She grinned at him.

Carrie watched him closely. Chi seemed even bigger now after working out. His swollen muscles flexed each time he raised the protein drink to his lips. She was calm again now that the thumping had stopped. Was he aware of her meltdown just a few minutes earlier?

Chi finished his drink and set the glass on the counter beside him. He appeared to be thinking as he and his mother locked eyes.

"No. As much as I'd love to, not tonight. I'm already behind on my next story. I need to stay here and write." Margret appeared disappointed. Chi continued. "But I will buy you two dinner at Tello's."

"Deal," Margret said boldly as she excitedly sat up straighter. "I know just the bottle of wine," she said looking at Carrie. Carrie gave Margret a weak smile and then her eyes shifted to Chi who was looking back. They locked eyes only for a moment before Carrie looked away.

"Just one bottle," he reminded Margret. "And you're walking, right?"

"Yeah, yeah," she responded waving her hand at him. "I wouldn't want to have to deal with your buddy Pete, the cop."

Chi grinned at her. "Right. Not a good thing. Walking would be better."

Carrie could not keep her eyes off of Chi. She would look at him and then look away before he could notice. This sweaty man in sweat soaked clothes was attractive. Very attractive. She had known a handful of bodybuilders or guys that worked out a lot in the gym. Many of them were larger than Chi, but Chi seemed to exude a manliness and power she hadn't seen in those other men.

"Alright, give me a sec," he said as he stepped into his room. He returned moments later with a credit card and handed it to his mother. "Just dinner," he said.

"Yes, of course," Margret replied. She stood, took the card from him, and tucked it into her front jean pocket. "And a movie," she said.

Chi squinted at her.

"Lighten up, sailor," she said as she walked past him towards the door. She turned to Carrie and gave her a tilt of her head to indicate it was time to leave.

Carrie stood, walked past Chi and his mother and stopped at the patio door. She turned at an angle to them and watched them as she held her hand on the door handle.

Chi grinned at his mother, held his arms open wide and stepped towards her. "OK, give me a hug then."

Margret stiff-armed him and backed away from him. "Don't you come near me all sweaty like that."

"Look at that. I'm buying you dinner and you won't even give me a hug," he said without smiling. "I see how you are."

"Yeah, well I gave birth to you. You owe me at least a dinner."

Chi chuckled. This was a game they had played many times. Margret looked at Carrie and gave her a wink.

"Susan will be home Wednesday," Chi told her. "Maybe we can all go out to dinner Thursday or Friday."

"Sounds like a plan," Margret responded. Carrie opened the patio door and let Margret step out and then followed closely behind her. Chi stood in the doorway and watched as Carrie and Margret climbed into Margret's car. He waved as Margret backed out of the driveway. His mother returned the wave. Carrie raised a tentative hand and waved with only the slightest of movements.

When they reached the main road Margret spoke up. "What happened back there?"

Carrie didn't respond but held her head down.

Margret tried again, "You were shaking like a leaf and didn't say a word the whole time we were there. What was that all about?"

"I'm sorry. I don't know." Carrie turned to look out her window. "That banging really bothered me."

"Why? I told you what it was. Chi does that all the time."

"I don't know. I'm sorry."

They drove in silence until they pulled into Margret's driveway. She put the car in park and sat motionless for a moment looking out the windshield. Carrie sat quietly waiting with her hands folded in her lap.

"Carrie, I don't know what happened to you but I can tell that whatever it was it was bad. What happened back at Chi's wasn't normal."

"I know."

"Can you tell me what happened to you?"

Carrie hung her head as Margret watched her. Tears welled up in her eyes. "No. Please," she said softly.

Margret put her hand on her back and rubbed her across the shoulder blades. "You know you're safe here, right?"

"I hope so."

"You are. Nothing's going to happen here."

"I know."

They sat there a few moments until Carrie could push back the tears. She wiped her face with her sleeve, sniffed and then looked into Margret's face. "Thank you," she told Margret.

Margret tilted her head. "For what?"

"For being my friend."

"Sweetie, I think I need you as much as you need me right now." She stopped rubbing her back and then patted her knee. "Come on. Let's go freshen up your makeup and then we'll go hit Tello's. I don't think Chi knows what he's in for when he gives a couple of women his credit card."

Carrie smiled. "But he said it was only for dinner."

"Yes, he did. But what he didn't say was how much food we could eat or how long that dinner should last." She laughed. "And we've got all night."

Ralph Nelson Willett

Chapter 11

Kevin stood at the high top table beside the chair. He faced the door on the opposite side of the room trying to hide his nervousness. Emiliano sat beside him seemingly much calmer than Kevin thought he should be. He knocked back the last of his second beer, fixated his eyes briefly on the far door, eased the glass down slowly and then looked at Emiliano. Emiliano was staring into his beer absent-mindedly. He was still nursing his first beer. It looked as if he was daydreaming. Kevin wanted to shake him awake, to make him feel the same tension he did.

"What time is it?" Kevin asked him.

Emiliano casually pulled his phone from his shirt pocket and checked the time, "Seven thirty-one," he replied returning the phone back to his pocket. "He'll be here."

The waitress brought over two more beers and set them on the table. Emiliano finished the one he had in three swallows and handed the empty glass to her. He thanked her as she took the empties away. Kevin said nothing. He glared at her, resenting the interruption.

"I don't like this," Kevin told him.

"Doesn't matter."

"Chainmail has never asked to see me like this before."

"Again, doesn't matter. But don't be thinking it'll be Chainmail coming. It won't be."

Kevin swore. "Then who's coming?"

"I've no idea. We'll see. Until then, just relax. Why you so jumpy?" Emiliano turned his head to face him.

"This doesn't feel right. It's not like when he wants us to take a run."

"You don't know what he wants. If you're righteous my brother, then you got nothing to worry about."

Kevin took two large swallows and set the glass down. "I'm clean. I've no idea why he..." He stopped mid-sentence as the front door opened. The man who stepped inside was large. Kevin guessed him to be at least six four and at least two hundred and forty pounds. He could almost see the chiseled muscle beneath the leather jacket he wore. The man paused at the door as he scanned the room, locked eyes briefly with Kevin and then continued his scan of the room. Kevin watched as he repeated the scan twice and then signaled outside. Two more men followed him in. The second one was much smaller, not much larger than Kevin, dressed indistinctively in jeans and a thin brown leather jacket covering a blue oxford shirt. The third man that stepped in was more like the first, large and muscular, scanning the room with a suspicious eye.

The smaller man and the first larger man walked quickly past Kevin and Emiliano and stopped at a door at the far side of the bar. The bartender met them at the door, unlocked it and returned to his station behind the bar. Nothing was said. The two stepped in, turned on the room lights revealing several tables inside and then closed the door behind them.

The third man stepped over to Kevin's table. Saying nothing, he motioned with his head toward the door at the end of the bar. Both Kevin and Emiliano began moving but the big man held his hand up towards Emiliano signaling him to sit back down. Kevin hesitated and the large man motioned him forward again. Kevin walked to the door with the large man following. At the door, Kevin stopped, turned and looked at the man following him as if asking for confirmation of his action. The man nodded. Kevin opened the door and stepped in. The man following him closed the door behind him but remained standing outside.

Kevin looked around the room. This appeared to be another bar. There were several round tables with chairs turned upside down on top of them and three or four with chairs tucked underneath. The shelves behind the bar were stocked with a hundred colorful bottles of liquors filled to various levels. There were a few high top tables but none of them had stools.

He saw the two men to his left as he entered. The smaller of the two was sitting at the far side of a table with the large man standing behind him to his right. He had unzipped his jacket revealing a weapon holstered under his left arm.

The man sitting at the table motioned him over to sit down. Kevin stepped over, pulled out a chair and sat down. He placed both hands on the table palms down.

"Hello, Kevin," the man said.

Kevin nodded.

"Do you know who I am?" the man asked.

"No."

"Chainmail sent me."

"OK."

"Chainmail is a bit concerned. It seems that someone in your pool has gone AWOL."

"What are you talking about?"

"Carrie. Where's Carrie, Kevin?" the man asked.

"She's left me."

"That's not what I asked you. I asked you where she is."

"She's tucked herself away for a while. I can find her if I need to. It's no big deal."

"That's not what Chainmail thinks. It seems to him that you been with this woman a long time. She knows things."

"She don't know anything," Kevin insisted. An angry tension began to rise in Kevin's voice. "She's too stupid to know anything."

The man lifted his chin up slightly at him and tightened his jaw. Kevin instantly regretted his tone and turned his eyes down to show it. The man continued. "Chainmail don't know what she knows. You've been making runs for us for some time. It's been good. We're family. But when we see someone leave the family we get a bit nervous. Know what I mean, Kevin?" Kevin nodded slowly. "It would be good if the family was together again, all us cousins."

Kevin let the words sink in for a moment and then nodded again. "OK, I'll bring her back in."

The man leaned back in his chair slightly and tilted his head up while looking at him. "Let me make a friendly suggestion," he said. "Bring her in...," he hesitated. "or take her out." The man let that register with Kevin. "We're OK with either one but we need to know what's going on with all our cousins." He let the words sink in for a moment more and then continued. "Kevin, if you can't take care of this, we will. If we have to, there won't be any loose ends. None."

Kevin bristled at the implied threat. "There's never been an issue between my crew and Chainmail. We've always done what you've asked and on time. We've always brought the stuff in and there ain't never been an issue. Why is this a problem now?"

"This isn't going to be a problem, right? You're going to take care of it."

"OK. I'll deal with it, but the next run, is it still ours?"

The man pulled out a cigarette, lit it and blew the smoke in his direction. He appeared to be thinking the question through. "Just take care of business," he said.

Kevin nodded. The man dismissed him with a wave of his hand. Kevin stood and left the room.

~~~~

Kevin and Emiliano sat across from each other at the dining table in Kevin's apartment. Empty beer bottles sat haphazardly on the table, countertop and floor. Emiliano had cleared a space in front of him, slouched back in his chair and rested his right forearm on the table. He watched Kevin as he alternated between taking nervous drags on his cigarette and small sips of his beer. Kevin's eyes shifted around the room anxiously as he tried to think through what he was going to do next.

"Tell him you don't know where she is and you need help finding her," Emiliano suggested.

"I can't," responded Kevin impatiently. "I've already told him I know how to find her. Anyways, I'm betting she's with her parents."

"OK, where's that?"

"I'm trying to remember. I need to find Amber. She'll know."

"What then?" asked Emiliano.

"Bring her back. I don't want to risk losing this next run. This will be enough coin for the rest of the year."

Emiliano shrugged. "What if she won't come back?"

Kevin faced Emiliano squarely. He hated that Emiliano could be so calm while he felt so nervous. "She'll come back," he said. "If she doesn't want to then I'll drag her back." He took another pull at his beer and set it back down on the table. He held the bottle with two fingers by its neck and rotated it in slow circles on its base. "Or I'll kill her," he said quietly.

Emiliano had seen Kevin like this before. He knew what Kevin said wasn't hyperbole. "Why kill her?"

Kevin wasn't in the mood for explanations or discussion. "Why you think I gotta explain anything to you?" Anger contorted his face but Emiliano didn't flinch.

"You don't gotta explain nothing," Emiliano replied calmly.

Kevin locked eyes with him and stared angrily. A long moment passed before Kevin looked away and calmed himself again. He drank his beer empty. "I want that run," he told Emiliano. "If Chainmail thinks she's a problem then she's gotta be fixed. She'll come home or we gotta fix her. That's all."

Emiliano nodded slowly thinking that through. "OK. How long we got?"

"I don't know. Maybe a month, maybe two, before we need to make the run. We'll do it just like last time."

"Yeah. That worked," Emiliano replied.

Kevin cracked open another beer and drank several swallows. "I want you to get ahold of Amber and find out where Carrie's at. Or find out where her parents are. Do that tonight and I'll take somebody and go get her tomorrow."

Emiliano nodded.

Kevin continued, "I'll make some calls tonight and see if anybody else knows."

~~~~

Kevin sat staring at his cell phone on the table. He was tired now. He had called a dozen people. No one had seen or heard from Carrie, knew where she was or where she might have gone. A couple of people suggested she might have gone back to be with her parents but no one had any idea where that would be.

Emiliano rang his cell.

"Did you find out where she is?" Kevin asked as he answered the phone.

"No. Amber doesn't know anything."

"She knows something," Kevin hissed into the phone.

"No. I worked her over pretty good. She don't know noth'n."

Kevin had seen Emiliano work over a woman before. If Amber had known something then she would have talked. He swore into the phone.

"OK, here's what I want," Kevin said. "Put the word out that I'm looking for her. Tell them I miss her and want her back and I'm sorry for everything that's happened and I want to make it right. I want everybody looking for her. Let them know that they'd be doing me a personal favor if they found her for me."

"OK," Emiliano responded. "But don't you think that Chainmail might figure out you have no idea where she is?"

"Let him figure it out," he growled back. "I ain't afraid of that. He'll know we're trying to find her and when we do we'll bring her in."

There was a silence on the phone. Emiliano spoke up. "Dude, what does she know?"

"Noth'n. She don't know noth'n. That chick was too dumb to make coffee let alone keep track of what we were doing and besides, I never told her noth'n."

"Yeah, but if she's with the cops you don't know what's she gonna say."

"She don't know nothing," Kevin repeated forcefully.

"Yeah. Got it," Emiliano replied.

"OK, start putting the word out," Kevin continued. "I'll meet you down at the bar."

He hung up the phone and pulled a cigar box from a kitchen drawer. Opening it he pulled out a small pipe and packed it with weed. Inhaling deeply as he held the flame of the lighter to the top of the bowl he held in the smoke for as long as he could and blew it out slowly. Sitting on the sofa he finished the weed. He sat staring out of the balcony door into the distance. He hated Carrie for leaving him in this mess. If he lost out on this run because she walked out on him, he'd kill her just for fun. First, he'd have to find her. There were only so many places she could go. He'd find her, he thought. Then he'd make her regret taking off.

Ralph Nelson Willett

Chapter 12

Margret was feeling the effects of the wine. She wasn't sure, but she thought that between the two of them they were just starting their third bottle. Or was it their fourth? They had arrived at Tello's at four and now it was almost seven. They had been here for three hours and were just now finishing their second meal order.

"See, I told you this is nice, didn't I?" Margret asked Carrie.

"Yes. It is nice. But isn't Chi going to be mad?"

"Maybe. But he'll get over it." Margret waved a dismissive hand at her. "He didn't say how much food we could order."

"He did say only one bottle of wine," Carrie reminded her.

"Yep," she answered. "He did say that. My son is pretty silly if you ask me."

Carrie grinned at her. "Your church doesn't have a problem with you drinking?"

Margret leaned back in her chair while looking at Carrie with a smirk. "I don't think anyone would be happy to know I've had this much, but other than that, no."

"Wow. In our church, if you ever drank anything you were going straight to hell."

"Seems like your church wanted to send a lot of people to hell. Let me tell you something, God ain't just hanging out waiting for you to screw up so he can punish you. Like, so you do something bad and he zaps you with lightning or something. He ain't like that."

"So, then what *is* he like?" Carrie asked.

"He's more like a father. Someone who wants to hang out with his kids, be proud of them and help them when they need it." Margaret saw the look on Carrie's face. "OK, he ain't like your father. You know that's not normal, right?"

"I suppose."

"God is more like a good father, more like my father. My father would teach us stuff and when we screwed up he'd help us fix it. All because he loved us and wanted the best for us. He never hung around just waiting and hoping we'd screw up so he could punish us."

"You know, Margret, using a father as an analogy for God doesn't really work for me. I can't relate to that."

"Yeah, I know. That's because you haven't seen what real men are like. Real men love their kids, take care of them and protect them," Margret said. "And their women too," she added quickly. "Real men aren't afraid to hold you, to pick you up when you fall down or screw up. They forgive you quickly and say I love you a lot. That's what real men do."

"I don't know any men like that."

"Yes, you do. You've met Chi. Chi's very much like his father."

"Well Chi isn't my boyfriend and I bet he's more the exception rather than the rule."

"Yep," said Margret. "That's where you're wrong. You've just been hanging out with the wrong men. I can tell you that every man out there makes mistakes just like every woman does but that doesn't mean they're bad people."

"You mean like my father," Carrie added quickly.

"Yes. Like your father *and* your boyfriend. You'll see. When you get to know what the men are like at church you'll see a difference."

"My father went to church," Carrie said frowning. "There were other men at that church that knew what was going on and they did nothing to help."

"Yeah, I'm sorry about that. But you know that's not normal, right?"

"You've said that. But that's the normal I've seen."

"That's what I mean," Margret told her. "You haven't seen what '*normal*' is."

There was silence between them as each sought words. Finally, Margret spoke up, "How did we get on this subject again? This is supposed to be fun."

"You mentioned that God was like a father," Carrie told her.

"Oh, yeah. That's right," Margret replied.

Carrie continued, "I can tell you that if God is anything like my father then I don't want anything to do with him. He can go ahead and send me straight to hell because I've been through hell. I already know what it's like."

Margret looked at her sadly for a moment and then a big grin spread slowly across her face.

"What?" asked Carrie.

"You said that if God is anything like your father then you don't want anything to do with him."

"Yeah? So?"

"What you didn't say is 'God doesn't exist'." Margret used air quotes to emphasize Carrie's statement.

Carrie looked slightly confused and then replied, "He doesn't exist."

"I don't know," Margret said grinning at her. "I think I might be getting through to you."

Carrie chuckled. "I think the *wine* is getting to you."

"Maybe," replied Margret grinning at her. "But I don't think so."

"OK, but don't you think it may be time for us to be headed back?"

"Not yet," Margret said while stiffening up. "We gotta order something to take home."

"You're kidding. I couldn't eat any more."

"You'll be hungry tomorrow. We'll just stick it in the fridge."

"I think if I were Chi, I'd be mad."

Margret grinned at her, "All I gotta do is bat my baby blues. Hey! That rhymed!" She giggled. "I'm his mama. He can't be mad at me. He's really just a big softy."

~~~~

They carried their take out orders the five blocks home and set it all on the table as they walked in the house. "Why did I ever agree to walking?" Margret asked.

"I think that had something to do with not being arrested."

"Oh, yeah," she said. "Want some more wine? I got more downstairs. You want some?"

"No thank you. I think I've had enough."

"Yeah. I suppose I should be done too." Margret plopped down in the rocking chair. "I should be done too," she repeated. She rocked back and forth a few times then added, "I may have overdid it this time."

"I didn't take you for a drinker," Carrie told her.

"I hardly drink anymore. Just after Scott died I drank a lot."

Carrie sat down on the sofa with her legs tucked under her facing Margret. Margret had slouched in the rocker, closed her eyes and was gently rocking back and forth. "I feel happy," she said as Carrie watched her quietly. "Wine maketh glad the heart. That's in the Bible somewhere. I can tell you that is true for me, for sure." She smiled as she rocked with her eyes closed. "It's days like this that make me feel happy. Know what I mean?" She opened her eyes and looked at Carrie.

Carrie nodded. "I'm glad you're happy."

"Aren't you happy?" Margret asked her.

"Yes. I suppose I am."

"You don't sound very convincing," Margret told her as she looked over at her.

"Well I haven't been happy in so long I'm not sure I know what it feels like."

"Oh, yeah," Margret replied. "I really feel sorry for you. Everyone deserves to be happy."

"Really? Why?" Carrie asked her.

Margret closed her eyes again as she rocked. "Why what?" she said softly.

"Why does everyone *deserve* to be happy?"

Margret stopped rocking, opened her eyes and again looked at Carrie. "Don't you think you deserve to be happy?"

"I don't know that anyone *deserves* to be happy." Carrie emphasized the word 'deserves' again.

"Why not?"

"I see a lot of happy people. Like you for instance. You're happy. But what did you do to *deserve* to be happy?"

"I didn't do anything. I just am."

"What about someone like me? What did I do to deserve to be unhappy?"

Margret didn't know how to answer. She thought for a moment then said, "I don't think you did anything to deserve to be unhappy. I don't think God meant for us to be unhappy. That's Satan's job. He's the one that wants us to be unhappy. But on the other hand, I think we do deserve to be happy."

"Why? How is it that we deserve to be happy?"

"Because we're children of the King. He wants us to be happy. He's not the one trying to make us so we're unhappy."

"I know. It's the devil," Carrie said coldly. "You said that, but if I don't believe in God what makes you think I'd believe in a devil?"

Sadness swept over Margret's face as she looked at her. "Carrie, I pray that God will open your eyes so that you can see him. He wants you to be happy. He wants you to experience his love. I think that once you open up to Him things will turn around for you. Heck, I think things are turning around for you right now. That's why you're here."

"Well I think someone is going to be very unhappy when he sees what we spent on dinner tonight," Carrie replied trying to change the subject.

Margret sighed with a broad smile. "No, he won't," she said as she resumed her rocking. "I know Chi. He already knows what I spent tonight. He gets a text message every time his card is used. He's probably just shaking his head and saying 'just how much can two women eat?'."

"Is he rich or something?"

"No, he ain't rich. He does really good for himself but he ain't rich. He just ain't worried that much about his money. Why else would he just hand over his card? And besides," Margret turned to give Carrie a mischievous grin, "he loves his mama."

Carrie nodded without expression.

"Hey," Margret began. "Wanna play some cards?"

"No thanks. If you wouldn't mind, I think I'd like to go in my room and just read a while. Is that OK?"

"Sure, sweetie. I think I might crash, too. I'll see you in the morning."

Carrie stood, pulled a Rachael Wallace book from the shelf and closed herself in her room. Margret sat in the rocker for several minutes longer, nearly drifting off to sleep. Finally rising from the rocker, she turned off the lights and went into her own room. Just before closing the door she checked the time on the wall clock. It was only just after eight o'clock.

Chapter 13

Carrie heard the sound of running water. "What is that?" she said out loud as she began to come out of a deep sleep. She looked around her bed and around the room. She saw nothing in the dim light but the sound grew louder. Thoughts of drowning flashed through her mind. Then she smelled smoke. It grew stronger as she desperately looked around the room from atop her bed, trying to find it's source. She heard a woman laughing but could not tell from which direction it was coming. Panic began to set in. She sat straight up in bed as she realized what the smoke meant. She yelled Margret's name to warn her.

Movement beyond the foot of her bed caught her attention and Carrie looked up to see her father. He stood with his shoulders sagging and his arms hanging loosely by his side. He looked at her with empty eyes. The laughter rose in a crescendo and then ended suddenly, leaving an echo in her ears.

"Dad, what are you doing here?" Carrie asked her father.

He stared back at her coldly. His eyes opened wider and turned a reflective black. His face remained expressionless. Raising an arm from his side slowly, he pointed at Carrie with an accusing finger.

The room suddenly burst into flames all around her. Carrie screamed. Her scream echoed back at her from all directions. The blanket on her bed caught fire along its edges. She screamed again as she felt the flame brush against her legs. Her father thrust his finger so close to her that she could see the dirt beneath his fingernail. The empty blackness of his eyes reflected the flames all around her.

She looked desperately for an escape but even the door was on fire. She screamed again as she twisted to look for an escape through the bedroom window. A face peered back at her from the darkness outside. It was pale, expressionless, with dead, empty eyes that also reflected the fire back at her in the same way her father's did. Again she screamed in terror at the sight of the face staring back at her.

She tried pulling the blankets up to her chest but it pulled the flames closer to her. She felt the burning on the side of her torso causing her to scream out again. Hands grabbed her by the shoulders from out of the flames and began shaking her violently, snapping her head back and forth. The face in the window behind her growled her name as her head shook loosely.

"Carrie! Carrie! Wake up!" The voice shifted from a growl to something more familiar. She screamed again as another face came into focus in front of her. She stared at the face uncomprehendingly. Another scream rose up from her throat. The fire disappeared and she looked around her room with panicked eyes to see if her father was still present. He wasn't.

"Carrie! Wake up!" Carrie tried to catch her breath as the panic began to subside. She was sitting up in bed. Margret was holding her by both shoulders trying to shake her from her sleep. She focused on Margret's face. Margret's worry was evident.

Margret stopped shaking Carrie as she saw her awareness return to her. Carrie stared at Margret for a moment as she became conscious of where she was. She leaned into Margret, placing her head on her shoulder and began to sob uncontrollably.

Wrapping her arms around her, Margret held her for several minutes, rocking her gently back and forth. "It's OK, honey," she repeated over and over again. "It's OK."

~~~~

Margret sat at the kitchen table sipping a mug of coffee as she watched Carrie sleeping on the sofa. She had been jolted out of sleep at four AM by Carrie's screaming. She quickly ran to her room where she found Carrie sitting upright with wide open, terrified eyes, screaming at the top of her lungs.

Carrie had moved into the living room and sat on the sofa after Margret calmed her down. Margret held her in her arms until the trembling stopped. Eventually, Carrie laid her head on Margret's lap and fell asleep again as Margaret gently stroked her hair. After an hour Margret placed Carrie's head on a pillow and covered her with a blanket.

Margret was done sleeping for the night. Being jolted awake by Carrie's screaming pumped her body full of adrenaline. It was now almost six and the sky was just beginning to become light as the sun rose beyond the eastern horizon. She had made herself a pot of coffee and now sat thinking through what happened. This was a new experience for her. None of her children had ever had night terrors. She didn't know anyone that did. She wasn't sure she entirely understood the event.

Margret opened her Bible in front of her and attempted to read but could not focus. Her thoughts continued to be on Carrie. Here was a young woman, younger than her own children, that had lived such a hard life. Some of it was not of her own choosing but then some of it was. Or was it? She wondered how much choice Carrie actually had in her situation. These were things Margret knew she didn't understand and didn't know how to relate to, being mentally tortured by her own father and then physically beaten by her boyfriend. Intellectually she knew these things happened but at no time had she ever met anyone who had this as a reality in their lives. Or if she did she wasn't aware of it, she thought.

Her eyes began to tear as she found herself watching Carrie as she slept on the sofa in the dim light. Soon tears began rolling down Margret's cheeks. She said a quick prayer as she watched her sleep. As the tears began to flood, she bowed her head, folded her hands on top of her opened Bible and began quietly praying out loud for her in earnest. She let the tears roll to the table making small puddles beneath her. After long seconds of prayer, she lifted her head and wiped her eyes with the palms of her hands.

She stood to retrieve a tissue from a box on the counter and noticed the room was brighter. She leaned back against the kitchen counter and wiped her face dry. Looking at Carrie she saw she had shifted positions. Glancing up at the clock she noticed that it was now just after seven. To Margret, it seemed she had prayed for only seconds but it had been almost an hour.

Chapter 14

The warmth of the sun coming into the living room from the kitchen woke Carrie just before nine. She sat up groggily and looked around. The memories of last night rushed back to her in an instant. Embarrassment flushed her as she thought about her panic and her screaming.

Margret stepped out of her room and noticed she was awake and sitting up. "Good morning," she told her.

"Hi," Carrie replied.

"You feeling better?"

"I suppose so."

Margret sat down in the rocker. "Do you remember what happened last night?"

Carrie looked at Margret with evident embarrassment. "Um, yes. I'm sorry. I don't know what happened. But thank you."

"For what?"

"For taking care of me."

"Oh, that's alright, Honey. I'm a mom. It's in my nature." Margret gave a dismissive wave that Carrie acknowledged with a slight smile. "Do you remember what you were dreaming?"

Carrie struggled to try and remember. "Yeah. Yeah, I think I do."

"What happened."

"I just remember that the room was on fire and my father was at the end of my bed pointing at me and yelling." She squinted her eyes down at the floor as she tried to remember. "Then there was that demon looking at me through the window."

Margret raised an eyebrow. "Demon?"

"Yeah. I've seen its face before in my dreams. That's why I remember. I only ever see its face. Real pale and its eyes look like they see you, but they're empty, no expression. Sometimes it sneers at me and other times he's just there, watching."

"How do you know it's a demon?"

Carrie picked her head up and looked Margret in the face. She appeared mildly surprised. "It wasn't a demon for real. There ain't no such thing. But that's what he reminded me of."

Margret slowly nodded as she thought through this information. Carrie continued, "The room door was on fire, and I was trapped. My blankets and everything were burning." She squinted down at the floor again as she tried to remember more of the dream. Margret said nothing.

"That's all I can remember," Carrie murmured as she looked down at the floor.

"Well, it was only a dream," Margret told her. "It's over now. Has that happened before?"

"Sort of. I don't remember waking up screaming before."

"I can tell you, you really scared me last night," Margret said.

"I'm sorry. I feel bad about it."

"It's not a problem, but I hope we don't have much more of that. I think before you go to bed tonight I'm going to bless your room."

Carrie smirked. "What are you going to do? Sprinkle holy water all over it?" she asked sarcastically.

"You know Carrie, you may not believe in these things, but I do. If it makes this old lady happy then just let me do it."

Carrie waved a hand at her palm up. "OK. No problem."

"Thank you. Now, what do you want for breakfast?"

~~~~

Margret sat at a high table in the Living Room Cafe drinking an iced coffee. Carrie had chosen to stay at home and read some more of Chi's romance novels. Carol, the volunteer barista, sat beside her. Margret had filled her in on the events of last night.

"I've got to tell you, Carol, I'm a bit worried about what I might have brought into my home," Margret told her.

Carol nodded as she listened. Margret continued, "I've no idea what type of spirits might be connected to this girl."

"Well, that is a possibility," Carol agreed. "But we do have protection in Jesus."

"I know, but I've never had to deal with anything like this before. I've never met anyone that's been so..." Margret sought the right word. "tormented."

"Do you want us to come and pray over her?"

"She wouldn't accept it. I told her I was going to pray over her room tonight before she went to bed. She almost laughed in my face."

"That doesn't mean we can't pray protection over your house. She doesn't have to even be there."

"I know," Margret said. "But if the spirit is attached to her it will just come right back." Margret's face was beginning to show her worry.

"How about we let God worry about that," Carol told her as she touched her forearm. Margret gave her a worried smile. "We can get a few people together, go to your house and pray over it while no one is there. But I think you'll have to be there. It's your house, and you're the authority over it."

Margaret thought this through. It did seem like the proper thing to do.

"We'll need someone to take her out for a while so we can meet you there," Carol said.

Margret looked surprised. "You mean like a date?"

"No. Not like a date. Maybe we can get a couple of women to take her out and do something with her for a while."

"Ah," Margret said as she nodded. "I see. Well, she's already met, Jess and Becky. Susan won't be back until tomorrow. Maybe we can get Becky and Rosie to take her out."

"It wouldn't hurt to ask," Carol said.

Margret pulled out her cell phone and paged through her contacts until she came up with Becky's. She was about to press the call button when she stopped and looked at Carol. She then put her cell phone back in her pocket. "I can't do that."

"What?" asked Carol.

"I can't take the risk of getting anyone else involved with any spirits. If they're attached to her then I wouldn't want those girls hanging out with her."

"OK. Then what do you suggest?"

"I'll ask Chi to take us out to dinner. I'll give you a key, and you can take care of it."

Carol looked away in contemplation. "I can do that," she replied.

Margret thought for a moment. "I think I'd like you to ask Chi's life group to help you out."

"OK, but why that group?"

"I don't know. It just came to me, but that's what I'd like you to do. And see if you can get Solomon Richards to go with you. I've heard he's been through this before."

Margret pulled out her phone again, leafed again through the contacts and pressed dial. She waited a moment and then said into it, "Hey, you're taking Carrie and me to Holland for Chinese food tonight."

Chapter 15

Chi pulled up in front of Margret's house at six. He climbed out and walked through the kitchen door.

"Bout time you got here," Margret told him.

"What? You said six. I'm right on time."

"If you're not early then you're late," she reminded him.

"Well, then I'm always going to be late. Get used it." He said as he gave her a hug.

He waved to Carrie sitting on the sofa reading one of his books. She waved back as she stood and stretched out her back.

"I wouldn't have thought it possible that you two could be hungry after all you ate last night," he told his mother.

"You didn't say how much I could eat," she said as she pulled out his credit card and handed it back to him. Chi tucked the card into his wallet and put it in his front pocket.

Carrie joined them in the kitchen and placed the paperback book she was reading on the counter. She saw Chi glance at it. "Interesting book," she said.

"Yeah? What makes it interesting?"

"Knowing it was you who wrote it. That's kind of funny."

"Funny? Why is that funny?" he asked her.

"Knowing you're a guy writing books for women."

"I write books for me. Women just like reading them."

"Wow," she said. "That makes you sound so gay."

Margret intervened. "That's enough, you two." She touched Chi's arm. "You two are starting to sound like you and Diane did when you both were in high school."

Chi smirked at her. "That's all I need is another sister."

Margret tossed Chi her car keys. "You're driving, sailor."

"Alright," he replied as he began to head out the door with Carrie following.

"I'll be right out. I need to take care of something first."

Margret waited until Chi and Carrie had walked out and then pulled her cell out. She dialed a number. A moment later she said, "Hi. It's me. We're leaving now. You have my permission to perform a cleansing. Thank you. Bye."

She tucked her cell phone into her purse and stood in the kitchen facing the dining room. She said a silent prayer to herself and then held her head high as she held her hand above her head, palm facing out. "To the spirits that may be in this house, you do not have my permission to be here. You will leave this house now." She held that position for a moment. A chill ran through her body. She shook it off. Lowering her hand and bowing her head she said aloud, "Jesus, please cleanse this house." She stayed there a moment longer and then joined Chi and Carrie in the car.

~~~~

Pete unlocked the kitchen door and let himself in with Rosie following close behind. Solomon Richards held the door as Becky entered just ahead of Jess. Solomon closed the door behind them as he came in. Chris and her husband tapped at the door. They let themselves in. Solomon pushed the door closed behind them.

They stood silently looking over what they could see of the house as they crowded into the kitchen between the island and the counter. They could hear the ticking of the kitchen clock on the wall, exaggerated in contrast with the silence.

"Let's get started," Pete said as he directed everyone toward the living room. They formed a circle holding hands, each bowing their heads. The silence remained, only punctuated by the ticking of the kitchen clock like a slow metronome. After several seconds Pete opened in an audible prayer. Quiet voices repeated "thank you, Jesus" as Pete spoke. Pete then stood silently praying, as Solomon picked up the prayer. Again, quiet voices repeated "thank you, Jesus" and "Praise you, Jesus."

The prayer continued for several minutes as each took a turn inviting in the presence of the Holy Spirit. At its conclusion, they released each other's hands and watched Solomon as he produced a small bottle of oil from his pocket. He blessed it and passed it to Pete who grasped the bottle between both hands, hiding it from view. Pete simply said, "Thank you,

Jesus." After giving it a light squeeze, he gave it to Rosie who said a brief prayer over it and then passed it to Becky. The process repeated several times until the bottle had passed around the circle returning it to Solomon.

Solomon brushed his gray hair back with one hand and walked quietly to the door that led to the basement. Everyone followed him down in turn. At the bottom of the stair, they collectively bowed their heads again, raising their hands, palm out, as Solomon prayed over the basement area.

As the remainder of the group prayed quietly, Solomon spoke with authority. "Any spirits that are here that are not of God I command you, under the authority given me as an heir of the Father, by the blood of Jesus Christ and by delegation of Margret Baroda, to leave this house and never return. You do not have permission to be here."

Solomon stood with his right arm stretched forward, his hand out. His face was grim and stern, projecting an absolute authority. He held that position for a moment. He next took the small bottle of oil, placed a small amount on his finger and used it to make the sign of the cross on the wall. He did the same for each wall in the basement. They repeated the process in the kitchen, then the living room and Margret's bedroom as they methodically worked their way through the home. They then moved into the small sewing room, crowding in and again repeated the process.

Solomon opened the door slowly to Carrie's room and entered. He hesitated just briefly before moving forward allowing the rest of the group to join him. The prayer began, and Solomon again commanded any spirits in the room to leave.

"Smell that?" It was Becky's voice speaking in a whisper. Solomon froze with his finger on the mouth of the small bottle of oil.

"Smoke," Rosie announced quietly.

"Is something burning," asked Jess.

They each looked around the room. The smell was faint but definite.

"No," Solomon said. "Anyone else feel the chill?"

"I do," replied Becky. "As soon as we walked in here I felt it."

"I feel it, too," Jess answered.

Solomon then repeated his command for any spirits in the room to leave and never to return three more times.

As the group prayed, he formed a small sign of the cross with the oil on each of the walls, the four-bed posts and then the headboard. He looked around the room again, moved to the window and placed one in the lower right corner of the window. He directed the group to leave. Just before he left the room, he placed a cross on the inside molding of the doorway. Closing the door behind him as he exited the room, he turned, put his hand on the door and leaned against it heavily. He said a quiet prayer over the door as the others watched. When he finished, he used the oil to place another small cross in the center of the door.

As a group, they stopped to look around the house and spread out between the living room and the kitchen. Rosie stood holding Pete's hand and said another prayer.

"Only one more thing we have to do," announced Solomon. "We have to do a once around on the outside of the house."

They left the house, and Pete locked the door behind them. They walked quietly in pairs as Solomon led them around the house. He painted a small cross on each of the outer walls as they walked around it and then on the front and back doors.

They formed a circle again in the driveway, and Solomon said a prayer asking God's protection for each of them. They then climbed into their cars and drove away.

~~~~

"OK, Mom, you can quit talking about that restaurant now. Yes, the food was good, but it wasn't that good." Chi was opening the kitchen door to let Margret and Carrie go in.

"Oh, come on, just because you think you're some world traveler doesn't mean you know good food," Margret teased him as he held the door for her.

"Yep. It's always good when I'm paying for it."

"That's right," Margret replied as she nearly skipped into the kitchen.

Carrie was smiling as she crossed the threshold and stopped, frozen in place. Chi looked down on top of her head as he stood holding the door open for her.

Margret turned to see the expression on Carrie's face. Carrie was slack jawed as her eyes darted around what she could see of the kitchen and living room.

"What's the matter with you?" Margret asked.

Carrie focused her eyes on Margret. She looked confused and dazed.

Margret took a step closer to her. "Are you OK?"

Carrie seemed to snap back alert. "Yeah, I'm alright." She wobbled and put her hand on the door frame to steady herself. Chi put his free arm under her arm to catch her if she fell.

"You don't look OK, honey. What's wrong?" Margret asked again.

Carrie took a second to answer, the smile was no longer there. Chi and Margret exchanged glances.

"I'm OK," Carrie repeated as she straightened herself out and shed her shoes. She walked into the living room and sat heavily in the rocker. She began to rock herself slowly back and forth as she stared straight ahead with a blank expression.

Margret kicked her shoes off and followed her into the living room. She stood in front of Carrie as she rocked herself.

"Carrie, you don't look so good. Can I get you something? Water maybe?" Margret looked at Chi to signal him for a glass of water.

"Thanks, Margret, but I'm fine."

Margret tilted her head as she watched Carrie. Carrie's eyes seemed to become vacant as if her mind was suddenly drifting away. She then began to tear up and quickly tears began to flow down her cheeks. Margret knelt beside her and held her hand.

"What's the matter?"

"I don't know," she whimpered. "I don't know what's wrong." She began to sob; her body shook as she gasped for air.

Margret put her arm around her, pulled her in, and looked up at Chi as he brought a glass of water for Carrie. Chi looked down on them as he stood beside them holding the glass. He looked baffled, not knowing what to say or do.

"Whatever it is, we can find a way to make it better," Margret told her.

"I don't know what's wrong," Carrie repeated as she tried to control the sobs. "I don't know why I'm like this. I don't know why I'm like this. I don't know why I'm crying."

Margret continued to hold her against her shoulder. She stroked the back of her head slowly and gently. The sobs began to quiet, but Carrie still trembled in her arms. Chi brought a box of tissues to them, and Margret handed her one. Carrie used it to wipe her eyes and nose.

"I'm sorry," Carrie said weakly.

"There's nothing to be sorry for, Honey," Margret told her.

"I'm so sorry," Carrie repeated.

"Oh, Honey, I don't know what you'd have to be sorry for."

Carrie remained quiet and finally spoke. "You treat me like your own daughter. Chi treats me like a sister. Why would you do that?"

"Maybe because we love you," Margret replied.

"Why would you love me. You don't know me." Her body shuddered in Margret's arms.

"Because God loves us. That makes it easy for us to love others."

Carrie remained silent. She wiped her eyes and nose again with a fresh tissue.

"There is no God," she said weakly.

Margret gave her a comforting squeeze. "Honey, now it sounds like your trying to convince yourself of that."

Ralph Nelson Willett

Chapter 16

The remainder of the week passed quietly. Carrie had no more nightmares and slept well, sometimes even beating Margret out of bed in the morning. Saturday she even made a bacon and pancake breakfast for the two of them before Margret was up.

To Margret, Carrie seemed much happier. Carrie was smiling much more and even laughing with her. Each of their walks downtown and to the beach seemed new and exciting. In the evening they would play card games or just read. Carrie had read her way through several of the Rachael Wallace romance books and once commented, "I can hardly believe it's Chi writing these. I can't picture that big muscle bound guy doing that type of thing."

"No one can," Margret replied. "That's what makes it so much fun."

Thursday Chi brought Susan over to introduce her to Carrie. The two of them instantly clicked as they sat talking.

Margret felt confident with her relationship with Carrie now. They had talked about where she could apply for jobs and where she might be able to find an apartment. Their conversations frequently broke out into laughter as they enjoyed each others company.

Saturday night as they both sat reading in the living room Margret said, "Chi's going to pick us up tomorrow about 10:30 so we can attend the 11:01 service."

Carrie looked up from her book and looked at Margret. It seemed to Margret that a sudden sadness returned to her.

"I'm sorry. I can't do that."

"Can't do what?"

"I'm sorry. I can't go to church with you."

"Why not? Why can't you? That's not our agreement."

"I know, but I can't. I'm sorry."

Margret stared at her with obvious hurt. Carrie looked away.

Margret said quietly, "You agreed that if you stayed here, you'd go to church with me on Sundays."

"I'm sorry, Margret. I just can't. This 'God' thing isn't going to work for me."

The look of hurt increased on Margret's face. "Please. Please don't do this to me."

"I'm not doing anything to you."

"Yes. Yes, you are. Don't you see? We made an agreement, and I kept my end. If you can't keep yours, then I have to ask you to leave. Please don't make me do that."

"Where am I going to go?"

"Please, Carrie. Don't make me do that."

Carrie was getting angry and spoke louder. "Look, you can't make me believe in a God that doesn't exist. You just can't. I'm not going someplace that's filled with hypocrites and liars."

"Carrie, please. Please don't make me do this. Please." Margret was pleading.

"I'm not making you do anything!" Carrie shouted at her.

Margret sat back in the rocker in resignation. "OK," she said quietly. "OK." She looked down vacantly at the floor. Carrie relaxed as the tension began to leave her.

Margret rocked almost imperceptibly as a minute passed. "I'll need you to leave on Monday."

"What?!" Carrie yelled as she sat up on the edge of the sofa. She stared angrily at Margret. Margret didn't respond. She continued staring at the floor with a sad, vacant look.

"Just because I won't go to church with you you're going to kick me out?"

Carrie waited, but Margret did not respond. When realizing that Margret was not going to say more, she stood quickly and walked angrily into her room.

~~~~

Sunday morning Margret ate breakfast alone at the kitchen table. She did not sleep well last night. Her mind raced as she tossed and turned, laying awake for hours. She worried about Carrie. Where would she go? Would she return to the same abuse she just came out of? Would she become homeless and live on the street? Margret did not know. Several times during the night she awoke and prayed as she lay in bed. Twice she cried. Was she doing the right thing?

While she ate her breakfast, she had seen Carrie get up once and go into the bathroom only to return angrily to her room a couple of minutes later without looking over to Margret. Margret had resigned herself to defeat. She was losing a friend.

She returned to her room, dressed for church and waited on her bed for time to pass until it was time to leave. When the clock reached 10:30 she left her room. She saw Susan's SUV pulling up in the drive with Chi in the passenger seat. Right on time, she thought. That's my sailor.

As Margret opened the kitchen door to leave, Carrie's room door opened and Carrie stepped out. She was wearing jeans, tennis shoes and a light blouse. Without exchanging words, Margret watched as Carrie walked past her by the door and walked outside. Anger was etched deeply into her face. As Margret left the house and locked the door behind her, a faint smile came to her face.

~~~~

Carrie was already irritated with this whole God thing, but being blackmailed into going to church did not help matters. Yes, that's what it was she thought, blackmail. Margret had blackmailed her into coming. She seethed inside. She'd find some way to pay her back for this. Margret said she was her friend and this is what she was going to do to her? She'd find a way to move out on her own, and put Margret, Chi and the others behind her as quickly as possible.

She stared out of the passenger side rear door window of the SUV avoiding looking at anyone and refusing any conversation. Susan and Margret bantered on about something, but Carrie tuned them out. The drizzling rain this morning seemed appropriate for the way she felt, sad, angry, cold and distant. She thought back to the last time she was in a church, a week before she graduated from high school. She sat between her father and mother as the preacher was yelling about something or another. He was always yelling about something. That's what preachers do, they yell. She hated the thought of going through that again today and resented Margret even more for it.

"Hell," she thought. "I'm going to hell. There's no need to tell me. I already know, so what's the point? Shout it. Go ahead and scream it. I don't care. Nothing can affect me anymore. I'm tougher than I was back in high school."

Susan pulled the SUV into the high school parking lot. Carrie sat up and looked around. She had been told that church was being held in the high school auditorium but had forgotten. She had expected a white-steepled building with tall stained glass windows. Her eyes darted around as she tried to see what type of people would go to a church like this. She counted. One. Two. She saw two women in skirts. Only two. In her mind, she wrestled with conflicting feelings that the dress code wasn't right and another that suggested she would be welcomed as she was.

Margret looked over at her. Carrie's jaw was clenched tightly, and her eyebrows angrily furrowed. She knew Carrie was unhappy about coming to church with them but didn't care. That was the agreement. She said a silent prayer that Carrie's heart would soften.

Walking towards the building Susan and Chi led the way holding hands together. Margret and Carrie followed close behind. Margret happened to look over and noticed Carrie watching Susan and Chi holding hands. "Would you like to hold my hand?" she winked at her.

"Stop it," Carrie hissed in an angry whisper.

As they entered the vestibule of the auditorium, they were greeted at the door by a couple that welcomed them in. The couple made a special point of saying hello to Carrie.

"Are you from South Haven?" the woman asked.

"No. I'm from Bishop Hill, Illinois."

"Never heard of that. Where's that at?"

"South and west of Chicago. Real small town. No one's heard of it."

"Just visiting?" the man asked her.

"I'm staying with Margret for a while." She pointed at Margret.

"It's great to have you with us," the woman told her. "Hey, Margret, be sure to take her to the info station and get her a welcome packet."

"Will do," Margret answered as she and Carrie began walking in.

They caught up again with Susan and Chi who were talking with two other couples. Carrie recognized Jessie, Becky, and Pete but didn't know the other woman. Pete saw Carrie, smiled broadly, held out his arm to her and invited her over to join them. "Good morning, Carrie. I'd like you to meet my wife, Rosie."

Rosie shook her hand. "Hi, Carrie." Rosie held a small baby. Carrie's eyes automatically drew to him. "This is Anthony." Rosie said then she nodded to the little girl standing beside her. "This is my daughter Chrissy." The little girl gave her a shy smile and a quick wave of her hand.

"Hi," Carrie said.

"You're looking better," Jessie said.

"Yeah. Margret's been taking care of me."

"That's what she does. Mama Margret." He smiled at Margret, and she smiled back. Jessie continued, "Today's service is going to be a little bit different. We've got a guest speaker today."

Oh great, thought Carrie. A special screamer. That's going to be just awesome. "OK," she said softly.

Margret tugged at her arm and directed her to a welcome station set up in the middle of the vestibule. An older woman stood behind it and smiled broadly as Margret and Carrie approached.

"Hi Tiffany," Margret said as she approached the table. "This is Carrie. She's here for the first time today."

The woman extended her hand out and shook Carrie's hand. Tiffany's eyes sparkled brightly. "Hi, Carrie. Welcome. I have something for first timers." She pulled a small gift bag off the counter and offered it to her. Carrie hesitated for just a moment as she looked at it and then cautiously accepted it from her. It was heavier than she expected. It was decorated with gift packing stuffed into it hiding its contents from view.

"Thank you," she said looking up. Carrie felt confused for some reason she could not explain and looked to Margret for reassurance.

Tiffany didn't seem to notice, "Do you live here in town?"

Carrie's attention was brought back to the smiling woman again. "Yes. I'm staying with Margret for a while."

"Ah. Where are you from originally?"

"A small town in Illinois."

"What brings you to South Haven?"

Margret intervened, "Hey, Tiff, sorry to interrupt, but I need to introduce Carrie to someone before the service starts."

"Oh, sure. Nice to meet you, Carrie."

Margret guided her away. Carrie still felt confused, awkward and perhaps a little afraid.

"I didn't think you'd want to answer a lot of questions," Margret told her. "When people come in it's normal for us to want to welcome them but I thought you may not want to tell your story just yet."

Carrie stopped and looked at her for a moment, "Thank you."

"No problem."

"Who did you want to introduce me to?"

"I don't know. We'll find somebody."

Carrie could not help but smile at Margret in spite of herself. She suddenly felt safe and relaxed a little. Margret led her into the auditorium. A music video was playing on the large screen up front with a timer counting down. The music was loud enough that Margret had to lean in and speak up for Carrie to hear her. "Where would you like to sit?"

Carrie looked around the auditorium. It divided into three sections. The right and left sides had rows of about six seats each. She guessed the middle section to have rows of thirty seats each. She looked behind them to the back of the auditorium. "I'd like to sit back there," she said pointing to the back.

"OK," Margret replied cheerfully as she immediately began walking to the back. Carrie followed behind. Margret reached the back row and moved as if to let Carrie move in ahead of her.

"I'd like to sit on the outside, please," Carrie told her.

"Oh, sure." Margret took the second seat in as Carrie sat beside her.

As the countdown continued, Carrie saw Chi and Susan enter the auditorium and look around. Susan saw them first, waved and pulled Chi along with her as they slid in the back row and sat down beside them. More and more people filled the seats ahead of them, and as the countdown reached the forty-five-second mark, the band stepped out on stage and took up their instruments. Carrie still felt a confusion she could not explain. So far this was not a church service she understood. People handed out gifts, there were music videos and a band on stage; this was not a church. She wasn't sure what it was, but it could not be a church.

The countdown hit zero, and the drums kicked in with a loud, heavy beat. The woman behind the keyboard told everyone to stand as "we begin to worship Jesus." The unfamiliar music was loud and upbeat. Carrie could feel the bass guitar and drums thumping in her chest. She could see people clapping along with the music including Susan who also sang along. Margret sang along with a big grin. Chi just stood, smiling. He saw her looking over at him. His eyes sparkled as he gave her a quick wink. She flushed and turned away.

"This was a far cry from any church I've been to before," thought Carrie. The church she had grown up in was smaller than this and the music they sang consisted of old hymns from the stone ages that droned on forever to an out of tune piano. Even thinking about having electric guitars on stage would, as her father put it, 'send you straight to hell.'

But she could not imagine that Margret was going to hell... or Chi. They had rescued her. She had seen Margret reading her Bible and praying when she did not know she was being watched. There was something real there.

'Something real there.' The words echoed through Carrie's mind above the music as it played. This wasn't real. She no longer believed in God. Even if there was a God, after what she'd been through, she did not want to have anything to do with any god that would let all that happen to her. Tension started to fill her body again as memories flooded back. Why would God, any god, let her be abused like she had been all her life?

She recognized that tension filling her body and spirit. It was defiance. That same defiance she felt when she closed herself off in her room, away from her father, as he screamed from downstairs about her many imperfections. "I don't need you, God," she yelled at him angrily in her mind. "I needed you then, and you weren't there. Now I don't need you. I can do this without you. You can leave me alone now!"

The band was playing the third song before she pulled herself out of bitter thoughts and into the present moment. The song was much slower and reverent. She looked again at Margret and Susan. They both held their hands up with their palms facing up and outward. Their faces lifted up, and their eyes closed as they sang along with the music with a slight sway. Chi had his head bowed and his eyes closed. He held his hands at waist level with palms facing up. He still didn't sing, and he did not sway like Margret and Susan, but he stood as if in prayer. Emotions in the room seemed to be running high, but Carrie only felt a strong sense of defiance. "I've prayed my last prayer," she said in her mind to a God she knew didn't exist. "It won't happen again."

Carrie pulled herself out of her own thoughts again and tried to refocus her attention. She crossed her arms over her chest and took a deep breath. She looked at the floor as anger began to rise up in her again. "There is no God," she said out loud, too quietly to be heard over the music.

As the band left the stage, another man stepped up. He wore faded jeans and a T-shirt that said: "These *are* my church clothes." Margret leaned over to Carrie and whispered: "That's Pastor Milan." Again this was something Carrie had not expected. She never thought of a pastor wearing anything other than a suit.

The pastor introduced the guest speaker, Matt Bodie, as he joined Pastor Milan on the stage.

The first thing that Carrie noticed was how young Matt Bodie was. The man could not have been much older than she was; twenty-four, maybe twenty-six at the oldest. He wore a baseball cap that was turned backwards and seemed to accentuate how tall and thin he was. He wore a T-shirt with big lettering that read "I'm Rapping For Jesus".

Music began to play with a heavy beat and Matt Bodie quickly began to step up and down the stage as he spoke rhythmically to the music into a microphone. It only took moments before the audience responded with clapping along with the beat. She saw some younger people pump their fist into the air along with the beat. A soft bounce could be seen throughout the congregation.

Carrie was baffled at the scene. Again, she thought, "This is not a church. I've no idea what this is but it is *not* a church." The song went on for a few minutes and then ended with the congregation applauding. The people sat down waiting for the man to speak. Carrie realized she hadn't heard a word of what was said in the lyrics of the song. Her attention was focused on everyone else around her. She looked at Susan as she settled into her seat. Susan smiled broadly and now seemed energized. Chi wore a faint smile as he slouched in his chair and held Susan's hand as he looked straight forward towards the stage. The so-called congregation seemed eager to hear what the man had to say.

Matt Bodie began to speak. He told a story of his early life and his struggles with the breakup of his parents, failing at school and a sexual assault by an older man. He spoke of his confusion, self loathing and shame. He told them of the pain that finally overwhelmed him to the point of making an attempt at ending his own life.

The room was quiet except for the sound of Matt Bodie's voice. Carrie looked around at the faces she could see. She saw looks of compassion everywhere around her. "This is nothing," she thought to herself incredulously. "I've had and seen more pain than this dude will ever see." She almost chuckled to herself.

The man continued sharing his story. Nearly dying from his suicide attempt he was befriended by a man who understood his pain. Bodie told of how this man reached into his life and helped him to see the wounds that ran so deep in his soul. Then Bodie told of how this man pointed him to Jesus, the one who could heal all of his wounds. Bodie told of how after accepting Jesus into his life things began to change. He was now beginning to put the hurt behind him and move on to something better; a complete and fulfilling life in Jesus Christ. His wounds were healed because someone took the time to point him to Jesus, the great Physician.

Carrie felt her stomach turn and she nearly sneered at the speaker on the stage. This man had no idea what real pain was. He had no clue what it was like to suffer for a lifetime like she had. For him to speak of a 'great physician', this Jesus, a God that doesn't exist, left her bereft of any sympathy for him at all.

The service ended with one more song by Matt Bodie. Rapping to the music he told his story again. The song tugged heavily at everyone's emotions. Now Carrie was just feeling annoyed as she looked around the room. Dozens of people were crying around the auditorium. If they weren't fully crying, then they were teary eyed. Was she expected to be that emotional too? She thought she would have actually preferred a screamer service over this weeper service. All these crying adults only served to make her more uncomfortable. As the song continued, a one-sided conversation began again between her and God, "Go ahead. Do whatever you need to, but you aren't going to get me crying." She tightened her jaw muscles as she jutted it out. She could not wait for the whole thing to be over.

Someone touched her arm startling her out of her thoughts. She turned to see a small black woman squatting beside her. Carrie had been so focused on her mental conversation with

God that she didn't notice the woman approach her. "Would you mind if I prayed for you?" the woman asked.

The conflicting feelings of wanting to be polite and absolute defiance ultimately resolved into a rude "Sure. Go ahead!" as Carrie spat the words out. The woman took no notice of the rudeness but knelt on both knees and placed both hands on Carrie's arm and began to pray out loud softly. The rapper continued his song. The words of the woman's prayer swept past her unnoticed as Carrie now continued her one-way conversation with God. "OK, See! You can't use this woman to get to me either. Do what ever you need to do, but you're not getting to me. I can do this all day long."

The rapper finished his final song just as the woman finished her prayer. Carrie only heard "in Jesus's name, amen." The woman then looked up into Carrie's eyes and returned a kind smile in exchange for the scowl that Carrie displayed. The woman stood and stepped quietly away just as the service ended. Carrie smiled to herself as she thought, "See, God, you failed. You didn't get to me." She smirked to herself and then almost laughed out loud as she reminded herself yet again that there is no God. She thought a moment about the one-way conversation she just had in her head, and told herself it was just a way to entertain her mind, a way to mentally escape this ridiculous environment.

~~~~

Chi, Susan, Margret, and Carrie met Pete and Rosie back in the vestibule to discuss lunch plans.

"I told Carrie we'd go to Tello's again," Margret said to her.

"We're out," Rosie said. "Nap time for the kids."

Just as Jessie and Becky stepped up to join the circle, Carrie felt a tap on her upper arm and turned to see the same small woman who had knelt and prayed for her in the auditorium. "Can I speak to you for a moment?" the woman asked.

Carrie wasn't sure what she felt at the moment. Was it fear? Was it annoyance? This woman was much smaller than her, nearly half her size, so she had no reason to be afraid. The woman had a kind smile and she tilted her head slightly to one side as she spoke to her. Carrie cautiously followed her, stepping back from the circle of friends, perplexed as to why the woman would want to talk to her at all. They only took a couple of steps away and then the woman stopped, faced her and looked up into her eyes.

"I was praying in the prayer room this morning," the woman told her. "The Lord showed me your face and told me you would be here."

Carrie's eyes opened slightly wider and she felt the beginnings of panic setting in. *"Not getting to me, God."*

"He wanted me to tell you something. He said to tell you that he has seen everything you have gone through and everything you have suffered. He wants you to know that he loves you very much."

Carrie stiffened. *"Not getting to me, God..."* Her eyes darted around the room above the woman's head. *"Not getting to me, God!"*

"There's more, Honey," the woman continued as she reached out and touched Carrie on the arm.

Carrie tried to maintain her emotional control as she focused her eyes on the woman. *"Not... Getting... To... Me..."*

"He wants me to tell you that your latter life will be ten times greater than your former life."

Carrie let out an audible "oh" as her stomach turned over. She raised both hands to her face, covering her nose and mouth. A flood of emotions overwhelmed her as she hid behind her hands. The tears began to rush down in a torrent. Her knees felt weak, and she thought she might fall to the floor. She felt hands take hold of her by both arms. Carrie looked to see who held her. Through the tears, she recognized Margret and Chi. They led her to a nearby bench and sat her down. Placing her elbows on her knees, and resting her head in her hands, she wept uncontrollably.

Chapter 17

Margret looked over at Carrie from the kitchen as Carrie sat in the rocking chair staring out of the window towards the backyard. When they left for church this morning, she looked angry, but now she just looked exhausted and sad. Her eyes seemed far away as she stared vacantly outside.

Jessie and Becky sat together on the sofa as Chi and Susan helped prepare a lunch of sandwiches for everyone. The silence was painful as no one knew what to say.

"Carrie, you OK?" Becky asked her quietly.

"Yeah, I'm fine," Carrie replied without emotion.

Becky exchanged glances with Jess and then with Susan. Carrie hadn't told them what the woman said to her in the church. When Carrie nearly fainted, and everyone gathered around her, the woman faded into the background and disappeared. It had taken several minutes before Carrie had calmed down enough for her to be able to leave the school with them.

"Alright, soup's on," Margret spoke loudly as Chi and Susan finished placing glasses of water around the table. Becky and Jess stood, but Carrie made no movement. Becky stood in front of her and held out her hand to help her up. Carrie turned from the window, looked up at her and then slowly took her hand. She stood slowly from the chair while looking expressionlessly into Becky's face. Carrie moved to the table as if she had resigned herself to fate.

Chi sat at the head of the formal dining room table with Susan to his right. Carrie sat next to her with her hands folded in her lap staring vacantly at the sandwich on her plate. Becky sat directly across from her. Margret, sitting at the opposite end of the table from Chi, held out her hands to both Becky and Carrie. Becky held Margret's hand, but Carrie made no attempt to move. The others all joined hands. Susan also held out her hand for Carrie, but again Carrie only sat staring down at her plate. Realizing that Carrie wasn't going to join hands with them, Margret bowed her head and said grace.

Everyone began to eat. There was none of the usual lunch chatter. They ate in silence. Carrie did not move.

"Carrie," Margret said. Carrie moved her head slowly to look at her. "Eat," Margret told her with a commanding voice. Carrie turned to her plate and slowly picked up half of her sliced sandwich and took only a nibble. She returned the sandwich back to her plate, folded her hands on her lap and chewed slowly while staring down. Everyone quietly watched her as she repeated this several times.

Margret finished her sandwich, leaned back in her chair turning towards Carrie. "OK," She said. "Tell me what happened."

Carrie turned her head to face Margret and then looked at the others around the table. Slowly she turned back to Margret. Carrie's eyes still had a distant look to them. Although Carrie was looking directly at her, Margret could tell that she could not see her.

"I don't know," she answered.

"No. You can't tell me that," Margret insisted. "I saw something happen. Mrs. Jackson said something to you and you crashed and burned. What happened?" Her tone was authoritative and commanding.

"I don't know," Carrie said again quietly while looking down.

"What did she tell you?"

Carrie thought for a moment. "She said God saw everything I've gone through and said to tell me my life was going to be ten times better than before." Margret did not respond. Carrie continued, "How did she know that? How did she know my life was bad? How could she know anything about me?" She snapped her head up as if suddenly having some great revelation and looked into Margret's eyes. "You must have told her."

"I didn't tell her nothing," Margret protested.

"Somebody told her." Carrie looked around the table at everyone else for their reactions.

"I don't think anyone told her anything," Chi replied. Susan nodded in agreement.

"Maybe it was God that told her," Margret said.

Carrie reached for her glass of water with a trembling hand and lifted it to her lips. Taking two swallows she then set the glass back down. "There is no God," she said just above a whisper.

Margret leaned in and touched her arm. "Now you sound like you're trying to convince yourself again," she said gently.

Carrie turned her head slowly, looked at Margret's hand touching her arm and then up into her face. "No, there isn't."

Margret pulled back and sat quietly looking at her.

"Carrie, can I tell you something?" Becky asked. She waited for a reaction from Carrie that she thought might not come. Finally, Carrie nodded at her. "When I was 15 I was raped by someone I knew." Becky let that sink in for a moment and then continued softly. "I didn't tell anyone for two years. It really messed me up. Everything fell apart around me. I said the same thing, 'If there was a God then why would he let that happen to me?' I didn't go to church or anything. I stayed home in my room most of the time. Then when I was seventeen, my parents took me to Florida with them on vacation. They decided to go to church that Sunday and made me come with them even though I didn't want to. While I was there, a woman came up to me and said 'I've got a word for you.' I never heard anyone say anything like that before. I didn't even know what that meant. She said 'God saw and has not forgotten.' Then she said 'The guilt is not yours. You need to tell.'"

Carrie watched Becky carefully.

Becky waited to see if Carrie was going to have any reaction. Carrie's expression had changed but nearly imperceptibly. Becky continued. "There was no way that woman could know anything about me. We never went to that church before and never did again. I broke down pretty much like you did today. That's when I told my parents. We went right home after that, and he was arrested. The police found out he had been abusing someone else, too. When I finally told someone, it probably saved the other girl's life, and maybe saved many more girls from being raped. He confessed and went to prison. The man is still in there and will be for a long time. It took two years of counseling for me to get through all that. Through it all, I found out that God does see, he does care, and he will take care of you. All that time I felt guilty and ashamed and couldn't tell anyone. But it wasn't my fault, and I don't think whatever happened to you was your fault either."

Carrie looked down at her plate. The others glanced at each other uncomfortably. Becky remained focused on Carrie.

"No," Carrie answered quietly.

"Can you tell us what happened?" Becky asked.

Carrie showed no reaction. After a moment she finally shook her head slowly. "No. I can't."

"Do you need to?"

Carrie seemed surprised at the question. "What?" she asked.

"Do you need to tell someone? We're here. You can tell us."

Carrie appeared to think about it then said, "No thank you."

"OK, but if you ever decide you want to talk to me about it, you can. I'll listen. And please don't forget that you can talk to Margret or Susan, too."

Carrie looked down at her plate and nodded. "OK," she replied. "Thank you."

Susan reached around Carrie's shoulders and gently pulled her into a hug. Carrie passively allowed the embrace.

After lunch, Carrie returned to the rocker and resumed staring vacantly out of the window. She rocked back and forth gently. Becky and Jess returned to the sofa in the living room. Chi and Susan joined them.

"Carrie," Susan began. "How about coming to life group with us tonight?"

Carrie responded without turning from the window, "OK." Everyone exchanged glances. Margret grinned at Susan. No one expected a positive response to the invitation. It surprised them.

"Awesome," Susan continued. "It starts at seven. Chi and I can come around and pick you up around 6:45."

"OK," she replied again with the same emotionless voice.

They remained together in the living room for several minutes. To Margret, every moment seemed unbearably uncomfortable. Jessie and Becky finally excused themselves and went home. Susan and Chi remained but shifted to the sofa. Chi found one of his books that Carrie had been reading sitting on the end table. He began to examine it as if he were checking it for defects.

"Nice book," Carrie said causing Chi to look up to see her watching him.

"Thank you."

"What makes you wanna write romance books?" she asked.

"Because people buy it. I make money."

Carrie put on a forced smile. "I wouldn't have known a man wrote that unless someone had told me."

"That's how I like it," Chi responded.

"Are you sure you're not gay?"

Chi didn't flinch at the insult. "Nope. Not gay." Susan smirked at him.

"You can't write a man's book?" Carrie asked.

"I write what sells. Romance sells."

"But you're not man enough to write a man's book?" she asked again.

It occurred to Chi that Carrie was trying to pick a fight with him. He decided not to bite. "Well, again, I write what sells. I gotta eat. When the market shifts to whatever a 'man's' book is then I'll write that. It will probably have lots of explosions, gun fights and karate."

"And women?" Carrie asked.

"Probably," Chi responded.

"But 'probably' means maybe not. Because you're gay."

Chi calmly set the book back down on the table and faced her. "Why are you trying to pick a fight with me, Carrie?"

"I'm not trying to pick a fight with you."

"OK, but don't you realize that you're being insulting?"

Carrie turned away and resumed looking out of the window. Margret and Susan both looked to Chi for his reaction. He shrugged his shoulders.

"What do I need to wear tonight," Carrie asked without turning from the window.

Susan responded, "You can wear what you're wearing now. It's casual. You can wear anything you want."

Carrie stood, walked into her room and closed the door.

~~~~

Carrie remained in her room the remainder of the afternoon. Chi and Susan left a couple of hours after lunch. At 6:35 Becky and Jessie returned to pick up Carrie for the life group meeting. "I thought Chi and Susan were picking Carrie up," Margret told them.

Becky answered her, "Susan called and asked that we stop in and pick her up. Something was going on at her house, and they needed to stay a bit longer. They'll still be at life group."

Margret knocked on Carrie's bedroom door. "Carrie, Becky and Jess are here to pick you up."

"OK," came the reply from behind the door. Margret stepped back into the kitchen while they waited. They watched as Carrie's bedroom door opened and Carrie emerged wearing a belted black miniskirt and a white tube top. Her midriff was bare, and she wore boots that came nearly to her knees. She had pulled her hair back into a ponytail and put on large hoop earrings. Her eyes were heavily made up with a dark blue eye shadow. She hesitated at her room door and looked between the three of them standing in the kitchen. Her tightly pursed lips made her look defiant.

Margret's mouth hung open as she looked Carrie over. Jessie's eyes also showed his surprise. Becky reacted as if nothing was unusual.

"You ready?" asked Becky brightly.

"Yes," replied Carrie a bit too loudly.

"OK, let's go."

Carrie looked at Margret as Margret regained her internal composure. Carrie's pursed lips became a smirk as she walked past her, joining Jessie and Becky at the door.

"Have fun you guys," Margret said as she waved them off.

Margret watched out of the kitchen window until their car drove off. Carrie had looked defiantly at her from the rear passenger seat as they pulled away. She stood back from the window feeling a sense of inner shock. The entire two weeks Carrie had been living with her, Carrie had never come close to dressing like that. The skirt was short enough that she wondered how she would sit down without exposing everything. Margret wondered why Carrie would do this and if there was anything she could do. She walked slowly into her bedroom and closed the door behind her. Kneeling at the edge of the bed, she folded her hands together, bowed her head and began to pray.

Ralph Nelson Willett

Chapter 18

Carrie had no idea what to expect when she agreed to come tonight but found she felt uncomfortable around so many people. She knew Chi and Susan, Jess and Becky and Pete and Rosie but there were at least a dozen more people here she didn't know. She now regretted coming.

They were meeting at someone's home. Even after twenty minutes she still did not know who this home belonged to. Chi had called this a Life Group. There were a handful of couples she could identify. The way everyone mingled it was difficult to see who the single people were, such as herself. She still felt as if she were a third wheel.

She stayed close to Jessie and Becky. Becky introduced her to some of the other women standing around talking. Trying to keep her story brief, she simplified it by only telling them she was staying with Chi's mother for a while. They all seemed to be around her age or only just a little older and everyone seemed genuinely happy to meet her. No one commented about how she dressed or even appeared to notice. Her attitude of defiance was fading quickly against the lack of any resistance.

Becky had told her they'd be eating here but she could not have imagined the variety of food that there was going to be. It was all lined up on the counter, salads, chili, a variety of breads, small cheeses wrapped up in meats and deserts. Paper plates were stacked up on one side along with plastic forks, spoons, knives and cups. She noticed that no one had begun to eat yet and did not understand why until one man stepped up to the counter, faced everyone and shouted loudly to get everyone's attention, "Hey, let's pray so we can eat." He then said a brief prayer of thanks over the food.

Becky placed her hand on Carrie's back and guided her towards the counter, "Let's eat." As she walked up and picked up a paper plate, she observed that it was only the women that were in line. The guys all held back, talking with each other. In Chicago, the women would have waited for the men to fill their plates first and to think that anyone would have said grace would have just been laughable.

"Carrie, you have to try some of these sweet potato quesadillas." Carrie looked behind her and saw a smiling woman she had met earlier, whose name she could not remember, looking at her.

"It's good?"

"They're great. Tina makes them. They've become a favorite here."

"Thanks. I'll give them a try." She added a couple of quesadilla triangles to her plate. She felt out of place and awkward. She had intentionally dressed to provoke but it didn't have the effect she expected... or wanted. She had thought that Chi and Susan would have objected to bringing her dressed as she was. But it was Jessie and Becky that came to pick her up, and they did not seem to care. Now she wondered to herself why she did it.

She watched what Becky did and tried to follow her example. She sampled the same foods that Becky did and she even prepared the food on her plate the same way Becky had. Carrie then followed her into the living room where a large circle of chairs had been set up. Becky sat down, and Carrie sat beside her on her right, crossing her legs uncomfortably. It wasn't long before another woman, who Carrie guessed to be maybe ten years older than herself, sat beside her and introduced herself.

"Hi, I'm Michelle."

"Hi. Carrie." She held her plate with her left hand and shook Michelle's hand with her right.

Becky spoke up, "Carrie is staying with Chi's mom for a while."

"Ah. So how do you know Margret?" Michelle asked.

Carrie wasn't sure how to answer or if she should answer at all but the smile on Michelle's face seemed kind, genuine and welcoming. "I just found myself without a place to stay for a while, and she was kind enough to let me stay with her." She looked for a way to deflect questions away from her. "So I take it you're a LifeBridge member too."

"Well we don't have actual formal memberships but yes, I've attended this church for a couple of years now. It's been great. Sometime I'll have to tell you my story when we have some more time. But the short version is God saved my life, and he did it through the people at church."

"OK. I think that's a story I'd like to hear sometime." Carrie attempted to give Michelle a smile. She had learned long ago how to present herself in such a way that would not put the other person off while still deflecting any serious conversation.

"I'd love to tell it," Michelle continued. "Let's get together this week, and I'll buy you a coffee."

Now Carrie felt trapped. This was a new experience for her. She had opened a door, and Michelle walked right through. Now she had to find a way to back out of it gracefully while not offending Michelle and then close that door behind her. She decided on delay, "Sure, when?"

"Are you free Tuesday night?"

"No. I'm sorry. This week I'm sort of tied up. I'll tell you what. How about you give me your number, and I'll give you a call when I can squeeze some time out?" Carrie still maintained her smile but furrowed her eyebrows just enough to appear to be thinking about how she'd clear her schedule.

Michelle nodded. "OK. We can do that. Or if you're not up for coffee then how about some Blue Moon ice cream?" She gave Carrie a bit of a mischievous grin which made Carrie return a genuine smile.

"That sounds even better. Margret bought me some for the first time just a week ago. I have to say I'm hooked."

"OK, I'll get you my number a little later on when I can get something to write it on. Are you from around South Haven?"

"No. I'm from a really small town in Illinois called Bishop Hill."

"How long you been here?"

"Not long. Just a couple of weeks."

"What brings you to South Haven?"

Carrie was becoming more uncomfortable with the questions. She knew Michelle was just trying to be friendly, but there were too many questions she did not want to answer. "I just needed a change. That's all."

"Well, welcome," Michelle said smiling at her. "I know you'll like it here. I do."

Jessie sat down on the other side of Becky. "Hey, Jess," Michelle said waving a hand. Jess was chewing a mouth full of food. He nodded at her and waved a fork.

After several minutes some of the men gathered the paper plates and trash from around the group and threw them out. Everyone took a seat within the circle of chairs as conversations bantered around them. A short man with a thick reddish beard sat down on the opposite side of the group from Carrie. He looked around the room giving everyone a warm smile. He locked eyes with Carrie for only a moment then crossed the room to introduce himself.

"Hi," he said. "I'm Bill."

"Hi. Carrie."

"Thank you for coming, Carrie. Is this your first life group?"

"Yeah. I've never been to one before," she told him.

"Well, welcome. I hope you enjoy it." Bill pointed across the room to Michelle who was talking to Rosie. "That's my wife, Michelle. Have you met her yet?"

"Yes, I did. She introduced herself to me a few minutes ago."

"Ah, OK. Good. Well, it's good to meet you, Carrie. I hope you enjoy the group."

"Thank you. I'm sure I will."

Bill returned to his seat next to Michelle and picked up a bible and notebook from the floor. After opening his notes, he drew everyone's attention and said: "OK, let's get started." Bill looked at Pete and asked, "Pete, will you open in prayer?"

The room quieted. Pete said a brief prayer thanking God for the opportunity for everyone to meet and to study his word. He invited the Holy Spirit to join them and lead the discussion and closed the prayer with "In Jesus's name, amen."

Bill glanced at his notebook and said, "Tonight we're going to be talking about God's mercy."

"Here we go again," thought Carrie to herself. "Now we're talking about a non-existent mercy from a non-existent God. How many people have died in the world today?" she asked herself. "One million? How many of those people were killed by some war or murdered in their sleep? How many people died of cancer? How many people were killed in car accidents or fires? If there is a God, then he doesn't show mercy."

Bill began, "In Romans 3:23 Paul says, 'All have sinned and fall short of the glory of God, and are justified freely by his grace through the redemption that came by Christ Jesus.' What this means is that all of us have fallen way short of the standards of righteousness that God wants us to live by. How can a perfect, holy God have the relationship he desires with us if he, being perfect, could not tolerate imperfection? It's because our imperfection has been covered, paid for by the death of Jesus Christ on the cross."

Carrie tried to listen dispassionately as Bill spoke. Bill talked about the mercy of God as it related to our sin. "We have sinned against God, but God has chosen to be patient with us and not give us the punishment we deserve." Bill then spoke of God's mercy as it relates to helping people who are hurting. He told about the mercy God showed the people of Israel when they were slaves in Egypt. He quoted the Bible regarding the mercy of the good Samaritan. He spoke of God's mercy when Jesus healed the blind, the lepers and the disabled. Bill then ended the study by talking about how "God has shown mercy to us by giving us freedom, peace, and health."

"Are there any prayer request?" Bill asked as he looked around the room.

Carrie turned inward as a wave of something she could not explain passed through her body like a mild shock. She began trembling for reasons she didn't understand. Her eyes began to moisten. Bill had talked about the mercy of God and the words echoed through her mind. 'The mercy of God...', 'The mercy of God...' All of her adult life she had rejected even the thought that there was a God specifically because she felt no mercy or love. Now that's exactly what she wanted from him: mercy. She heard voices offering their prayer request to the group, but the words floated over her without registering. Memories rushed in. Memories she tried to suppress for so long. They hit her in waves as she remembered her father screaming at her day after day and her mother's inability to help her as she crumbled into herself. Memories of holding on until she finally left Bishop Hill with no plan, no money and nowhere to go.

Carrie found arms around her as the final break came. Tears broke free, streaking bright blue makeup down her face. She was trembling as Susan and Becky held her tightly. With her head bowed, she was leaning against Susan as the tears dropped onto her arms. She crossed her arms over Susan's and

Becky's and squeezed them to her. The remainder of the group had gathered around her and began placing their hands on her back and shoulders, praying quietly for her still not knowing what was consuming her.

Michelle knelt in front of her with a box of tissues and handed her one. Carrie wiped her eyes and nose, laid the tissue on her lap and then took another. She repeated the process again. Looking into Michelle's face, she saw that tears had begun to trickle down her cheeks as well.

"I'm sorry," Carrie whimpered softly.

"There's nothing to be sorry for, Carrie," Michelle said. "Nothing at all."

"I don't believe in God." Carrie barely got the words out through the sobbing. She tried to calm herself. She wiped her eyes and face again as she continued, "How is there mercy for me?" Again she broke down as she forced her words out of her clenched throat. She tucked her head into Susan's arms and wept. "I'm so sorry, I'm so sorry," she repeated.

Susan held her head gently to her and then brushed her hair back with her hand. "There's nothing to be sorry for. We're here for you."

Michelle put her hands on Carrie's knee, bowed her head and began praying silently for her. There was a quiet murmuring of prayer from the group as several people prayed quietly for her. As Carrie calmed herself, Michelle looked up into her face, "Carrie, can you tell us what's going on?"

Carrie stared at Michelle with unfocused eyes and remained silent for several moments as she tried to relax her throat enough to speak again. The murmuring of the prayers began to quiet as everyone tuned in to listen. Finally, she spoke, "I don't believe in God anymore."

"I know, Hon," said Michelle. "But can you tell me what's going on."

Carrie fought her inner battles wondering if she should tell these people, people she hardly knew, some of the darkest secrets of her life. She looked over at Becky and then around to some of the other faces she could see. Some cried sympathetic tears like Michelle had, others had not, but on all the faces around her she saw compassion.

"I ran away," she began. As she spoke, Chi moved around and knelt on one knee in front of her and Susan.

"What did you run away from, Honey?" asked Michelle.

"Everything. Kevin. Chicago." She hesitated. "My life," she whispered. She took control of her voice again and said, "My dad only ever screamed at me, so I left home as soon as I graduated high school and went to Chicago. I met a guy and stayed with him for a while. Two years. He was mostly nice, but then he lost me." She closed her eyes and squeezed them tightly, pushing out tears that streamed down her face. She opened her mouth to speak but could not. Chi reached over and put his hand on her knee, she looked at him then held his hand for a moment, giving it a squeeze. She tried again to speak, and the words came out in a hoarse whisper. "He lost me in a card game." Her body spasmed again as Susan held her tightly.

Tears flooded down her face again. She never intended to tell anyone anything about herself, but now she found she could not stop. Her life forced its way out into the open, to be exposed. "I'm so sorry," she whimpered again.

"It's alright, Carrie," said Susan. "We love you. It's alright."

Carrie pulled herself together and tried to continue. She opened her mouth to speak, again found she couldn't and waited longer as she tried to compose herself. Finally, she took two deep breaths and began again, "Kevin wasn't so nice. He was mean. I stayed with him for four years. I tried to leave once. I went to a woman's shelter. But he found me there and took me back home. He knows people. They let him take me home. They were supposed to protect me but they didn't. He kept me locked up for three weeks." Her eyes now shifted to some far away point beyond the floor. Moments passed as everyone waited for her continue.

"He'd come home drunk and hit me for no reason at all. Sometimes because I didn't have dinner ready for him when he got home, other times because he didn't want what I made. But I had no place to go. He'd find me. He'd always find me. I had no place to go."

Chi looked over at Pete standing behind the girls. He could see anger rising in his eyes. Chi knew that as a cop, Pete would want to try to do something and do it now. Chi could see Pete's jaw muscles tighten, tense and flex. Chi tilted his chin up just slightly. The movement caught Pete's attention. Pete looked him in the eye. Chi shook his head so slightly that if Pete had not been looking directly at him, he would not have seen it. Pete nodded his understanding and calmed himself. Now was not the time for action. There would be time later, but at the moment it was more important to hear Carrie, to listen.

Carrie continued, "He killed a man once. I know he did. He didn't talk about it, but I know what he did." She continued to stare vacantly at the floor. "They had some deal going on that went bad, so Kevin found him and killed him."

"He made me sleep with a guy a couple of times. I'm not a whore." She looked up at Michelle with pleading eyes, horrified at what she just told these strangers. "He made me do it. I'm not a whore," she added quickly.

Michelle nodded back, "I know."

"The night before I ran away he came home late. It was my birthday. He promised to take me out for dinner, but he came home late. He was drunk. All I did was ask him where he'd been and if we were still going out for dinner. He got mad. Said it wasn't any of my business and beat me up bad. I thought he was going to kill me. I stayed in bed until he left for work and then put all my stuff in my car and drove. He had a short shift that day, so I didn't have long."

She then looked at Chi, "Then my car broke down." Chi nodded at her.

Carrie sat up straight as Susan and Becky released their arms from around her. She took another tissue from Michelle and wiped her eyes again and then blew her nose. "I'm so sorry; I didn't mean to dump all that on you."

Michelle took her left hand and held it. "Carrie, have you been abused like this all your life?" Carrie nodded. "Was your mother abused like that too?"

Carrie thought for a moment. That was something that had never occurred to her. "My dad never hit my mom that I know of. He just yelled a lot. I was always going to hell for some reason or another."

"You know that's another form of abuse, don't you?"

"I suppose."

"Do you realize that is not normal?" asked Michelle.

"Yes, I suppose."

"What about your grandmother? Was she abused too?"

"I never knew my grandmother. My grandfather murdered her before I was born. He died in prison," Carrie told her.

"I see." Michelle hesitated for a moment looking down and then looked up again. "Carrie, you've fallen into a type of bondage; A generational bondage that has you tied to a cycle of abuse. Do you know you can be freed from that bondage?"

Carrie looked at her through teary eyes. She felt confused. She wanted to be free from a lifetime of torment but what power did this woman have that could make that kind of change in her life?

Michelle continued, "Carrie, there is a God, and he sent his son Jesus to free us all from bondage. The bondage of our own sin and the bondage of the type you're in right now. There's a rich and satisfying life in Jesus Christ just waiting for you. You heard Jeff speak about God's mercy tonight. I'd like to pray God's mercy over you, right now, that he break that bondage of abuse in your life so that you can be free."

Carrie was looking at her with a mixture of hope and doubt and then looked down again. "I don't believe in God anymore." It was almost whispered.

"God isn't limited by your belief. He's much greater than that. Carrie, we want to pray over you. Will you let us do that for you?"

Carrie hesitated only a moment and then nodded slowly. Standing, Michelle motioned for everyone to gather tightly around Carrie again. As she placed her hands on Carrie's head, everyone moved in and gently put a hand on her shoulders and back. They began softly praying.

Michelle led the prayer, "Our Heavenly Father, we come to you tonight in the name of Jesus, our Savior, the one who died for us so that we may live. We bring before you Carrie, who has lived all her life in bondage, the bondage of abuse and torment. We pray Father God that tonight you break these chains. Break these chains and release her from this bondage that has been passed down to her from generation to generation. Cast these spirits that condemn her away, never to return. Free her, Father God, for we know that you love her and we plead your mercy on her. Those of us gathered here tonight agree on this, and we ask this in the name of Jesus Christ. Amen."

Carrie was crying again as she looked up into Michelle's eyes. Michelle helped her to stand as she gave her a hug. Carrie then saw Becky waiting to her left with tears in her eyes, and she reached over and embraced her. Jessie stepped in and wrapped his arms around them both. Susan and Chi were next as they both held her. Relief swept through her and something more, something she could not remember feeling before tonight but still she knew exactly what it was. It was love.

Ralph Nelson Willett

Chapter 19

Margret sat in the rocker reading her Bible as Carrie entered the door with Susan and Chi following closely behind her. Margret could see that the thick blue makeup was nearly completely removed now. Carrie stopped to glance at Margret contritely for a moment and then walked directly into her room. Chi closed the outside door behind them as he and Susan stepped into the kitchen.

"How'd things go?" asked Margret.

Chi and Susan sat on the sofa. Chi leaned back with his arm laying on the backrest behind Susan. Susan sat on the edge and faced Margret.

"I think Carrie had a breakthrough tonight," Susan told her.

"What kind of breakthrough?"

"I'm not sure, but she told us what was going on and let all of us pray for her."

Margret raised her eyebrows and looked at Chi. Chi nodded his agreement. "OK, so what happened?" Margret asked.

"It looks like a generational curse, probably a spirit. She said her grandfather killed her grandmother, and that she and her mother were constantly verbally abused by her father. After she moved to Chicago to get away from it, it got worse."

"Worse how?" asked Margret.

"Well, aside from being beaten up it sounds like her boyfriend pimped her out."

"Oh," Margret responded in surprise.

"Her first boyfriend gambled and lost her to the last guy she was with in a card game."

"Oh no." Margret put her hand on her mouth and looked away.

"This is the first time she's been able to get away. She tried a woman's shelter once, but somehow he was able to drag her back."

Chi added, "That would explain why she was so adamant about not going to a women's shelter when we found her."

They sat quietly for a while. Margret absorbed this new information, not knowing what more to say. Susan leaned back into Chi's arm. A few minutes later Carrie emerged from her room wearing jeans and a t-shirt. She had completely removed the makeup. She sat down on the sofa next to Susan in a mild slouch.

"How are ya, Carrie?" Margret asked.

"Fine," she replied quietly. She was looking down at the floor in front of her then looked up at Margret. "Margret, I'm sorry."

"Sorry for what, Honey?"

"I'm sorry that I haven't been really nice to you. You've been so good to me, and I didn't treat you very well."

"Carrie, I don't know what you're talking about. You've been fine. After all you've gone through I'd expect some things."

Carrie looked down at the floor and spoke again after a moment. "Did Chi tell you what happened?"

"Susan told me you let everyone pray for you."

"Yeah, I did." She looked at Susan and Chi. "Thank you for that."

"You're welcome," Susan said smiling at her.

Carrie looked back down at the floor. She looked like she had more to say. Everyone waited. Without looking up she said, "I really didn't think you'd all let me go tonight since I was dressed like a whore." She looked up at Margret wide-eyed and quickly added, "I'm not a whore."

"I know."

"I just really didn't want to go. I wanted everyone to stop bugging me about this church thing. Quit bugging me about God." She looked down at the floor again and murmured, "Now I'm not so sure."

Susan put her arm around her and pulled her in. "You know we love you, right?" she asked.

"Why? Why would you love me?"

"Because God first loved us," Susan replied. "It's easy to pass on love when you know God's love."

Carrie remained quiet for a moment. Her eyes remained unfocused on the floor. "That's easy for you to say. You've had an easy life."

Susan gave her another squeeze. "I know. God has blessed me but it hurts me to know what you've been through. I can't imagine. But that doesn't mean that God doesn't love you. I think that's why you're here, to get you out of that."

"That's what Margret said," Carrie replied.

"I think it's true," Susan said. "This can be the beginning of your new life. Free from the curse."

Carrie looked up and turned to Susan. "Do you really think it's a curse?"

"From what you told us, it's followed your family at least from your grandmother."

"My great grandfather was mean too. My great grandmother committed suicide."

Susan nodded and gave her another squeeze. "I'd say that's a generational curse, like Michelle said."

Carrie thought for a moment and then asked, "Is it over?"

"We can pray that it is, that you're released from it. If you accept it then, yeah, I think it's over."

Carrie resumed her vacant stare at the floor. The room was quiet as no one spoke. A long moment passed before Carrie spoke softly, "I accept it."

~~~~

Carrie was waiting at the breakfast table when Margret emerged from her room. She was sitting at the table drinking a cup of coffee and smiled broadly at the sight of Margret. Carrie stood. "What would you like for breakfast?" she asked Margret. "I'm making it."

"You are?" asked Margret surprised. "Nice. Pancakes?"

"Awesome. Chocolate chip pancakes? I was hoping you'd ask for that."

"Uh, sure," Margret said in bewilderment.

Margret sat down at the table; Carrie brought her a mug of coffee. "You look pretty chipper," Margret told her.

"I slept good last night. Woke up early. I've been waiting for you."

Margret watched as Carrie busied herself mixing the batter and preparing the pan and plates. She seemed excited as she moved from counter to sink to stove. The transformation seemed surprising to Margret. The young woman who only days before moved in such a way that it appeared that the weight of the world was on her shoulders, now moved lightly and quickly around as she smiled.

Carrie set the table for the two of them, placed a big plate of hot pancakes in the center of the table and sat down. She held out her hands to Margret with a big smile. As Margret reached out and took her hands, Carrie said, "I'll say grace." She bowed her head and said "Thank you God for this food. Amen." She looked up at Margret who appeared stunned.

"What?" Carrie asked.

"You. You're different."

"Yeah. I feel different." She buttered her pancakes and poured hot syrup over them. Margret moved slower while keeping an eye on her. "What you want to do today?" Carrie asked while chewing.

Margret hesitated. This sudden change seemed too drastic to be real. "I don't know," she responded. "What do you have in mind?"

"I'm up for some Blue Moon ice cream."

"OK," Margret replied tentatively.

"Then we can walk to the beach again," Carrie continued.

"OK."

Margret began eating her pancakes slowly as she watched Carrie bubble. "You said grace," Margret commented.

Carrie looked up from her plate with a smile and asked "Is that OK?" and took a large bite.

"Of course," replied Margret. "But why? I mean, you said you didn't believe in God, and now you just prayed."

"Things are different now," she replied. "After last night things are different. I can feel it. Now I know there is a God."

"Wow," replied Margret stunned. "That's awesome."

"And I had some good dreams last night for the first time I can remember."

"Good dreams?"

"Yeah," Carrie said. "I haven't had a good dream in forever but last night I did. I woke up twice because I was happy. Is that weird?"

"Well, I'd say that's different. Better than waking up with nightmares. I can't say I've ever woken up because I was 'happy'. What were you dreaming about?"

Carrie thought for a moment. "I can't remember everything, but there was one where I saw my mother back at our farm. She was happy and twirling around in the sun. She saw me and waved me over to her. She was smiling so big, and we started twirling around together. That's when I woke up."

"Well that's interesting," Margret told her. "You must be thinking about your mother some."

"I was thinking when I woke up that I should call her, tell her I'm still alive. I'd like to talk with her."

"Be careful. If you called, what would you do if your dad answered the phone?"

"Hang up. I don't want to talk with him. I know when he'd be out and Mom should be home."

"OK, but be careful," Margaret told her.

"I will. Can I use your phone this afternoon?"

"Sure. No problem."

~~~~

It was late morning when they returned home after walking downtown and to the beach. The weather was turning dark, and Margret and Carrie expected it to start raining at any moment as they heard a distant thunder to the south of them.

They heard the phone ringing just as Margret was unlocking the door. Margret rushed in to answer it before the answering machine picked up. "Hello," she said into it. She looked at Carrie as she listened to the caller. "Sure, one sec," she said into it. She held the phone out towards Carrie. "It's for you."

Carrie took the phone and hesitantly put it to her ear. "Hello?"

"Hi Carrie, this is Bill Wallace from Sand and Sun. Have you got a second?"

"Yes."

"I heard you might be looking for a job. I need someone part time to help out in the afternoons with paperwork and light filing. Would you be interested?"

Carrie was instantly excited. "Yes. I'd be interested." She couldn't hide the excitement in her voice.

"It's only part time, maybe fifteen to twenty hours a week. You OK with that?"

"Yes, that's great!"

"Can you start this afternoon around one?"

"Sure I can! I'll be there."

"Great, Margret can give you directions. We're within walking distance of Margret's house."

"Awesome. Thank you. Thank you so much." Carrie was nearly shouting into the phone.

"OK, great. We'll see you then," Bill told her.

"Can I ask you how you heard about me? Are you the same 'Bill' from Life Group?" Carrie asked.

"No. That's my brother in-law. You met Michelle last night. She's my sister."

"Oh, yes. Thank you. Thank you. I'll see you at one."

She handed the phone back to Margret. "I got a job." She laughed, clasped her hands together holding them tightly to her chest and spun herself around gleefully.

"At Sand and Sun?"

"Yeah." Carrie seemed happily stunned.

"That's wonderful! See how God works?" Margret asked.

"Yeah, that's not what I expected. I start at one. Can you tell me how to get there?"

"Well, it looks like it's going to rain," Margret replied. "How about I drive you over there the first time?"

"What should I wear?" Carrie asked Margret. "I don't have any clothes for an office."

"Knowing Bill," Margret answered, "You'll fit in with just about anything you'll wear. But I'd suggest jeans and a nice blouse."

Carrie disappeared into her room and emerged only seconds later with an inquisitive look on her face. "Margret?" she asked. "What is Sand and Sun?"

"It's a used car dealership, Hon," Margret replied.

Carrie pulled her hands up under her chin and spun herself around again. "I've got a job!" She then rushed back into her room. Margret couldn't help but let out a quiet laugh.

About a half hour later Carrie emerged again. She had put on some light makeup covering the remainder of her bruising, and had dressed in jeans and a blue short sleeved blouse.

Margret could see the excitement in her eyes. "Very nice," she told her. "You've got about an hour and a half to wait. What are you going to do while you're waiting?"

"I don't know. Maybe I'll dance," Carrie told her. "I'm pretty excited." She raised her arms above her head and twirled around again.

"I can see," Margret said. "You got ready early enough. It's raining so you can't go outside now."

Carrie sat down in the rocker. She grinned broadly at Margret sitting on the sofa but didn't say anything. "Looks like things are turning around for you," Margret told her.

"I hope so. This job is the best thing I've had happen in a while. You know, I had a job once working on an assembly line when I was with Kevin."

"Oh yeah? What happened?" Margret asked her.

"Kevin got lit one afternoon and came to the shop. He walked right in the back door, saw me talking to my supervisor and he got all jealous. Punched him. Three other guys tackled him and started beating him up, so I tried to stop them from hurting him. I got fired."

"Oh. I'm sorry."

"The cops took him away, but nothing ever came of it. I think if they hadn't taken him to jail he would have beat me up again. As it was, he was pretty sore from when those three guys beat on him."

"So you didn't get another job?" Margret asked her.

"I couldn't. It was better if I just stayed home. Every once in a while, Kevin would get mad that we didn't have any money and he'd want me to go to work but when I started looking he'd get mad that I was looking. Then he'd just do some deals and get some money in, and he'd be happy, and everything would be fine for a while."

"What kind of deals?"

Carrie rocked back and forth a few times looking away from Margret. Her smile faded rapidly. "I really don't want to talk about Kevin anymore."

"OK. No problem."

"I'm just excited to have a job," Carrie said as the broad smile returned. "I'll get to meet more people. Maybe make some friends."

"That would be good. Do you have any friends back in Chicago?"

"One. Amber. But I don't dare call her. It's better if she doesn't know where I am. We'd get together when Kevin was at work. She was really smart. She just had a problem."

"What kind of problem?"

"Coke. She did a lot of it. She was actually really smart. Smarter than me but couldn't shake it."

"Did you ever do drugs?" Margret asked.

"Yeah. When I got hurt, it helped."

"But you're not addicted."

"No. I'm not. I don't know why I'm not." She looked at Margaret. "I probably should be, you know?"

"Well, maybe God protected you from that."

"Maybe. I don't know. Does he do that?" Carrie asked.

"I think God can do anything."

"I hope she's doing OK," she told Margret. "She'd be the first person Kevin would ask if he wanted to find me."

"Would he hurt her?"

"I don't know. Maybe. I guess it depends on how bad Kevin wants to find me. That's why it's better if she doesn't know where I am."

They sat there quietly for a couple of minutes. Carrie still seemed excited even through the sadness she felt for her friend. Margret felt sorry that the conversation led down the path it did. There was still so much she did not know about Carrie that was slowly being revealed to her.

Carrie reached over to the end table and retrieved a Rachael Wallace romance book she had been reading, opened it to a bookmarked page and began to read. She found herself to be too excited to read and returned the book to the table.

Carrie looked up and saw Margret watching her. Carrie gave her a broad smile. "This is my fourth one," she said as she tapped the cover of the book on the end table. "I'm kind of hooked. It's too bad you don't read any of them."

"What's been your favorite so far?" Margret asked her.

"The first one I read, Love's Obsession."

"That one I *did* read. It was good."

"Yeah. I liked it. I could relate to the main character."

"Which one was that?"

"Shelly. I think I'm a lot like Shelly. Hurt but OK, dreaming about a better life. I wish I could find someone that was obsessed with me the same way the guy was with her."

"Chi writes a good story," Margret said nodding.

"Yes, he does. I still find it funny that a guy writes these," Carrie chuckled.

"I think Susan may be a big part of his inspiration," Margret said smiling at her. "He's obsessed with her."

"Yeah. They look so natural together. You can tell Chi loves her."

"Yes he does," Margret agreed.

The light rain that had been coming down suddenly shifted to a hard drenching rain. Watching out of the living room window towards the back yard, they could see the wind was blowing hard enough to blow the rain nearly sideways. Leaves and small branches blew across the back yard.

"Wow," said Carrie as she raised her voice to be heard over the rain hitting the windows. "It's really coming down."

Margret stood and checked the windows around the house to be sure they were closed. When she returned, she found Carrie rocking slowly, the book resting in her lap, staring out of the window with a contented smile. It came to Margret's mind that Carrie had now found peace.

"All safe and secure," Margret told her regarding the windows.

"Yes, it is," Carrie replied quietly. "Yes, it is."

Chapter 20

Carrie was still excited after Margret picked her up from work at five o'clock. They ate at The Winery restaurant to celebrate. Carrie told her all about what she did and the people there. Margret knew everyone she had met since they all attended church together. Carrie chattered excitedly all evening right up until she went to bed around eleven. Margret was happy and excited for her. It reminded her of when her daughter Diane got her first job when she was still in high school, when she was sixteen.

Tuesday morning Carrie emerged from her room groggily. "Good morning, sunshine," Margret said to her as Carrie approached the kitchen table. "How'd you sleep?"

"Not so good. I kept waking up thinking about my new job. I was just too excited to sleep."

"You'll get used to it. I promise," Margret told her.

After breakfast Carrie cleaned the table off, putting all the dishes into the dishwasher and wiping down the table and counter. The two cups of coffee she drank made her feel better, and she was becoming excited again to go to work. She sat down on the rocker and tried reading.

"I need to go out for some groceries," Margret told her. "Wanna come?"

"Thank you. But would you mind if I just stayed here?"

"That's fine. I'll only be gone about an hour."

Carrie watched her leave as she rocked slowly back and forth. She had laid the book back on the end table and resumed to idly watching out towards the backyard. She felt contented. Something she hadn't felt in a long time. She closed her eyes, folded her hands and spoke just above a whisper. "Thank you, Jesus, for bringing me here. Thank you for Margret and Chi and Susan. Thank you for Jess and Becky and Michelle and thank you for my new job." She sat quietly for a moment with her eyes closed. Her mother came to mind. "And Jesus, I pray that you'll protect my mother. Get her out of this generational curse, too." After sitting quietly for several more moments, she added, "Amen."

She opened her eyes and watched out over the back yard again. She suddenly missed her mother, and the urge to talk to her became overwhelming. She retrieved the cordless house phone and returned to the rocker. She noticed that her hand was shaking as she thought about making the call. She was nervous. This call would be the first time she had spoken to her mother in almost seven years. A thought came to her mind that her mother may not even be alive any longer. The thought made her even more anxious.

Checking the kitchen clock for the time, she saw that it was almost 9:30. That would make it 8:30 Chicago time. If her father kept the same habits, he would be out in the barn or out in the field tending to something. Her mother would be in taking care of the house. She said a quick prayer, "Dear Jesus, please let the call go good. Please don't let my father be home." She then mustered all the internal strength she had and dialed her parents home phone.

One ring. Hearing the ring gave her butterflies in her stomach. Two rings and the butterflies became a tight knot. She felt the shaking increase in her hands. Three rings and she suddenly felt cold chills run through her body. Four rings and she felt relief knowing that the answering machine would pick up.

"Please leave a message, <beep>" It was Carrie's father's voice, very abrupt, gruff, and direct. That was the same message that was on the phone when she left over six years ago. A debate raged through her mind as she tried to decide if she was going to leave a message or not. What if her father heard it? A second passed as the machine waited for her to speak. Two seconds, a near lifetime raced by. Three seconds and suddenly she felt sure that the machine was going to hang up on her.

"Hi, Mom." She hesitated. "I just wanted to let you know that I'm alright and everything is..."

The phone clicked. "Hi, Carrie." It was her mother's voice, soft, gentle and quiet. It took a moment for Carrie to overcome her initial shock at hearing her mother's voice. "Carrie?" her mother inquired. "You there?"

"Hi, Mama."

"Hi, Carrie. How are you?"

"I'm good. How you doing?"

"OK, I guess. Pretty much same as it always was. I just miss you."

"I miss you too, Mama."

"Where are you at?"

"I'm in Michigan."

"Where abouts?"

"I'd rather not say. I'm sorry."

"That's OK. I understand. Your father is doing good."

"Does he ever talk about me?"

"No. He doesn't. I'm sorry."

"It's OK, Mom. I understand but are you really doing OK?"

"Yeah. I'm fine. You don't need to worry about me. I wanna know how you're doing."

"It's all good, Mom. I got a good job, and I have lots of friends, and I'm happy."

"That's good. Are you married?"

"No. I'm not married. No boyfriend either."

"What about kids?"

Carrie bristled at the question. She knew what the question suggested for her mother. It implied that her mom thought Carrie was sleeping around. She tried to contain her anger. "No. I don't have any children. I said I wasn't married."

"I know. These days you just never know." There was a moment of silence as it seemed neither one knew what to say.

Then her mother asked, "But Carrie, why are you calling after all this time?"

Carrie took her time answering. Why did she feel the need to call? "Because I miss you. I miss our conversations and things. I even miss doing the dishes with you."

"Seven years is a long time," her mother said.

"I know. Almost seven years."

"You've missed us all seven years and never called?"

Carrie became more tense at the question. "I missed *you*, Mom. I was afraid to call. I didn't leave on good terms."

There was a long delay. Her mother continued, "You left me alone."

"I know," Carrie replied quietly. "Is it still as bad?"

"It's not so bad. I have a roof over my head and everything I need. Your father takes good care of me."

"Good care of you? Like when I was there?"

"Carrie, your father has his faults, but he's a good man, a Godly man. He's trying to do what's right."

"Mother, he abused you. He abused me."

"No, Carrie. He never abused us. He's just trying to be sure we live like the Bible tells us to."

"No." Carrie's voice was growing louder, and she began to speak more rapidly. "The Bible never said to scream at us like that. Where does it say that?"

"God wants us to live holy lives. Your father takes his responsibilities for our family very seriously. Can't you see that?"

"No, Mom, I can't. You don't deserve to be treated like that. I don't either. I *won't* be treated like that."

"He never hurt you, Carrie. He never hurt you."

"What are you talking about? He hurt me all the time. All that yelling and telling me I was going to hell. That's abuse." There was a long silence on the phone. Carrie could hear her mother's breathing beginning to become labored. "Mom, don't you see that what he did to me was emotional abuse? He may have never hit me, but he did abuse me. He abused you."

The long silence continued. Carrie waited. "Carrie," her mother began slowly. "It's probably best you don't come around."

Carrie lowered her voice and spoke quietly. "I know, Mom. I wasn't planning to."

"You probably shouldn't call again either."

"OK," Carrie said hoarsely. Her eyes began to tear.

"Goodbye, Carrie."

Carrie waited. Her throat was tight. She could not get more words out. There was a distinct click as her mother disconnected the phone. A moment later she heard a dial tone. She set the phone on the end table and began to cry. "Why, God? Why can't I have my mother?"

The excitement of the job distracted Carrie from the phone call for the remainder of the week. She enjoyed what she was doing and even took extra time to learn about the cars on the lot. She watched the only saleswoman closely as she met with customers and showed them cars. The woman took a liking to her and took time to explain to her how car sales worked. Carrie could envision herself as a saleswoman. The thought excited her even more.

Friday evening Chi had called, and he and Susan offered to take her and Margret to Kalamazoo for lunch and then a movie. "You're not gonna try taking us to one of those *cheap* restaurants again are you?" Margret teased into the phone as she winked at Carrie. They both eagerly accepted the invitation.

Saturday before noon they both spent extra time dressing up. Margret lent Carrie a pair of her high heeled boots that came up over her calf. She wore the same jeans and short sleeved blouse she had worn Monday on her first day at work. Margret helped her with her makeup, and when Carrie examined herself in a full-length mirror, she found that she felt beautiful. A feeling she wasn't used to.

"You really look nice," Margret told her.

"Thank you," was all Carrie could say.

Susan and Chi walked in earlier than expected and Susan also noted how nice Carrie looked. Chi looked her over and nodded in agreement. Carrie felt herself blush.

"Y'all ready?" Chi asked.

"Waiting on you," Margret said grinning at him. They began walking to the door when Margret stopped as she looked out the window. "Who's this?" She asked. Everyone stopped to look out of the kitchen window. A tall man in heavy work boots, jeans, a thick denim shirt and a denim jacket was moving quickly up the sidewalk to the house. A woman in a plain ankle-length dress followed a few steps behind him. Her waist length hair was pulled back into a long ponytail that swayed back and forth with each step as she tried to keep up with the man's quick pace. She walked with her head bowed slightly.

"That's my dad," Carrie said with panic forming in her voice. She reached instinctively for Margret's hand. "How'd he find me?"

"Do you want to talk to him?" Chi asked. "You don't have to. I can make him go away."

Carrie thought for a moment. The man rang the doorbell then knocked at the door roughly.

"Yeah. If you guys stay here, I can talk to them."

"OK," Chi replied. "You go sit in the living room. I'll let them in."

Margret pulled the rocker out and set it facing the sofa as far away from it as she could to add distance between them. Carrie sat in it looking frightened but determined. Margret and Susan stood by the kitchen island as the man knocked again, louder this time. Chi, seeing that everyone was ready, opened the door.

"Can I help you?" he asked.

The man that met Chi at the door stood at least three inches taller than he did. Although Chi had expected him to be older for some reason, he guessed his age to be only in his early forties. The man appeared to be very muscular and in good shape. His hair was cut in a flattop, military style and his face was clean shaven. The woman with him stood three feet behind him with her hands folded, hanging down in front of her. She looked down demurely.

"I'm looking for my daughter, Carrie."

"And you are?"

"I just said she's my daughter," he said gruffly. "That would make me her father."

"OK," Chi replied calmly. "and does her father have a name?"

"You can call me Mr. Rhodes and who are you?"

"You may call me Mr. Baroda," Chi replied. "One second." Carrie's father could see her sitting in the rocker from where he stood. Chi turned just enough to call over his shoulder while keeping an eye on Rhodes. "Carrie, you have a visitor," he called out loudly. "Are you receiving today?" Rhodes moved to take a step inward, but Chi held up a finger stopping him. Rhodes glared at him.

"Yes. He can come in," Carrie replied nervously.

Chi led them into the living room and indicated they should sit on the sofa facing Carrie. Chi stepped back to the kitchen island, and leaned back against it. He crossed his arms and waited. Rhodes flashed an angry look at him, but Chi displayed no emotion.

"Hi, Dad," Carrie said. "How did you find me?"

"Why? You think I'm stupid? It was easy enough to look up this address on the internet from the caller ID."

Carrie didn't respond.

"I've come to take you home," Rhodes told her.

"I am home," Carrie replied.

"No, I mean to where you belong. You need to come home and get right with God."

Carrie looked at her mother who appeared embarrassed and defeated. "No, Dad. I'm staying here. I am right with God. I have a good job, and all my friends are here. I'm staying here." Her voice projected confidence.

Rhodes anger flashed on his face. "Look at you. You're dressed like a man and are you wearing... makeup? Your face looks like a whore but the rest of you is dressed like a man. Are you a cross dresser or are you gay now?"

Carrie appeared to shrink slightly in her chair under her father's glare and vocal attack. Rhodes continued, "Are you sleeping around like a whore, too? Are you sleeping with him?" he asked while nodding his head towards Chi. His voice was getting louder. "You need to get your life right with God, or you'll end up going straight to hell."

"I'm not going to hell, Daddy. God loves me." The strength in her voice was beginning to fade.

Margret looked at Chi. His face showed none of the anger he was holding under his control.

"Straight to hell!" Rhodes nearly shouted. "You've abandoned your family, you abandoned your mother, you abandoned me.

You're too young to be out on your own doing God knows what."

"I'm twenty-four," Carrie replied weakly.

"You're not old enough," he nearly shouted. "Look how these people have influenced you. You're wearing pants and boots, and you cut your hair. You painted your face like a common whore. I'm taking you home so you can get right with God."

"Well, I've heard enough," Chi said as he stepped between Carrie and her father. "It's time for you to leave."

Rhodes nearly launched himself into the air as he stood quickly. He stopped just inches in front of Chi looking down at him intimidatingly. "I'm taking my daughter with me," he said in a low growl.

"You're leaving. Carrie is staying," Chi said without flinching.

Rhodes screwed up his face in anger. "You don't want to mess with me, boy."

"You're leaving," Chi repeated.

The blow to Chi's midsection was fast and hard. Chi tightened his stomach muscles and let out a controlled yelp to counteract the sudden inward pressure. The result was that the blow had no more effect than hitting a padded brick wall. Chi was immovable. The second hooking swing came from Rhodes left hand towards the right side of Chi's jaw. Chi easily blocked the blow with his forearm. Rhodes swung another hooking punch with his right hand towards Chi's jaw. Again Chi blocked it. This time Chi extended his arm, reached around Rhodes' elbow pulling it under his own arm. The move forced Rhodes off balance. Chi stepped and reached in with his right hand under Rhodes' left arm and around his back as he slammed his hip into the man's midsection. Rhodes' feet flew in the air as Chi threw him over his hip, slamming him down to the floor hard on his shoulder. Chi held Rhodes' right arm as he squatted down behind his back. He placed his knees on Rhodes' ribs and neck, pulled the elbow up into his midsection and held Rhodes' in submission by folding his wrist painfully into itself.

Rhodes yelled out a drawn out "Ahhhhhh" as the shock of hitting the floor and the pain on his wrist came to bear. Carrie's mother moved, looking as if she was going to intervene but stopped short as she saw Margret take a step towards her. Margret shook her head at her, and Mrs. Rhodes stepped back.

Rhodes swore. "Let go of me."

Chi applied more pressure to the wrist and Rhodes cried out again.

"Here's what we're going to do," said Chi calmly. "I'm going to walk you to your car, and you're going to drive home. Do you understand?"

Rhodes swore at him again. "Let go of me."

"The only acceptable response here is 'yes sir,'" Chi told him as he applied more pressure to the wrist; again Rhodes cried out in pain. "Do you understand?" Chi asked him.

There was no response. More pressure was applied. "Yes, sir!" Rhodes screamed.

"Again, I'm going to escort you and your lovely wife to your car, and you're going to return home. Do you understand?"

"Let go!" More pressure. "Yes, sir! Yes, sir!"

"OK, I'm going to release you and stand back to let you get up. Then we're going to move out to your car. If you try anything, anything at all, I will break your arm. Am I clear?"

"Yes, sir," Rhodes nearly whimpered.

Chi quickly used his free hand to check the small of Rhodes' back for a weapon and then his pockets. Rhodes grunted in pain. Finding nothing, Chi slowly released the wrist, stood up and moved back out of reach. Carrie had moved from the rocker and was now standing on the far side of the kitchen island with Susan.

Rhodes sat up on the floor and flexed his wrist. He stared at Chi angrily. Chi stared down at him with a granite face displaying almost no emotion at all. Rhodes stood cautiously. He slowly looked at everyone in the room, his eyes fixating momentarily on Carrie. He said nothing to her. He then moved quickly out of the door. Carrie's mother nearly ran to keep up. Chi followed at a safe distance behind them.

Chi waited on the sidewalk as Rhodes led his wife to the car parked at the curb. He unlocked the door using his key fob, opened the door for her and let her in as he glared angrily at Chi. Rhodes closed the door behind his wife and stood momentarily to stare at Chi. His eyes held a fiery rage. Chi appeared immovable as he returned the stare.

Rhodes began walking slowly around the back of his car as he kept an eye on Chi. As he came around the back, the trunk lock popped. Rhodes threw open the trunk quickly and pulled out a baseball bat. Chi was on him in an instant, closing the gap, and meeting him chest to chest. Rhodes only had enough time to pull the bat back with one hand in a vain attempt to swing, but Chi was on him before he could make a forward motion with it.

Rhodes was off balance with the impact of Chi running squarely into him. Chi hooked a leg around Rhodes' leg and shoved himself upward and forward into Rhodes. Rhodes feet again left the ground as he fell backward. He landed solidly on his back on the pavement. Chi landed with all his weight on top of him. There was a loud snap as two of Rhodes' ribs broke. Chi reached his left arm under Rhodes' neck, grabbed his own wrist and used it as leverage to drive his right fist like a ram into Rhodes' jaw. The pressure of Chi's fist driving the jaw against his bicep caused the jaw to break with a dull thud as it crushed it inward. Rhodes screamed in pain. Chi quickly sat up and mounted him with his knees on either side of Rhodes' chest just under his armpits. Rhodes, still holding the bat, tried to swing but Chi struck first, striking his nose with the palm if his hand by driving it directly down. The nose broke in a splash of blood. Another strike with the palm against the cheek and then another. Rhodes raised both arms in a weak attempt to push him off. Chi took hold of Rhodes' right wrist with his right hand, pulled his arm out straight and then broke it at the elbow with a swift strike of his forearm.

Rhodes now lay screaming in pain unable to defend himself from further damage should Chi choose to inflict it. What felt like minutes to Rhodes took less than ten seconds. Chi waited to see what Rhodes would try next.

"Please. Please stop," whimpered Rhodes.

Chi did not reply. He sat on top of him while Rhodes lay helplessly on his back.

"Please, no more. Please." Blood trickled down his face in rivulets from his nose. Both eyes were quickly beginning to swell shut. "I'll go home now. I'll go home. I promise."

"No. You won't," replied Chi calmly.

~~~~

Pete Sender stood in front of his supervisor behind the ambulance. "The two neighbors that witnessed it both said that the guy came at Chi with a bat."

The police supervisor nodded. "Pete, I know he's your friend, but he really messed this guy up."

"I know," Pete responded. They both looked at Chi sitting in the rear seat of the police interceptor. Pete looked back at his supervisor. "But the man did attack him in the house and then attacked him with a bat."

The supervisor took a moment to look into Pete's eyes. "Broken jaw... broken ribs... broken arm... What he did to that man was way over the top." A grin spread across his face slowly. "I'm just glad this guy is on our side."

Pete smiled back, relieved that his boss had apparently decided no charges were to be placed against his friend. "Yeah. He's a good guy, but attacking him isn't the best idea. So what are we going to do?"

"Well, between you and I, for the protection of Mr. Baroda, we're going to have to arrest Rhodes. But Chi will have to file charges."

"I don't think that will be a problem."

"OK, let Mr. Baroda out and let's see what he wants to do."

Pete opened the door to the Interceptor, and Chi stepped out.

"I suggest you file charges, Chi," Pete told him.

They both looked over to the open ambulance where two paramedics were working on securing Rhodes inside. They could hear outbursts of swearing coming from him as he berated them.

"Yes," Chi agreed. "I'll press charges."

Chapter 21

Kevin's cell rang waking him out of a sound sleep. His head hurt and the ringing of the phone made him instantly angry. The sunlight pouring in through the window let him know it was already mid-morning Saturday. He swore in the phone loudly as he answered it.

"Hey, it's Jowuan," the voice from the phone said.

He swore into the phone again. "Jowuan, who?"

"Does your woman drive a blue Malibu?"

"Yeah, why?" again he swore into the phone.

"Gotta dent in the left rear quarter panel?"

Kevin suddenly realized what the call was about. He sat up quickly on the edge of the sofa. "Yeah, it does."

"Dude, I think I found it for you."

"Where's she at?"

"Her car is parked outside a maintenance garage in South Haven. We just happened to be driving by when we saw it. Heard you were looking for her."

"Yeah. Yeah, I am. Where's South Haven?"

"Up just north of Benton Harbor in Michigan. Not that far. Bout 2 hours."

He swore softly into the phone as his mind raced to try and remember who she might know in Michigan. He could not think of anyone. "Yeah. I think I know where it is. Did you see her?"

"No, man. Didn't see her. I thought it might be her car because it's the only one with Illinois license plates on the lot."

"See if you can find out where she is. You'd be doing me a big favor."

"Cool. What do you want me to do if I find her?"

"Call me. I'll come up and get her."

~~~~

Jowuan watched the car repair shop for several minutes from across the street where he was parked alongside the road. Kamar sat in the passenger seat sipping an energy drink. "He wants us to try and find her," Jowuan said as he set his cell on the console of the Camaro. He swore. "This is gonna cut into our cruise."

"So what you wanna do?" asked Kamar. "We can't just sit here."

"Nah. We can't sit here. He ain't paying us," replied Jowuan.

"So what you wanna do?" repeated Kamar.

"Let me think on it a second." Jowuan sat staring at the service center. He could see three people working in various service bays and wondered who he could not see. "Maybe we should just go ask them."

"Dude, these white country people ain't gonna answer any questions from us about a white girl."

"We'll see." Jowuan put the car in drive and pulled out again onto the divided highway. He had looped around once when he first saw the car and now was going to do it again. He found the nearest turnaround and headed back toward the auto repair shop. He parked his car behind the Malibu and stepped out. He looked the car over briefly as Kamar joined him.

"Let's go see," Jowuan told him.

They walked into the waiting room of the auto shop. Someone stepped in and greeted them.

"G'morning. Can I help you?" the man asked.

"Yeah. Hey, my man. The woman that owns that Malibu can you tell me where she's at?"

The man looked out at the car. "No. Sorry. That car was here when I started working here two weeks ago."

"Dude, the car actually belongs to a friend of mine and his girlfriend ran off with it. He'd like it back," he told the man.

"OK, hold on. Let me get my boss."

The man stepped out of the room leaving the two of them there. Jessie joined them a couple of minutes later.

"Sorry for the wait. Can I help you?" Jessie asked.

"Yeah, my man, you can. That's my friend's car. His girlfriend ran off with it and he'd like it back."

"Oh, I see," Jessie replied with a surprised look on his face.

"Yeah, it came in about 3 weeks back. Cops found it by the side of the road and asked me to pick it up. It's not running." Jessie looked over the two men standing in front of him.

"It's like this, my friend would like to talk to her. Do you have any idea where she might be at?"

"No. Sorry. I don't," Jessie told him. "The cops just asked me to hold onto it while they try and locate the owner. I'm about to tell them to get it off of my lot. I'm not a junkyard."

"What's wrong with it?"

"I didn't put much time into checking it out because I wasn't asked to. But it appears that it's the system computer."

"How much it cost to fix it?" asked Kamar.

"If it's what I think it is it will cost about three thousand dollars."

Kamar swore. "Nah, that ain't right."

"Like I said I didn't put much time into checking it out. Could be something else."

Jowuan spoke up again. "So you don't know where the woman is?"

"No. I don't. My guess is she just abandoned it when it broke down and somebody picked her up."

"OK, thanks, my man. I'll let my friend know you have his car. He's gonna want to come get it."

"Sure. Let him know that there's going to be a seventy dollar towing fee."

Kamar glowered at him from behind his sunglasses. Jowuan smiled. "I will," he said. "Thank you."

Jessie watched as the two of them stepped over to the Malibu again. Jowuan pulled out his cell and took a picture while Kamar climbed back in the passenger seat. When Jowuan got back in the car Kamar asked, "What you wanna do?"

"He ain't paying us," Jowuan told him. "I don't need no favors from him. I'll just call him and say that the mechanic didn't know who owned the car and didn't see nobody. If he wants more he can come do his own investigations."

Jowuan sent the picture of the car to Kevin via text message. Kevin called him as soon as he received it.

"What'd you find out?" Kevin asked.

"The dude in the shop said the car was found by the cops by the side of the road. He don't know no more."

"Can you ask around some more? Maybe someone else in town has seen her. Check the bars."

"Nah, man. I ain't got time for that. We headed north and we gotta get to my grandma's house."

"You'd be doing me a personal favor, Jowuan."

Jowuan swore into the phone. "I said I ain't got time to be hunt'n down your woman. You come up and find her." Kevin swore at him. Jowuan angrily hung up the phone. Putting the car in gear he said, "We ain't got time for this mess." He then drove off again headed north.

~~~~

Jessie watched until the Camaro drove off and then called Pete.

"Hey, Pete," he said into the phone. "I just had a couple of visitors looking for Carrie. They saw her car parked in my lot."

"Oh, shoot," Pete replied. "We should have hidden the car. What'd you tell them?"

"I said the cops found it abandoned and asked me to bring it here. I said I didn't know anything more than that."

"OK, I'm coming around to your place. Be there in a couple."

It only took a couple of minutes before Pete pulled up in the police interceptor. He left it running as he stepped in to talk to Jessie. He wrote the description of the two men in a small notebook and tucked it back into his pocket. He then asked to speak with the mechanic that first talked with them.

"I don't know anything about the car," the man told Pete. "That's why I went and got Jess. They said the car was stolen."

Pete confirmed the description that Jessie had given him of the two men and the car with the mechanic.

"Jess, if you wouldn't mind, let me talk to everybody together. It won't take but a second."

Jessie gathered the mechanics in front of a car in the left bay. "I just want to tell you that if anybody comes asking about that car I want to know about it right away."

"What do we tell them if someone asks?" one of the mechanics asked.

"You tell them I found the car abandoned and asked Jessie to hold it while we try to find the owner." Pete looked each one in the face. The delay added emphasis to what he said. "That's it. That's all you know. Then you call me. Does everyone understand?"

Each mechanic, including Jessie, nodded in agreement. "Alright, thank you." The mechanics went back to where they were working. Pete turned to Jessie. "I need you to put this car somewhere out of sight. Can you do that?"

"Yeah. I can put it out behind my uncle's barn out on 68th."

"Does it run?" asked Pete.

"Yeah. I fixed it using parts from the junk yard. Chi told me not to tell anyone. He didn't think it was a good idea for Carrie to be taking off so he didn't want me to tell anyone it's running."

"Good plan," Pete told him. "I'll call Chi and let him know what happened. Then I need to see if these guys are still in town."

"Alright. I'll take the car out this afternoon. I'll get Chi to help me out."

"Cool. Alright. Thanks, Jess," he said as he started toward the door.

"No problem. By the way, is the car in her name or not?"

Pete stopped and looked at him. "Yes, it is. It's registered in her name and her name is on the tags."

Jessie nodded at him. Pete left the shop, climbed back in his car and called Chi.

~~~~

Chi wasn't happy at hearing someone was looking for Carrie. He had been working on the third revision of another book when Pete called him. Now his mind was completely distracted from the story. He thought through the possibilities. Someone was looking and they had gotten close. He wondered what would have happened if they would have actually found Carrie. She was with his mother and that put his mother at risk. He didn't like that.

For several minutes he sat staring at his computer screen without actually seeing it. Finally, he stood and walked into his bedroom and into his walk-in closet. He pulled a wooden box from the top shelf and carried it to his bed setting it on top of it. The box was locked with a brass padlock. Pulling his key ring from his pocket he selected a small key and opened the lock with it. He lifted the lid slowly and stared at its contents.

For long moments he stood at the side of his bed staring at a Beretta 9MM pistol in its holster. He reached into the box and stroked the leather slowly as he let his eyes go unfocused. This is not what he wanted to do. He stopped, closed his eyes and said a prayer.

With the prayer complete, he hung his head and opened his eyes, looking down. Chi remained there thinking for a moment before he withdrew the weapon from its holster and laid it on a shelf. He unbuckled his belt and strapped the holster on in the center of his back. It tucked away in his jeans. He then re-holstered his weapon and pulled his T-shirt over it, completely concealing it from view.

Ralph Nelson Willett

Chapter 22

Carrie's mother sat behind her father and his court-appointed lawyer. Rhodes leaned back in his chair slouching. His right arm hung against his body in a cast. He wore an orange jumpsuit and his ankles were chained together. The lawyer was using an iPad to make notes.

Carrie sat with Margret in the back of the courtroom on the prosecution side. Chi was required to wait outside the courtroom. Carrie saw that her mother had glanced at her as she came in and sat down, but her mother turned away without acknowledging her.

The bailiff announced the judge as he entered the courtroom. Everyone in attendance stood. The judge opened a file. After looking through the documents briefly, he asked the prosecution to present his case. The charge was assault and battery.

"How does the defendant plea?" The judge asked Rhodes' lawyer.

"Guilty, your honor."

Margret and Carrie looked at each other. They had not expected a guilty plea."

"Mr. Rhodes, do you agree with the guilty plea?"

Rhodes let his anger show. "Yes, I did it," he said through his wired jaw while staring angrily at the judge.

"Very well. I understand that the injuries you sustained were a result of this attack?"

"Yes, your honor," replied his attorney. "Your Honor, Mr. Rhodes has a farm in Illinois that requires his presence. In light of the injuries he sustained, we would like to request leniency and recommend a suspended sentence."

"Does the prosecution object?" inquired the judge.

"No objections, Your Honor," was the reply.

"Very well, Mr. Rhodes, I sentence you to 90 days in the Van Buren County jail. Suspended. Mr. Rhodes, I hope..."

"I don't recognize your authority to sentence me to anything," shouted Rhodes. With his jaw frozen in place, he hissed through his teeth. "Only God can sentence me. You do not have the authority to sentence me to anything."

His lawyer leaned over to him and whispered loudly, "Shut up! You got a suspended sentence."

The judge appeared surprised at the outburst. "Mr. Rhodes, in this courtroom, I am God's representative. I suggest you accept what you've been given."

Rhodes swore at the judge. "Only God can judge me. Yes, I did it. Yes, I may be guilty in your eyes, but in God's eyes I did what was right."

The judge's eyes flashed angrily at Rhodes. "Mr. Rhodes, be careful or the next thing you say will have you serving that suspended sentence."

Rhodes screamed at the top of his lungs one drawn out "Ahhhhhhhh" as he shook his head side to side. He took a deep breath again and shouted at the judge, "You have no right. You're only man's representative here on earth. My God is greater than you and you have no right to judge me!"

"Your sentence in now activated!" the judge shouted at him, banging his gaval.

Rhodes swore at him again. He was starting to foam at the mouth.

"One hundred twenty days," the judge ordered.

"Ahhhhhhh!" Rhodes screamed again. He reached down with his good hand below the edge of the table and turned the table over violently towards the judge. His attorney stepped back in fear. Strings of angry cursing spewed out from Rhodes as spittle flung outward from between his wired teeth.

"One year!" shouted the judge. "Bailiff, remove this man!"

The two deputies had already moved in. Rhodes took a swing at the nearest one. The deputy leaned back from the punch letting it pass him. He then moved into Rhodes and blocked him from retracting his arm for another punch. The second deputy placed a handcuff on his wrist and attempted to bring it down to cuff it to a chain wrapped around his waist. Rhodes tried to shake the deputies off violently. The chains around his ankles hobbled his steps so he squatted slightly and then pushed up hard against the deputy attempting to handcuff him to the waist chain. The deputy lost his balance, and Rhodes continued to drive hard into him to send him backward causing him to fall to the floor. The second deputy held tightly blocking his good arm from being effective. He tried to drag Rhodes to the floor, but the bigger man held his stance and continued to attempt to shake him off. Rhodes tried to head butt him, but the deputy held his own head tightly behind Rhodes' shoulder leaving no room to be hit.

The deputy that had fallen to the floor removed his pepper spray as he stood. He gave it a quick shake and sprayed it directly in Rhodes' eyes. Rhodes screamed out in pain and his eyes involuntarily slammed closed. Again the deputy attempted to handcuff the free arm and still Rhodes violently resisted.

Rhodes spasmed suddenly and violently, falling to the floor. The second deputy stood over him holding the taser gun, glowering at him angrily as Rhodes continued to spasm. When the shaking stopped, Rhodes lay groaning. Both deputies stood back momentarily, breathless. They then rolled him over onto his back and handcuffed his free hand to the waist chain. The taser had caused Rhodes to release his bladder involuntarily causing a growing wet stain to appear around his groin area.

The deputies stood him up and began to move him out of the courtroom. As they came to the rear of the room, he saw Carrie. Anger contorted his face again. "You did this to me!" he shouted. "You did this to me! You're gonna burn in hell, you whore! You'll be Satan's whore then! You'll be Satan's own whore!"

Rhodes was led out, and the courtroom became silent.

When the courtroom began to clear, Chi stepped in and joined his mother and Carrie. They both appeared stunned and speechless. "I saw them bring him out. Looks like they tasered him."

"How'd you know?" Margret asked.

"They walked him right by me. I've seen what happens when a man gets tased."

"Did you hear everything that happened in here?"

"I just heard shouting."

"The judge gave him a 90 day suspended sentence, and then he went nuts. It ended up being a whole year," Margret told him.

Chi smiled. "Cool."

Carrie's mother approached them tentatively. The three of them stopped to look at her as she came near. "Hi," she said meekly.

"Hi, Mom," Carrie said. "You OK?"

Mrs. Rhodes instantly began to tear. "No," she said.

Carrie moved in and hugged her. Her mother didn't respond initially, letting her arms hang by her side but eventually she wrapped her arms around her daughter and wept.

"Is it over?" she asked Carrie.

"At least for a year, Mom. That will give you a chance. Would you like to stay with us for a while?"

Carrie's mother rested her head on the taller shoulder of her daughter. She remained there as Carrie rocked her gently side to side. "I can't, Carrie. I need to take care of the farm. Your father will be angry if I don't take care of the farm while he's gone."

"Mama, you don't need to do anything but take care of yourself."

"I know. But I love your father. He takes care of me. Now he needs me to take care of the farm, so that's what I'm going to do."

"Mama, he doesn't love you." Carrie was pleading. "You know that. He doesn't love anyone."

"No. Your father loves me."

"God loves you, Mama. Just like he loves me. He's not that mean God that Dad kept telling us about. God, the real God, loves us."

"Carrie, I can't leave your father. I just can't. I know what you think, but I can't do it. He's a good man."

"Oh, Mama. Please don't do this. It's so much better out here. There's real love here. I go to a good church, and you can come too."

Carrie's mother pulled back from her embrace. She wiped her eyes. Her face began to show defiance. "I'm not leaving your father. That's the end of this. I love him, and he loves me. I need to be there for him when he gets out."

"OK, Mama. Maybe I can come visit, and we can talk some more. Or maybe you can come to South Haven. You have a year to think about it."

"I've decided. There's nothing more to say. You can come visit if you want but we won't be talking about me leaving your father. Understood?"

Carrie nodded. "OK. But I'm going to pray that God releases you too."

Her mother blinked at her. She didn't understand. "What does that mean? It's your father that's in jail. I'm not."

"Mama, we have been under a curse. It's called a 'generational curse.' It's come down to you and me at least from my great grandfather. I've been released from it. I'm going to pray that you are too."

"There's no such thing," her mother said as she looked at her blankly.

"Yes, there is. I know that now. I can see it clearly. I'm free. I want you to be free too."

Her mother stared at her dumbfounded. "What have they been teaching you?"

"It's true. A generational curse."

"Oh, Carrie. You've been blinded by the devil."

"I'm sorry, Mama. I've seen the devil. I've seen him in my father and a boyfriend I had. I once was blind, but now I see. I hope you'll see it sometime soon."

Her mother shook her head. "I'll pray for you, Carrie."

"I'll pray for you, Mama."

They looked at each other for a long moment. "I have to go," Carrie's mother said softly.

"OK, Mom. Can I call you?"

"Sure, Carrie. We can talk."

Chapter 23

"Margret, do you know where my car is?" Carrie asked.

"Nope. You'll need to see if Chi knows," Margret replied. "Do you know if it's been fixed?"

"I don't think so. I only now just got the money to fix it."

"Well, tomorrow you can ask Chi or Jess at church," Margret told her. "One of them will know. Getting tired of walking to work?"

"Well, no. But I think I'd like to have my car back. Plus it's starting to get cold. I don't want to have to ask you to drive me to work every day in the winter."

The weather was turning cold. Carrie now measured time by how long ago her father had gone to jail: it had been a month. One month ago he went to jail. In eleven months he'd be out. It was now the first week of November, and it was getting colder.

~~~~

"Hey, Jess, Becky," Carrie greeted them in the church vestibule.

"Hey, Carrie," replied Becky with a broad smile. "How are you doing? Coming to life group tonight?"

"Of course. I haven't missed yet. I'm doing good." She turned to Jessie. "Jess, do you still have my car?"

"Yes. Sort of. But I think you'll need to talk to Chi."

"Why? I can pay for it now."

Jessie cleared his throat and pointed to Chi and Susan walking in the door. "Talk to Chi. He'll explain." Carrie turned to meet them.

"Hi, Carrie," greeted Susan reaching out to her and touching her hand.

"Hi, Susan. Hi, Chi. Chi, where's my car?" Carrie greeted them both with exuberance.

"Well hello, Carrie. Straight to the point today, I see," Chi responded. Her bubbling caused him to smile at her.

"Of course."

"Jess told you to talk to me, didn't he," Chi stated.

"Where's my car, Chi?" Carrie asked again.

"There was a problem with it."

"What's wrong? I got money now. I can pay to have it fixed."

Chi's face went blank. The smile escaped him. "It's already been repaired, Carrie."

Carrie looked puzzled. "What's going on, Chi?" The bounce that Carrie had when greeting them had vanished.

"Let's go sit down for a second." Carrie now began to look worried. She followed him to a nearby bench. He sat down next to her while Susan stood by him. "Somebody saw your car at Jessie's shop and stopped to ask about you?"

"When?" she asked.

"A little over a month ago. Some guys saw the car parked at Jessie's place and stopped in and asked Jess about it."

"What'd they look like?"

"Two black guys in a Camaro. That's all I know. They told Jessie that it belonged to a friend of theirs and he wanted it back."

"It's mine."

"We know. But someone is looking for you. Jess told them that the police asked him to tow it off the street because it was abandoned. He told them he didn't know who owned it."

Carrie looked worried now. Her eyes darted around the room. "So Kevin knows I'm in South Haven," she said trying to keep her voice calm.

"We don't know what he knows," Chi told her.

"Where's my car now?"

"It's behind Jessie's uncle's barn. It's hidden so no one can see it. We can get it anytime you want." Chi reached over and held Carrie's hand with both of his. Panic flashed through

Carrie's eyes but faded quickly as she let Chi hold her hand tightly.

"I don't want it. I don't want him to find me." A low level of fear could be heard in her voice.

"Pete's been keeping an eye out for anyone that might look suspicious, but that's kind of hard to do. He doesn't have any idea what to look for."

"Why didn't you tell me?"

"I didn't think there was a good reason to worry you."

"You didn't think? You didn't think?" Carrie pulled her hand out from between Chi's. Her anger now flowed through her words. "Of course I'm going to be worried. You don't know Kevin. If he wants to, he'll find me. I need to know if he's looking for me."

"I'm sorry. Maybe I should have told you. We've all had our eyes open, and we haven't seen those guys around again."

"If Kevin finds me, he'll kill me."

"He won't find you," Chi assured her.

"How can you say that, Chi? He found my car. Why do you think he can't find me?"

Chi nodded. Carrie was correct. There was no reason to presume that Kevin wasn't looking for her or that if he wanted to, he could not find her. "I'm sorry, Carrie. I've made a mistake in not telling you."

Carrie's eyes darted around the floor as she thought about what she should do. She suddenly relaxed and looked calm again. Chi looked at Susan who raised an eyebrow at him.

"He won't find me," Carrie said smiling and reaching out to touch Chi's arm. "I've been released. God will take care of him. I'm fine."

She stood up. "But I think I better get a different car. I'll talk to Bill tomorrow and see what I can do." She walked away from Chi and Susan as they watched. Carrie's effervescence returned as she nearly skipped away from them.

Ralph Nelson Willett

Chapter 24

"What kind of stupid name is 'Chainmail'?" Kevin asked Emiliano as he exhaled the smoke from the small pipe he had inhaled it from. "It sounds stupid."

"You shouldn't be talking like that," Emiliano replied calmly as he knocked the ash out of the finished pipe. "You don't know who's listening."

"Nobody's listening," he shouted at the wall on the opposite side of his living room. "I told him I'd find her and I will."

"We can't keep driving up there and just looking around. We got things to do."

Kevin backhanded him lightly on the arm. "What we gotta do? Huh? What we gotta do?"

"Stuff, man," Emiliano responded. "Stuff."

Kevin swore. "Yeah. We got stuff." He drank the beer he was holding, finishing it quickly with large gulps. He pulled another can from the plastic ring of the six pack on his coffee table. He popped it open and slouched down some more on the sofa. A dark shadow crossed his face as he spoke quietly. "We gotta find her. That's the stuff we gotta do." He guzzled the beer, emptying the can and pulled another one out of it's ring. "Chainmail says we gotta find Carrie so we'll keep going up there till we find her. Then we'll bring her back. Maybe pass her around a bit for some cash. That will teach her to split."

"We can't keep wasting time just driving around up there," Emiliano said again. "She may not even be there. She could be dead as far as we know."

"Wouldn't that be something," Kevin said with a crooked smile. "We spend all this time looking for her so we can kill her and she's already dead."

Emiliano took a large drink from his can then said without emotion, "So you decided to kill her."

"Maybe. I ain't decided yet. If she gives me trouble, then I will."

Emiliano said nothing.

Kevin sat up with a burst of energy. He nearly shouted, "I'll bring her head back and lay it on the table right in front of Chainmail and say 'There! See that, dude? She's dead. I took care of business'." He hit his chest hard with his fist. "Me! I took care of business." He took another large drink from his can of beer. "I took care of it," he said as the energy drained from him again.

"That would be funny, man," Emiliano laughed. "Laying her head right on his table. I'd love to see his face."

Kevin collapsed back again on the sofa and slouched deeply. They sat quietly for a few moments as they both sipped their beers. "I gotta find her," Kevin said almost inaudibly.

Emiliano brushed his hair back behind his shoulders with one hand. "Have you asked her mom?" he asked.

"I don't know where her mom is."

"We know she's from some small hick town. Somebody's got to know her mom."

Kevin suddenly sat bolt upright full of energy again. "Yeah! Bishop Hill!" He swore. "I just remembered. Bishop Hill! We can go up there and ask around for her. Find her parents. Beat it out of them if we have to, but they'll know."

"Dude, you ain't gotta ask no one. Just look 'em up on the internet."

~~~~

The GPS said Kevin only had another mile to go before he reached the Rhodes farm. He waited in the SUV at the end of the main drag of Bishop Hill, Illinois as he rehearsed in his mind what he was going to say: "Mr. Rhodes, my name is Charles Riker. I'm looking for Carrie Rhodes. Is she here? No? Well, would you happen to know where I can find her? I represent her last employer. She was injured about a month ago, and I've been authorized to offer her a rather large settlement. How much? Well, I'm sorry Mr. Rhodes, that is confidential but trust me on this, it is substantial. Thank you, Mr. Rhodes. Can I have her number, too, so I can call her and let her know I'm coming? Thank you, Mr. Rhodes."

The scenario played out over and over again in his mind to the point where he could see no other way it could happen. He even wore a suit so that he'd better fit the part. The suit was confining. He felt completely awkward and out of place.

Checking himself in the mirror he could see that his tie still wasn't right. After several attempts, he resorted to a clip-on tie because he didn't know how to tie the knot in a real one. But he did look the part, he thought. Even with his long hair he still could pass as a representative of a corporation.

Driving the final mile to the farm, he passed field after field of brown corn and other crops he could not identify. When the GPS said he had arrived at the farm, he found an old, opened rusty gate that at one time had guarded a long driveway. The drive now consisted of two ruts on either side of a grassy hump running down the length of its center. The drive led up to a barn with red faded paint and rotting boards. It appeared to have not been painted in decades. Missing shingles left gaps that glared like gaping holes in its roof.

The house didn't appear much better. Its siding seemed to be a type of white slate laid out in overlapping squares. A large fenced pen that came up within feet of the house held four cows that grazed lazily in the open air. As the SUV approached, chickens scattered noisily out of the way.

He parked where the driveway ended at the back door of the house. A rusting pickup truck was parked up on blocks nearby. He could see a newer car parked closer to the barn. He climbed short steps to the back screen door and knocked on its frame. He listened. No response. He knocked again. Still, no answer. He looked behind the house and saw the barn door open. He headed there next. As he approached it, a large dog laying by the door, looked up at him but did not move.

"Hello?" He shouted into the barn.

"Hello?" came a faint reply from deep inside the barn a second later.

"Hello? I'm looking for Carrie Rhodes?" he shouted back.

Mrs. Rhodes came into view from behind a wall. She was wiping her hands on a rag.

"What can I help you with?" she asked.

"I'm looking for Carrie Rhodes."

"She's up in Michigan."

"Michigan. Really?"

"Yes, Sir. South Haven, Michigan."

"Would you have her address?"

"Yeah. I have to go in the house to get it. Follow me."

Kevin could not believe his luck. This woman was giving up the details without asking a single question of him. This could not be easier, Kevin thought to himself. He followed her to the back door. She held the door for him and let him in through the mud room and into the kitchen.

"Wait here. I'll get it. Would you like something to drink?"

"No thank you, Ma'am. Is Mr. Rhodes here?"

"No, he's not. He's up in Michigan, too. I'll be right back." She left the room as Kevin waited, standing by the table. He was smiling to himself and nearly chuckled out loud. If he had wanted to rob her, it could not have been easier. Shoot, he thought, if he wanted to do anything at all, including kill her, it couldn't get any easier. His mind raced through the possibilities. They were far out in the country. No one else was around. No one to see anything. No one to hear anything. No one to do anything.

She returned moments later and handed him a small piece of paper she had torn from a small notebook. He looked at it. On it was written an address in South Haven as well as the telephone number.

"Thank you, Ma'am," he said.

"You're welcome. Is there anything else I can do for you?"

Kevin thought about the question for a moment. His mind raced again through the possibilities. Flashes of violence rushed through his thoughts as he felt the adrenaline beginning to surge through him. He hesitated only for a moment and then looked her in the eye. "Uh, no thank you, Ma'am," he said with a smile. "You've been a great help." He turned, left the house, climbed into the SUV and drove away.

Chapter 25

"You're not serious," Emiliano told Kevin. "She didn't want to know why you wanted her address?"

"She didn't ask a single question. She just let me in her house and then gave me that piece of paper with her address and phone number on it."

"That wouldn't happen in Chicago," Emiliano replied.

"I know," Kevin said incredulously. "She must be as stupid as they come."

Emiliano took a shallow drink of his beer. Both he and Kevin slouched on his sofa. Kevin held a cigarette in one hand and a beer in the other. The ashes from the cigarette fell onto his jeans. "Maybe when this is all over we can pay her another visit. See if she's got any cash," Kevin said after taking several swallows. "Might not be worth the gas money, though. It didn't look like she had anything." He was silent for a moment then added, "Could be fun, though. It was all I could do to not have a bunch of fun right then and there."

"Where was her father?" Emiliano asked.

"Didn't see him. I asked her. She said he was in Michigan, too. He could be with Carrie. Who cares?" Kevin finished off his beer and then sat up to the coffee table. He opened the bag of weed on the table and packed a small pipe with it. He held the lighter to it and inhaled the smoke deeply. He held his breath and handed the pipe to Emiliano who repeated the process.

Kevin continued. "They had this dumb dog, too. It just looked at me when I came by it. It didn't bark or nut'n. Didn't so much as wag his tail. I would have thought it was dead except it looked at me. Didn't care who I was or what I wanted. I could have beat that woman to death, and I don't think that dog would have so much as sat up and sniffed my butt."

Emiliano took another long toke on the pipe and returned it to Kevin. He held his breath for as long as he could and then smoothly and slowly let it out, blowing it upward. He took another swig from his beer. "So what you wanna do now?" he asked Kevin.

Kevin was holding his breath for several seconds and then exhaled in a sudden burst. "We're gonna bring the chick back. I'll make her regret taking off. Then we're gonna go see Chainmail." Kevin took a long drink from his beer and handed the pipe back to Emiliano. "We can start putting the crew together and making plans. We're gonna get that run. It better not have happened yet. That would piss me off."

Emiliano held the lighter to the pipe bowl as he inhaled, paused, then inhaled deeper still, in two short inhalations as he tried to bring the smoke as deeply into his lungs as was humanly possible. He held his breath and closed his eyes as the veins in his neck began to bulge. When he finally exhaled, he coughed several times before he could breathe normally again.

"You going up to get her?" Emiliano asked.

"No. I'll send the Jackson boys up. They wanna be part of the crew so let's see what they can do. Should be pretty easy. Just a quick snatch and back."

"What if she's with somebody?"

"Like who? Her dad? A dude? So what? If anybody gets in the way, we'll make him regret he was ever born." Kevin grinned and then giggled. With the weed, he was now finding himself to be funny. "Regret he was ever born." He laughed again. Emiliano chuckled at Kevin. "Regret he was ever born," Kevin repeated again while laughing.

Emiliano began laughing with Kevin. "Why is that funny?" he asked Kevin.

"I don't know. Just is."

~~~~

Chi knew something was wrong the second he turned the corner onto his mother's street. Perhaps it wasn't that he 'knew' it but more like he felt it. He slowed his truck as his eyes darted around the neighborhood. The streets were dark except for street lights that gave a yellowish glow to the parked cars. He had a nagging feeling in the pit of his stomach that would not let him drive home until he drove past his mother's house. He knew why the instant he saw the Buick parked in front of the house.

The older model Buick wore a metal flake purple paint with a white vinyl roof. It had large chrome wheels with thin tires. The windows were tinted nearly opaque, but it was the front license plate that churned his stomach. It was an Illinois plate.

He clenched his jaw as he examined the house. The light by the kitchen door was not turned on, unusual for this time of night. All the curtains were drawn, but he could see the interior lights bleeding through from the edges of the windows. He parked his truck in front of the neighbor's house and without touching it he consciously verified he could feel his Beretta tucked in behind his back. He then reached into his glove compartment and removed a .38 hammerless revolver. He tucked it into his jacket pocket, exited the truck and closed the door quietly.

Stepping up the sidewalk moving forward to the house, he heard the Buick making small popping sounds as it's engine cooled. The sound let him know the car hadn't been there long. Stepping up to the kitchen door, he tested the door handle. It was locked.

He stood at the door for a moment weighing his options. He heard voices from behind the door, but could not make out the words. Deciding on a course of action, he quietly put his key in the lock, hesitated just a moment and then quickly opened the door and stepped in.

"Hey, Mom!" he yelled out as he entered the kitchen quickly. He surprised the two men in the living room. One of them had been kneeling above Carrie as she lay face down on the floor. He was wrapping duct tape around her head and mouth, gagging her. The tape had already secured her wrists behind her. He saw his mother's legs on the far side of the rocker as she lay on her stomach but her face was hidden from view.

The man squatting over Carrie stood quickly and drew his weapon on Chi, pointing it at his head. The second man also pulled a pistol, holding it with two hands, pointing directly at Chi's head.

"Close the door," the first man said quietly and calmly while stepping towards him.

Chi feigned panic and raised both hands up to his head level. "What do you want?" Chi asked trying to sound frightened.

"Close the door," the man hissed again.

Chi closed the door with his foot by swinging it behind him. The man stepped closer putting the barrel of the weapon against his forehead. The second man lowered his weapon but kept his eyes firmly on Chi.

"If you want money it's in my wallet." Chi pointed downwards with his left hand towards his left hip pocket. "Do you want me to get it or do you want to get it?"

The man's eyes shifted to look down in the direction where Chi was pointing. Chi had asked the man to make a choice. The fact that the man took his eyes off of Chi and having to make a decision, had given Chi the split microsecond he needed. He ducked out of line from the barrel of the weapon while at the same time hitting and holding the man's wrist with his left hand. His right had grabbed the side of the weapon and bent it back, up and against the man's wrist. The pistol discharged as Chi took one step back removing it from the grip of the surprised assailant's hand.

Chi now held the weapon. He quickly pointed it at the second man as the man tried to bring his pistol around to bear on Chi again. Chi fired twice in rapid succession hitting him in the chest. The man stumbled backward as his weapon fell to the floor. Chi then returned the weapon to bear on the first man, who was recovering from his surprise. The man took one small step toward Chi just as Chi shot him twice in the chest. The look of pain and shock were quickly wiped away as Chi fired once more into the man's head. He fell to the floor instantly dead. Chi turned his weapon back on the second man, who was still standing The man used his hands to try to stop the blood from flowing from the holes Chi had introduced into his chest.

The man fell forward to his knees and looked up at Chi. Blood foamed from his mouth. He slowly attempted to reach for his weapon laying on the floor beside him. Chi gently kicked it away.

Chi squatted down in front of him and looked him in the eyes with a stone cold, emotionless stare. The man's chest made a wet sucking sound as he tried to inhale. Blood foamed around his lips and nose. He looked Chi in the eyes and held them there one last moment before he faded away. Chi moved sideways out of the way as the man fell forward onto his face.

Chi now moved quickly to Carrie as he said loudly to her, "Is anyone else in the house?" Carrie shook her head. Her eyes were wide and panicked. Chi quickly did a check of the two bedrooms with his weapon and then returned to where his mother lay on the floor. She hadn't moved. He knelt beside her. Blood was flowing from her nose and down her cheek. Chi checked her pulse by laying his fingers on her neck. She was alive. He checked her quickly for any other wounds and found nothing more.

Moving to Carrie, he set the weapon aside, pulled out his pocket knife, snapped it open with a flick and cut the tape holding Carrie's wrists. Carrie rolled over to her side and sat up. She found the edge of the tape around her head and began to unwrap it. Her hair stuck to it, but Carrie angrily pulled the tape off taking small clumps of hair with it. She finished tearing the tape from her face and removed a sock from her mouth.

Carrie looked around at the two dead men. Blood and brain matter splattered the walls behind where the bullets exited the first man's skull. Blood was now pooling on the floor beside them. Anger rose in her until it burst through. She nearly sprinted to the second man and began pounding her fist down angrily on the back of his head. She then stood quickly, leaped in two steps across the floor to a floor lamp, rushed back with it to the second man as its cord yanked free from the socket. She then rammed the base of the lamp straight down onto the man's head. Chi watched her expressionlessly only a moment, then turned his attention to his unconscious mother. Carrie expended all of her anger and broke down in tears.

Chi checked his mother, then rolled her onto her side. He placed a pillow under her head to keep it level. He then called 911.

~~~~

It was three o'clock the next afternoon by the time the police released Chi from custody. His mother and Carrie waited for him at his house, sitting on his sofa. They each wore jeans and one of his sweatshirts that appeared massive on them. They both looked terrified and exhausted.

"So what's going on?" Margret asked him.

"I'm fine. My attorney is dealing with things. How are you two doing?" He placed containers of take-out food on the table.

Margret had swelling and bruising around both eyes. She had difficulty opening one of them. "We're OK," she answered. "But neither of us can sleep."

"Yeah. I didn't get any sleep either." He spread open the containers revealing chicken dinners and then set the table with plates and glasses of water. "Come get something to eat," he instructed."

"I'm not hungry," Carrie replied.

"I know. But you need to eat. Come over and sit down."

Chi sat at the table and waited for them. Margret stood first and began walking slowly to the table with Carrie following behind. After sitting, Chi said grace and then added almost as an afterthought, "and thank you, Jesus, for protecting us. Amen."

Chi dug out the mashed potatoes from the styrofoam container and flopped it heavily onto his plate. He then pulled out the fried chicken breast and set it on his plate. Margret and Carrie sat looking at the containers in front of them without moving. "Eat," demanded Chi calmly. They both reluctantly removed their food from the styrofoam containers and placed it on their plates. Carrie dipped her fork into her potatoes slowly and took a small bite.

"How long were you in E.R.?" he asked Margret.

"About two hours after the ambulance finally got me there. Mostly just waiting. They did an x-ray and said I'm fine then said to watch for a concussion."

"They wanted to keep your mom overnight," Carrie added. "So they could watch for signs of a concussion but she wouldn't stay. You should have seen your mom," Carrie continued excitedly. "She jumped on one of them. It was crazy. The guy had a hard time getting her off of him."

"I think that's when he hit me," Margret added. "I can't remember."

Carrie continued as she excitedly explained to Margret what happened, "He hit you once, and you started falling backward. When you caught your balance you started back after him, that's when he hit you again and knocked you out."

Margret looked up at Chi as she leaned in, smiled and put a fork full of potatoes in her mouth.

"They won't be hitting anyone ever again," Chi said calmly.

They ate quietly for a few moments. Margaret broke the quiet asking "When can we get back in the house?"

"I don't know yet. As soon as the investigation is over, I suppose. My lawyer will let us know. Then we need to get the blood cleaned up and patch the bullet holes." He thought for a moment. "I don't think I want you going back there for a while."

"Why not?" asked Margret and Carrie at the same time.

"Because we don't know who these guys were or how they found you. Someone isn't going to be happy I dispatched these guys. I think that will make it too dangerous to be there until we can sort it all out."

"Did Pete say anything?" Margret asked.

"No. Pete wasn't allowed near the investigation because he's my friend. The state boys took this one."

"Do you think you'll go to jail?" asked Carrie.

"It doesn't look like it and my lawyer doesn't believe this is a problem. The facts are pretty clear that this was a home invasion and they hurt the two of you. They put a gun to my head, therefore, making it justifiable homicide. In any case, I think if I were going to be in jail I'd already be there."

"I didn't know who those guys were," Carrie said. "I would have thought that if Kevin knew where I was, he would have come and got me himself. That's what he did last time when he pulled me from that shelter."

"How did you know to stop by?" Margret asked Chi.

"Just a weird feeling I had that I needed to drive by. I couldn't shake it. So I was on my way home from Holland and decided to come by. I knew something was up when I saw the car."

Carrie sat up straight, excitedly. "God told you," she said giddily as she smiled. She was beaming.

Chi and Margret looked at her for a moment. It was only a couple of weeks ago she insisted there was no God and now she credited God for miraculously sending Chi to save them. Chi nodded at her and continued eating.

Chi's cell chirped. He checked it. "Susan's coming up the drive." He ate several more bites before walking to the door to meet her. She came in, wrapped her arms around him and buried her head in his chest. Chi could see she had been crying. She said nothing.

"We're OK, Hun," he told her. She sniffled as she held him. He rubbed her back trying to reassure her.

"You could have been killed," she said not looking at him.

"Yes. I could have been, but I wasn't."

She pulled back from him and looked him in the eyes. Chi could see that her eyes were bloodshot and red from crying. "How can you be so stoic about this?" she asked him.

He gave her a faint smile. "I'm a guy," he replied.

"You killed two guys, and that doesn't bother you?"

"Yeah, Hon. It does bother me," he said soothingly. "That's not something I would *choose* to do, but I did what I had to do. That's it." He turned trying to guide her to his kitchen table. "Come sit down with us. Have you had anything to eat?"

She walked with him to the table and sat down. "I'm not hungry."

"Like I told Mom and Carrie, you need to eat, and there's plenty." He set a plate in front of her along with a glass of water. She sat staring at her plate. "Are you OK, Margret?" she finally asked without looking up.

"Yeah. I'm fine. I've had a black eye before."

Carrie chimed in, "I get to play makeup artist on Margret like she did with me."

"You're too happy about that, Carrie," Margret told her without smiling. She turned again to Susan. "When did you find out what happened?"

"This morning, early, when Chi called and told me. It's all over the news now." She was quiet and continued to look down at her plate. Chi sat down beside her and dished out some potatoes and put a piece of fried chicken on her plate.

"Eat," he told her. She began to nibble at a chicken leg slowly.

"What's the news saying?" Carrie asked.

"Just that there was a shooting that left two people dead and that Chi was involved. They haven't identified the victims yet."

"Victims?" Chi questioned. "Did they mean the two guys or us?"

"The two guys, I think," Susan answered. "I saw something on the TV this morning where the police chief was being interviewed in front of Margret's house. He said it appeared to be a home invasion."

"It was," Chi said.

Susan looked at Chi. "Who were they, Chi?" She then turned to Carrie. Her look was accusatory.

"I didn't know them," Carrie protested.

"We don't have any idea who they were," Chi answered. "Their license plates said Illinois."

"Then they were after Carrie," Susan said flatly as she looked at Carrie. "From Chicago. They were there to kill Carrie,"

"No, I don't think so," Chi replied. "They were trying to kidnap her."

Susan kept her eyes on Carrie. She hesitated briefly and then added, "You almost ruined our lives."

Chi's and Margret's response was nearly instantaneous as they said in unison, "Susan!" The pain in Carrie's eyes was evident.

Susan said nothing more. She remained focused on Carrie. Her eyes began to tear.

"Babe, that's not how it is," Chi told her. "Carrie isn't the one that invaded Mom's house."

"She's not?" Susan questioned in a manner that implied that she thought that maybe she was.

"No, she's not," Chi answered. "Some bad people came in, and I took care of it."

Carrie spoke, "Susan, I'm sorry. I don't know what to say. But it was God that brought Chi over to rescue us."

Susan looked over to Chi who nodded his agreement and then she turned to Carrie. "But you don't believe in God."

"I do now," she insisted. "How can I not? It was God that brought me here, and it was God who told Chi to come to Margret's last night. If God is saving me through you, then he's not going to let anything happen to you, Margret or Chi either."

Susan had been holding a chicken leg. She set it back down on her plate and then slowly wiped her hands contemplatively with a paper napkin. Everyone watched her. She turned to Chi, "I'm scared."

Chi slid his chair closer to her and put his arms around her as she began to cry. "I know, babe," he said. "We all are."

Ralph Nelson Willett

Chapter 26

Kevin rocked back and forth nervously inhaling one cigarette after another. Emiliano wasn't answering his calls or his texts. He should be here, he thought. He faced the door from the high-top table he sat at. He checked his phone frequently for the time or a text from Emiliano. Something was wrong. He could feel it. The Jackson brothers hadn't returned when planned. They hadn't called or sent him a text to let him know what happened. They were now almost thirty-six hours late. There was no information about finding Carrie or not. The phone call that told him Chainmail wanted to see him spiked panic that he fought to suppress.

The waitress brought him another beer he hadn't asked for. Kevin quickly drank half of it before setting it down and checking his phone again. He glanced around the bar. Very few people were inside, in fact, it was almost empty. This added to his discomfort.

A large man entered the bar, stopped at the door and scanned the room. He locked eyes with Kevin then stepped in further. A second large man followed behind him. Kevin noticed the waitress and the woman behind the bar exit through a door behind the counter. Seeing them walk out only added to his anxiety.

The two men walked to Kevin's table. The first man he saw enter the bar pointed to the door leading into the side room where Kevin knew the second bar was. Kevin left the table and walked to the door with the men behind him. He reached the door and turned it's handle expecting it to be locked, even hoping it was locked; it wasn't. After opening it slowly just a crack, the second large man pushed it opened and then roughly shoved Kevin through. Without touching it Kevin mentally assured himself that his weapon was tucked securely in the small of his back.

The door closed behind him leaving the room completely dark. He heard a snap of a light switch and rows of lamps over the tables came to life. The first big man pointed to a round table at the far end of the empty bar. The table had chairs turned upside down on top of it. Kevin pulled one down, set it on its legs, sat on it and waited. He felt shaky and wanted another cigarette.

The second big man stood to his left while the first one stood two steps behind him.

"Where's your boss?" Kevin asked.

The second man took out his cell, dialed a number and put it to his ear. A moment passed before he said into the cell, "He's here." Another moment passed. He took the cell phone from his ear, put it on speaker phone and set it in front of Kevin.

"Kevin," the voice said in a cheerful tone.

"I'm here," Kevin replied.

"Hey, Kevin, we've got a problem."

"I don't know who you are," Kevin said trying not to sound nervous.

"It's Chainmail," came the cheerful reply.

So Chainmail wasn't going to show up in person today either, he thought. "Hey," he greeted. "What's the problem?"

"You sent a couple of my boys up to South Haven to get your woman."

"I didn't know they were your boys. They never told me that."

"You sent my boys up to do what you should have done."

"They never told me they worked for you," Kevin insisted.

"They did, Kevin. You got them killed," Chainmail said with the pleasantness leaving his voice.

Kevin was silent as his mind raced to process this new information. "What happened? I don't know anything about this."

Chainmail's voice was calm and measured. "You sent them into a trap. Someone was waiting for them."

"I don't know anything about this," Kevin blurted. "Who did it?"

Chainmail swore at him without raising his voice. "You did."

"I didn't do anything!" Kevin's voice was growing louder with panic. "They agreed to go bring Carrie back here."

"They're not coming back, Kevin," Chainmail said in a measured voice.

Kevin's panic was rising quickly. "Look, I'll go up and get her myself. I can be back by tonight."

"No need. I'm going to take care of it."

Kevin's mind raced. He thought of the run that was supposed to happen at the end of the month. "Does that mean you're going to give the run to someone else?"

"Kevin. Kevin," Chainmail said calmly. "We told you that if we took care of this, we wouldn't leave any loose ends. That includes you, Kevin."

The words sank in quickly. Kevin looked at the man standing to his left. Kevin's eyes widened as the man tilted his head and a grin spread slowly across his face. An arm reached around his neck from behind and pulled him backward out of his chair, knocking it over. The man behind him had reached around his neck, placing the crook of his right elbow in front. He put his right hand in the crook of his left arm, grabbed the back of Kevin's head with his left hand and squeezed tightly. Kevin grabbed the man's arms with both hands in a futile attempt at escape. The pressure on the carotid arteries blocked the blood flow to Kevin's brain. His world blacked out in mere seconds, and he went limp and unconscious in the man's arms.

The man that had been standing to Kevin's left picked up the chair and stood it back on its legs. Kevin was dragged limply around and placed back in it. The man holding Kevin rested Kevin's head on the table face down. He stepped behind him again, grabbed Kevin's jacket at the center of his back and held him in place with one hand. He used his other hand to remove Kevin's pistol and tucked it in his own jacket pocket.

Kevin's arms hung limply downward. His breathing was clearly visible as his diaphragm expanded and contracted with each breath he took. He let out a quiet groan. His arms began to twitch as the blood flow was restored to his brain. The man to his left stood next to him, raised his hand up and drove his hand down sharply striking Kevin at the base of his neck with the heel of his hand. There was a loud snap as his neck broke. Kevin's head arched unnaturally backward as he fell forward under the table. The breathing stopped.

The two men looked down at him impassionately. "Done," said the man to the left as he picked up his phone.

"Fine," Chainmail's voice said from the speaker phone. "Go find something to do for a while."

The two men walked out, turning off the lights before opening the door and then quietly closing the door behind them. As they walked past the bar, one of them rapped his knuckles on the polished wood twice. No one noticed them enter the bar. No one saw them leave. The waitress and the bartender returned.

Ralph Nelson Willett

Chapter 27

Margret listened to distant thunder as the fall winds began to blow a storm eastward. She guessed the storm would reach them sometime within the next half hour to forty-five minutes. As she looked over the trees, she could see the sky flash brightly. "One one thousand, two one thousand, three one thousand, four one thousand, five..." She reached twenty-five before she heard the rumble of the thunder. She guessed the lighting to be around five miles away. Maybe it will reach us sooner, she thought.

Chi came out of the house and joined her on the porch looking towards the west. She looked up at him and then turned back again. "Storm's coming," she said.

"Yes."

"Did you talk to Susan today?"

"Just got off the phone with her. She's alright. We're going out again tomorrow."

"Things got messed up, didn't they?" Margret asked him. "How long before things settle down?"

"Don't know. Hopefully, we're done," Chi replied. "With her boyfriend gone, hopefully, that's the end."

Both the chief of police and Pete came out together to see them yesterday afternoon to give them the news. The Chicago police had contacted them to let them know that Kevin had been found dead from what they described to them as an apparent accident. The police also checked Emiliano's apartment. They found pools of blood, but Emiliano was still missing, and the police suspected he would also turn up dead by reason of another 'accident' somewhere.

"When can I go home?" Margret asked.

"The place has been cleaned up, and the bullet holes patched in the walls and roof. I suppose you can go home as soon as you want." Chi hesitated and then added, "But I think I'd dig out Dad's old pistol if I were you."

"Yeah, I'm gonna do that. I just hate the thought of using it, though," Margret told him.

"You'll do what you have to do. Just like always," Chi replied.

The sky flashed again. Margret counted out loud for Chi's benefit. "Seven miles," she said as she took a step towards the door. Margret stopped and looked up into Chi's face. "At least we can say it wasn't a boring summer," she told him.

"We can say that," Chi replied with a grin. "Yes we can."

Margret walked into the house with Chi following behind her. She shed the hooded sweatshirt she was wearing and then walked downstairs to join Carrie. Carrie was sitting in an easy chair watching TV. She smiled at Margret as she came down the stairs.

Chi had insisted that they stay downstairs as much as possible. The basement level of the house was nearly as nice as the upstairs. It was almost like an extra apartment beneath the main floor. The stairs were hidden behind a door that one would assume to be only a closet when it was closed. The two women shared the bed in the same room Carrie had used the first night she met Chi.

Chi slept on a cot in the workout room where he could watch several flat screen security monitors. Carrie had been amazed the first time she saw the security setup in the room and wondered why Chi would have such a sophisticated setup for his home. He had camera views completely around his house and in each of the common rooms inside. An alert would be sent to his iPhone if certain boundaries were crossed. One of the things that surprised Carrie was that Chi could also monitor the only entrance into the subdivision.

Apparently, the State Police had also taken an interest in his security setup, wondering why someone would need such a sophisticated system for his home. Chi and his lawyer explained that just after Chi left the Navy he had planned on opening a security company, and made a hobby out of testing equipment to learn about it and see if he wanted to carry the product. After showing the investigators the documents where he registered a name for his security company they apparently were satisfied.

Margret had told Carrie once when they had come to Chi's house for a visit, while he was working out downstairs, that he probably knew they were coming as soon as they entered the subdivision. Now she understood how that was possible.

There was now a stainless steel hammerless revolver sitting on the end table next to Carrie. It lay incongruously next to the Bible Carrie had been reading. Chi had shown both Carrie and

Margret how to use it. Everyone hoped that they would never have to.

They heard Chi close the stairway door and watched as he stepped around the corner seconds later. He had taken to wearing a holstered Glock semi-automatic pistol at his side while in the house. While outside, he concealed it. "Buttoned up for the night," he told them as Margret sat down and reclined in the second recliner.

"You can't hear the thunder down here," Margret commented.

"What thunder?" Carrie asked.

"See. There's a storm coming, and you had no clue," Margret answered.

Chi spoke up, "It's pretty quiet down here. There's sound proofing insulation through this whole place."

"Did you put that in or was it here when you bought it?" Carrie asked him.

"I put it in. I like it quiet." Chi entered the workout room and closed the door behind him.

Margret and Carrie watched TV until eleven, killed the lights and headed to bed. Margret peered out of the egress window and could see that it was raining lightly. Most of the storm had passed, and they hadn't heard a thing. She turned out the small table lamp on the nightstand next to her and crawled into the bed they shared.

~~~~

"Mom. Mom." Margret was awakened by Chi's hushed voice as he shook her gently.

"What's wrong?" she asked.

"We've got company. Get up."

"Who?" she asked as she sat up. Carrie was waking up groggily.

"No one good. I need you out of here."

Margret gasped as her mind came to full alertness.

"Where do we go?" whispered Carrie.

"Out the window." He looked at a video on his cell. "It's clear. Move."

Margret quickly put on a pair of sandals as Carrie met her and Chi by the window. She put her hand on the latch and then froze. "What about the alarm?" The window was alarmed to squeal when intruders from the outside approached. A proximity alert tripped the alarm if someone stepped in the egress.

"I've disabled the egress alarms until I can get you out of here. I need you to cross the street and go down that trail I showed you deep into the woods. Keep going until you get to the other side then turn left. You'll hit the next woods. Take the pistol and stay there until I come get you."

Margret held the revolver, opened the window and let Carrie exit first. She climbed the walls of the egress and helped Margret up and out. Together they ran quietly across the small backyard and crossed the street. They found the trail and made their way along it in the dark as Chi had instructed them.

Chi re-enabled the egress alarm with his cell. He had 15 seconds to leave and be out of the egress before the alarm was triggered. Chi stepped into the egress and quickly closed the window behind him. He grabbed the edge of the wall and pulled himself out without using the steps. Rolling out, Chi somersaulted into a run. He slipped quickly into the woods.

A small man was quietly trying to pick the lock to Chi's side door. He had successfully opened the door handle lock but was now struggling with the deadbolt. He swore at it. It was dark. They had unscrewed the porch light.

"Hurry it up," the large man next to him whispered harshly. The small man swore again. The large man scanned the area for any movement or any indication they may be spotted. He could see the black SUV parked directly in front of the house. Two more men, dressed in black, stood by the side of it, holding assault rifles by their sides trying to minimize the view if someone should see them.

"I can't get this one," the man picking the lock said.

"Why not?"

"I haven't seen this kind before. It's got a tumbler I can't figure out. Just break the door in and get it over with." His whisper was getting louder with his frustration.

The big man glowered down at him as he thought through his options. "Alright, we switch to the alternate plan." The smaller man quickly gathered his tools and tucked them away in a small pouch. Together they jogged back to the SUV.

"What's wrong?" one of the men by the SUV asked.

"Alternate plan," the large man said as he approached them. All four men quickly moved to the back of the SUV and opened it's rear doors. They pulled out two large coolers, set them on the ground and opened them to reveal several bottles filled with gasoline with rags sticking out of the top. They quickly laid out several military-style rifles along with a dozen magazines on the floor of the SUV. After verifying that each rifle was loaded and ready they split up into two-man teams. Each man carried a rifle strapped to his shoulder. One man carried a cooler. The other man carried a three pound hammer and a Molotov Cocktail. They moved window to window as the man with the hammer smashed it in. The second man lit the rag on fire and the man with the hammer would throw the bottle inside.

An external alarm bell clanged loudly with the first window breaking. It echoed loudly through the neighborhood, announcing their presence. The men ignored it.

The fire began to spread rapidly inside. The two teams moved quickly. After breaking each of the upper floor windows, they did the same to the three egress windows until all of the gasoline bombs had been tossed in.

The house alarm continued to clang as they ran back to the SUV and retrieved rifles. The four men lined up behind the SUV and opened fire, pouring bullet after bullet into the house. The powerful rifles projected the shots through the exterior walls and insulation, through the drywall and on through the outside wall on the far side of the house.

Expending their first magazines, they reloaded and began again. The flames were now raging through the house. Lights came on in neighboring homes, but the men ignored them also. Each man emptied their second magazine into the house and reloaded again.

The man on the far left saw from the corner of his eye the man on the far right stumble forward. He turned his head just as the next man to the right began to fall. He saw a dark figure bearing his weapon onto the head of the man next to him as the man continued to fire his rifle into the house. A light flashed from the dark figure, and the third man's face splattered outward. The man on the far left turned to bring his weapon around quickly, but a bright light flashed through his eyes. He crumbled to the ground.

Three of the four men now lay face down on the pavement. The fourth man had fallen to his side in the fetal position. Chi calmly stepped to the first man and kicked his weapon away from him while pointing his weapon at the man's head. He checked each man as he picked up the rifles and tossed them into the yard. A single bullet to the head had silenced each of them quickly.

Moving quickly, Chi walked to the driver's side rear door of the SUV and verified no one was inside. He repeated the process with the front door. Chi reached into the SUV and turned the headlamps on. He walked once around the vehicle as he did a visual check of the area surrounding him. Confident that the area was now secure, he walked to the front of the SUV, set his pistol on the ground, took three steps back and knelt on the pavement to wait for the police.

Chapter 28

Chi sat stiffly and soberly next to his attorney William Flag. The room was bare except for a heavy wooden table and four wooden chairs that creaked when you moved in them. There were no windows in the room, reminding Chi of a large concrete closet. The fluorescent lighting made the room almost painfully bright. Flag's briefcase remained closed in front of him, and he impatiently tapped his yellow pad with his pen.

Two Michigan State Police troopers that Chi guessed to be a few years younger than he was had transported Chi to the St. Joseph, Michigan FBI office. They had the look of having just graduated from the academy and seemed nervous.

Once seated in the small office, two FBI agents had peppered Chi with questions, but Chi remained calm and silent until joined by Flag. Chi and Flag talked privately for about an hour before the agents joined them and the questions were repeated. This time he answered cautiously while being monitored carefully by Flag. He was advised not to answer only a few times as the events of the night unfolded.

A third agent had entered the room and requested that the other agents join him in the hall. The agents never returned. That was six hours ago making it almost twenty-four hours since the attack. Flag was beginning to look exhausted. Chi felt weary.

The door opened, and an older agent sat down across the table from them. He leaned back in his chair and began reading notes from within an opened manila folder.

"Are you going to press charges or are you going to release my client?" Flag demanded to know.

There was no response or acknowledgment from the agent as he continued to turn pages within the folder. A minute passed, and again Flag repeated the question, and again he was ignored. Chi now seemed completely alert as he watched the agent carefully. Another minute passed. Flag again demanded to know, "Are you going to release us?"

The agent looked at Flag over the folder without raising his head, closed the folder, placed it flat on the table and folded his hands over it as he leaned in turning directly to Chi. He held his gaze for a moment then said, "It appears they didn't know who you are, Commander."

Flag turned to Chi with a questioning look and then back at the agent. "What does that mean?"

The agent turned to Flag. "I'm ATF special agent Van Dyke. There will be no charges at this time."

Chi had no reaction.

"ATF?" questioned Flag. "Why is the ATF involved."

"Because of the weapons they used," Chi said flatly without turning to Flag. "Fast and Furious?" Chi asked the agent. The agent only glanced at him but ignored his question.

"Are we free to go?" asked Flag.

"Yes. You're free to go."

Both Chi and Flag stood. The agent leaned back in his chair again and spoke to Chi. "Commander, I'd like to talk with you privately, if I may."

"No!" shouted Flag instantly at Van Dyke.

Van Dyke did not react to Flag. Chi stopped and looked directly at him. They held each other's stare for a moment. "OK," Chi answered.

"No you will not!" Flag shouted at Chi defiantly.

Chi turned and faced Flag. "Yes."

Flags face became red with anger. He turned to the door and left hurriedly. He turned back just before closing the door and said, "I'm right out here. Do not, do not, do not answer any questions." He closed the door hard behind him. Chi sat down again and waited.

"My son served with you," Van Dyke said.

"Who's your son?"

"James Van Dyke."

A closed mouth smile spread slowly across Chi's face. "Fireball," Chi said with only the slightest hint of emotion.

The Agent nodded at him. "When I saw your file I called him and dragged him out of bed. He told me a bit about you." Chi did not react, his face appeared like stone. "He told me why you opted out." Again, no reaction from Chi. "Let me tell you what's going on. Your mother brought Carrie Rhodes in as soon as Ms. Rhodes knew the FBI was taking the case. She was trying to protect you. It's no wonder they wanted her so badly. She's a wealth of information; names, dates, locations. I met with her earlier today. She has a phenomenal memory, and I think she still has a lot to tell us."

The thin smile left Chi's face as a spark of anger flashed through is eyes. He stared for a moment at Van Dyke then stood, walked to the door and waved Flag back in. Flag glared at Van Dyke as he joined them again at the table. The agent was clearly unhappy that Chi brought his attorney back into the room.

"Carrie Rhodes is in the FBI's custody. I would like you to represent her," Chi told Flag.

"I'm representing *you*," Flag reminded him. "It's not a good idea for me to represent the both of you."

"I know, but for now I'd like you to represent her."

"OK," Flag replied with resignation.

Chi turned back to Van Dyke. "Please continue."

Van Dyke's eyes steeled with anger at him. He and Chi held their stare for several moments. "Alright. Carrie Rhodes came in yesterday. She has intimate knowledge and details of activities that we have active investigations into. Enough so that current undercover investigations that have been ongoing for the last eighteen months could be cut short by as much as a year." Van Dyke took a moment to let that settle with Chi and Flag. He then continued, "She's being taken into protective custody and is being moved to a safe house within the next two days."

"What does she know?" asked Flag.

"Names, date, places, materials. Just about everything we could ask for. Ms. Rhodes' life will be at risk."

"It already has been," Chi said.

"Yes, Commander. We know. Now I need to ask *you*, do you have someplace you can go to lay low for a while? You, your mother and your fiance?"

"I believe so. I'll have to make a phone call, but I think I do."

"OK, make that phone call. If it doesn't work out, then I'm prepared to offer the three of you protective custody."

"Understood."

~~~~

Chi sat at the picnic table overlooking Little Sheldon Lake, the smaller of the twin lakes in the upper portion of lower Michigan. He straddled the bench and held Susan as she leaned against him with her legs stretched out. Chi had his arms wrapped around her and rested his chin on her shoulder. The morning sun had risen but that was just a technicality as it was still down behind the trees. They cast a shadow across the lake as steam rose from it when the warmth of the water met the cold air.

They were now wearing their winter coats. Susan wore a knitted hat and mittens while Chi had on his black leather gloves. From here they could see the far side of the lake through the shadows and rising mist. There was only one other cabin on the lake, and it stood dark and vacant almost directly across from them. Had this been summer he expected that both of these houses would be alive with people already even at this time of the morning, but this first week of December found the three of them alone.

Chi heard the rear cabin door open, and he glanced over his shoulder. Margret was bringing a small tray with steaming mugs of coffee to them. She met them at the table, handed one to each of them, sat down and took a sip of her own.

"Thank you, Margret," Susan told her.

"Yes, thank you," Chi agreed.

"You're welcome," Margret told them.

They sat quietly watching the mist rise from the water. "I expected we'd have a foot of snow already up here," Margret told them. "Thank God for global warming."

Susan chuckled at her.

The only sounds to be heard were the small lapping waves against the shore. Chi had been here with Pete while they were both still in High School. In the spring the sounds of birds and insects would have seemed deafening compared to the silence of these late fall months.

Pete's grandfather built this cabin, and it had been used for almost three generations of families as they shared it for summer get-aways. It would have been winterized by this time with all the pipes drained, and storm windows put back on as protection against winter freezing, but the Sender family kept it open for their use.

Chi's cell buzzed and chirped. He pulled it out and checked it.

"Someone's coming," he told them calmly. "Get in the house."

Susan and Margret stood and quickly moved back to the cabin just shy of a run and closed the door behind them. The crunching of the tires on the driveway stones could be heard as Chi waited for the vehicle to come around the bend into view. He was now standing, waiting for who ever was coming. His right hand reflexively moved to his holstered weapon.

A red Chevy Impala pulled almost silently into view. Chi could see three people in the car but could not make out who they were through the windows. It pulled up slowly next to his Subaru and parked. As soon as the car stopped, the rear passenger side door opened, and a woman stepped out and looked at him over the roof of the car smiling broadly and waving her hand wildly at the wrist.

"Carrie!" Margaret shouted as she ran out of the cabin to meet her. Carrie rushed to her, and they met just feet in front of the car. They hugged each other and Margret gave her a kiss on the cheek. Carrie's eyes had begun to tear up as they hugged in a joyous reunion. Susan stepped out of the house and ran lightly in a skipping run to join them.

The driver's side door opened and Agent Van Dyke stepped out. Chi waited for the agent to join him near the table. As they shook hands, they turned to stand shoulder to shoulder so that they both faced the women. Carrie was looking at Susan's left hand nearly squealing with joy.

"I understand congratulations are in order," Van Dyke said.

"Yes, thank you. Considering the circumstances, it was better to get married sooner than later."

"I understand."

"The problem is we've had to spend our honeymoon with my mother in the next room. That's not the best thing that could have happened." Van Dyke grinned at him. Chi smiled and continued. "It's a good thing Mom likes to take long walks on the trail around the lake."

The agent laughed. "Just like the pioneer days, I suppose."

"I've no idea what they did in the pioneer days."

"Are you going to have a formal wedding later?" the agent asked.

"Yes. We're thinking about what we want to do now. Not much actual planning we can do at the moment."

The agent waved to the third man in the Impala. An older man with a long overcoat stepped out and began walking over to them. He stepped up and held out his hand for Chi to shake.

"Commander, I'd like you to meet General Thompson, retired."

"It's good to meet you, General. But please call me Chi. I'm not in the military any longer."

"It's good to meet you, Mr. Baroda."

"Please, Chi."

"OK, Chi."

The agent spoke up, "Let's sit down at the table for a few minutes. Is that OK or would you prefer to step inside?"

"Out here is fine with me," Chi said as they all moved to the picnic table. Van Dyke and Thompson sat across the table from Chi.

"The General would like to talk to you about something, but first I'd like to fill you in," the agent started. "I don't know if you've heard the news or not but over the last two days there have been several arrest thanks to the information that Ms. Rhodes provided. One hundred thirty-two people in Chicago, sixteen in Detroit, twelve in Philly and forty arrested in Dallas with three dead. Two hundred and three people in total. Four caches of military grade weapons were seized along with an estimated thirty million in heroin, cocaine, and marijuana. A major smuggling ring has been disrupted here in the states as well as a disruption of a major source in Mexico. Mostly thanks to the information that Ms. Rhodes was able to provide."

"I wouldn't have guessed she knew that much," Chi said.

"Neither did we but when she started talking it became apparent that she knew a lot of the intimate details of these organizations. It seems her boyfriend didn't think much of her and didn't know when he should keep his mouth shut. Then her friend Amber told her a lot of things. Ms. Rhodes has an incredible memory."

Chi continued to listen. General Thompson seemed to watch Chi carefully as Chi absorbed the details.

Agent Van Dyke continued. "The main group in all this is called 'Los Hombre's de la Tabla'."

"Men of the table," Chi repeated in English.

"That's right. It originated out of Juarez Mexico but moved operations to Chicago. The lead man is named Diego Sanchez. He pretty much stayed out of the spotlight and let his brother Juan Sanchez, who goes by the name Chainmail, run the day to day.

"These guys were very successful partly because they always found a way to deflect things if something went bad. This is where Carrie's boyfriend comes in. He ran a small crew of six people. He was very skilled at smuggling and logistics. What the Sanchez brothers would do was to get things ready in Juarez to come to the US, and then he would tell one of the crews he had a run for them coming up. Then he'd listen. If word came back around to him from the street about the run, that meant he had a leak, and he'd postpone it and assign it to another crew. He had several crews willing to do these. The Sanchez brothers paid the crews very well for these runs. If something happened, he could legitimately say that these guys didn't belong to his group. Only one crew was ever caught in the act. There was a shootout at the border, and all six men and one woman involved were killed, so we got nothing out of them.

"But it seems Carrie's boyfriend talked too much within her earshot because she knew about all his runs. Date's, time's, who and where they were delivered to, but it wasn't just Kevin. Her friend, Amber Meyers told her a lot of things. Ms. Meyers was a low-level prostitute dealing with a lot of the members of other crews and several of the Sanchez boys. It appears that these guys couldn't keep the pillow talk down. She's dead now. Kevin's partner, Emiliano beat her badly trying to find Carrie. She overdosed on heroin the next day.

"That's when Kevin decided to pay Carrie's parents a visit. He didn't know about the incident up in Michigan with her father. Kevin drives up and her mom thinks he's some government agent involved with what happened with Mr. Rhodes. She tells him exactly where to find Carrie without so much as flinching. That might have saved her life, though, since I believe that Kevin was prepared to kill her if she didn't tell him where Carrie was.

"Kevin's death was not an accident. I don't think anyone ever thought it was, but there were a couple of Chicago's finest that helped to cover the murder. A couple of Chainmail's thugs broke his neck. But here's something you may find ironic, Emiliano, the thug who walked all over people, ended up being ground up and mixed in with cement that was used to create a decorative sidewalk at a business in Joliet."

Chi gave him a questioning look.

"No kidding. It was a beautiful red sidewalk. Somebody spilled and DNA was extracted from bone fragments found in the concrete." The agent nearly laughed but instead looked out over the steaming lake for a moment. The general looked at Van Dyke without showing any emotion.

Van Dyke continued. "If it wouldn't have been for Ms. Rhodes, the undercover investigation would have had to go on for at least another year, and I doubt it would have been as clean and exhaustive. Because of Ms. Rhodes, we dismantled a major gang, drug, and weapons ring, both domestically and in Mexico. I think it's safe to say that she saved perhaps thousands of lives."

Chi nodded thoughtfully. "That was a God thing," he said.

"Well I don't believe in that stuff, but I can see your point" Van Dyke replied.

Chi stiffened and spoke rapidly. "My Point?" he asked. "Here's my point: If Carrie's father had treated her well she would not have run to Chicago. If her first boyfriend in Chicago didn't gamble her away in a *card game*, she would not have been with Kevin. If Kevin had treated her like he loved her, then she wouldn't have run from him. If she hadn't run from him, her car would not have '*just happened*' to break down right where I was at the time or Carrie probably would not have survived. If it weren't for her calling her mother because she missed her, they would not have come up to try and get her. If her father hadn't attacked me, he might have been home when Kevin showed up, and he may not have told him where she was. And *that* may have gotten them both killed. If Kevin hadn't been told where Carrie was, then he wouldn't have sent two men up to get her. If I hadn't had a *feeling* that I needed to drive by my mom's house that night, Carrie would have disappeared into Chicago and probably never been seen again. If I hadn't been trained how to disarm a man in that exact situation, then perhaps I would have been *the dead man*. If I hadn't killed them, then they wouldn't have sent four more men with assault weapons up to kill me. If they hadn't tried to kill me, then I wouldn't have killed them. Again, I was trained for just that type of thing. If I hadn't killed them, then Carrie would not have felt that she needed to come and rescue me from jail and without that, *you* would have had nothing. And you yourself said that without Carrie, then perhaps thousands could have died.

"No, it *is* a God thing," Chi continued. "Too many pieces had to fall together at just the right time in just the right places. I don't know how you can't believe that this was a God thing after you see how everything fits together."

Van Dyke nodded slowly as he processed what Chi had said. Looking at General Thompson Chi could see a thin smile had crossed his face.

"OK," Van Dyke said. "I get it. There's some more. Carrie's father is dead. He died in his sleep in the Van Buren County jail. The autopsy showed he died of a massive heart attack. His arteries had one hundred percent blockage. But when they opened him up they found he also had severe stomach ulcerations and cirrhosis of the liver. It looked like the man was living on borrowed time and his time ran out. He was only forty-four, but he was tore up on the inside like he was ninety.

"Carrie, of course, didn't want to have anything to do with him and her mother asked that his ashes be shipped down to her. I understand there won't be a memorial. Nobody liked him enough to come apparently. That was three weeks ago."

"So she's free," Chi said.

"Yes. We don't need to hold Carrie any longer, but I think she should still keep a low profile."

"That's not what I mean. She's now free from everyone that tortured her."

"Yeah, I'd agree. She's been released from all that."

They sat quietly for a few moments letting it all sink in. "OK, Chi," Van Dyke continued. "There's another reason I'm here. General Thompson would like to talk to you."

"About what?" asked Chi calmly as he faced the general.

Thompson leaned in. "Well, Comm..."

Chi interrupted him, "Chi."

"Yes. Well, Chi, I represent an organization that needs a man of your skills and professionalism. We work internationally with agencies all over the world. My understanding is you speak three languages other than your native English, and that, along with your previous training, makes you a very valuable asset."

"Not interested."

"Before you turn it down, I have to say that your country needs you. There are some very bad people doing some very bad things that require men such as yourself that know how to deal with them. The men we need would be saving American lives and not just American but the lives of innocent men, women and children across the globe."

"Not interested. I know what that would mean, and I'm not interested."

"What do you think that means, Chi?" the general asked.

"It starts with being away from my wife for long periods of time and ends with me killing people. I'm not interested." There was a moment of silence. Chi asked, "What department did you say you represent?"

"I didn't."

"But you are part of the ATF, or you wouldn't be here with Agent Van Dyke."

"No. We're not affiliated with the ATF. I can't say more than that."

"CIA?"

"No."

The two men held each other's stare for a long moment. The general broke the silence. "We saw how you dispatched six men. You dealt with them in a very efficient and professional manner. This is what we need. Along with that comes many privileges."

Chi leaned on one elbow facing him. He hesitated and then quietly but sternly said, "You're looking for an assassin."

"No, I'm not."

Chi's voice took on the authoritative tone again as he raised his voice slightly. "General, you're playing a game with me, and I can't say that I like it. You say that you need my skills, comment on how efficiently I 'dispatched' six men, and then you say you're not looking for an assassin. You have to know that I don't trust you already."

"You have no reason to trust me. What you do have reason to consider is the protection of your country. I'm telling you that we need you. You are not an assassin. I'm not looking for one. I am looking for someone with the intelligence and skills to be able to walk into risky situations and keep his wits about him. Then, if something goes wrong, has the ability and agility to get out of it, fight his way out of it if needed. That person would be working with a team of like-minded professionals."

"Now you're looking for James Bond."

"Almost, but this is the real world."

Chi looked at Van Dyke. "Is Fireball part of this?"

"I can't say," replied Van Dyke.

The general added, "I will say that you would be leading and working with some of the best people the United States has ever produced. You're one of those."

The general was quiet for a moment and then spoke with a lower tone. "You can't tell me that the action you were just involved in didn't stir something in you. You can't tell me that didn't fire up your adrenaline and excite you. Like it or not, you *are* a professional with exceptional professional skills.

Your country needs men exactly like you at this moment. Writing romance novels doesn't serve anyone but you."

Chi turned towards the house. The women had moved inside. He took off his gloves and rubbed his hands together and blew into them. The general spoke to him again while Chi looked away towards the house. "I know you're a believer. I know what church you go to. Let me tell you this: I am also." Chi turned to look him in the eyes. Again they held their stare, as Chi evaluated the General's statement. The general continued, "King David was a man after God's own heart. God used him to defend Israel. The people praised him for killing tens of thousands, and God blessed him. We need a David working for our country now. You understand that I can't fill you in on the details now but what I can do is to ask you to visit me in Virginia where I can get you the necessary clearances and give you much more detail. I think once you see what's going on then you'll want to serve with us. More than that, I think you'll find that you'll *need* to serve with us. All I'm asking today is that you commit to checking this out and listening to us."

"I won't commit to anything today."

"That's alright. I can give you more time to think about it."

Chi looked back at the house again and spoke softly while looking away from them. "I just got married. I don't want to leave my wife." He sat a moment in contemplation then added, "I thought I was through with that life. I *wanted* to be through with it."

The general lowered his voice and spoke softly, "Chi, you can't tell me you're happy writing romance novels. That's not who you are and never has been."

Chi lowered his head and slowly ran his ungloved hand over his hair. He then stood in a slow, smooth movement. "Gentlemen, let's go see what the ladies are up to."

The two men joined him as he walked slowly towards the house.

~The End~

I'd Love to Hear from You!

Thank you so much for spending your time with me. I greatly appreciate the feedback from readers. If you enjoyed this book, please consider leaving a short review on Amazon.

Here's the link to let us know what you thought of the book.
www.NorthernOvationMedia.com/therelease/review

Thank you so much,
Ralph Nelson Willett
****

Want Free Books?

From time to time Ralph gives away free copies of his new releases. But his promotions are highly temporary. If you'd like to be notified when he's giving his kindle books away for free, please consider signing up at the following link:
www.NorthernOvationMedia.com/freebooks

Stay In Touch With Ralph Nelson Willett

Stay in touch with the author via:

Facebook:
www.Facebook.com/RalphNelsonWillett/

Twitter:
www.twitter.com/northernovation

Email
AuthorRalphNelsonWillett@gmail.com

If you enjoyed The Release – Escape From Torment, please post a review on Amazon.

Other Books By Ralph Nelson Willett
Available on Amazon

The Rose Stone

In this christian short story, Rosanne struggles with suicidal thoughts, addiction, and unwanted pregnancy. A small stone, a token from her past, reminds her of the love of her family; a love she once walked away from. In a ruined life and far from home, Rosanne reaches out in desperation for the help she needs. Now a God she rejects reaches into her life through that same small stone, guiding her back home, both physically and emotionally.

The Rose Stone will have you feeling the pain and desperation of a young woman who once had it all but now fights to stay alive. The story takes you in deep as you hear the voices that condemn her, struggle with her as she stumbles and you'll cry with her as she escapes her personal demons. Although it's fiction, this may be a story of someone you know; it may even be you. It's a story of how God can use even the smallest and most common things to rescue a life. In Rosanne's life, it's all touched by a single stone; The Rose Stone.

The Summer Tourist

The Summer Tourist - A Contemporary Christian Romance
Tina reflected on how she had been used by the man she loved. The crushing weight of his deception overwhelmed her, leaving only her pain. Standing in front of the lighthouse, she raises tear-filled eyes toward Chicago and whispers, *"I am not your summer diversion."*

She holds the sparkling bracelet he had given her over the water. The final emotional release of letting him go was to turn her hand slowly and let it fall away.

Could she ever trust again? Would an old flame return to love her once more?

The Summer Tourist, A Christian Romance, is set in the city of South Haven MI with its sandy Lake Michigan beaches and iconic lighthouse. As part of the Haven Series, this book examines love and love lost. Can a love and trust ever be restored?

Made in the USA
Columbia, SC
29 April 2019